Phaedra

Phaedra

❨ *A Novel* ❩

Laura Shepperson

alcove
press

Copyright © 2023 by Laura Joan Shepperson

All rights reserved.

Published in the United States by Alcove Press, an imprint of The Quick Brown Fox & Company LLC.

Alcove Press and its logo are trademarks of The Quick Brown Fox & Company LLC.

Library of Congress Catalog-in-Publication data available upon request.

ISBN (hardcover): 978-1-63910-153-5
ISBN (ebook): 978-1-63910-154-2

Cover design by Andrew Davis

Printed in the United States.

www.alcovepress.com

Alcove Press
34 West 27th St., 10th Floor
New York, NY 10001

First Edition: January 2023

10 9 8 7 6 5 4 3 2 1

For Amelia

ta tou dramatos prosopa
Dramatis Personae

Crete

Residents

Phaedra—princess of Crete
Minos—king of Crete and father of Phaedra
Pasiphaë—queen of Crete and mother of Phaedra
Ariadne—princess of Crete and sister of Phaedra
Kandake—maid to Pasiphaë
Helia—bull leaper
The Minotaur—reputed monster who lives in the laby-
    rinth under the palace

Visitors

Xenethippe—Athenian tribute
Theseus—prince of Athens and son of Aegeus, disguised
    as a tribute
Pirithous—Theseus's captain and friend

Athens

Residents

Aegeus—king of Athens
Hippolytus—prince of Athens, son of Theseus and
    grandson of Aegeus
Trypho—adviser to the king

Cassandra—maidservant to Medea

Criton—a prosecutor

Visitors

Medea—princess of Colchis, ex-wife of the hero Jason; reputed to be a witch

Agneta—her maidservant

A woman like this can you embrace? Can you be left in the same chamber with her and not feel fear, and enjoy the slumber of the silent night? Surely, she must have forced you to bear the yoke, just as she forced the bulls, and has you subdued by the same means she uses with fierce dragons. Add that she wishes her name writ in the record of your own and your heroes' exploits, and the wife obscures the glory of the husband.

—Ovid, *Heroides VI*, 95–101
(trans. by Grant Showerman, 1914)

PROLOGUE

The Bard

"Gather round, welcome guests and good citizens of Athens, gather round. I have a tale to tell you, one close to your heart. It's about your brave king, Theseus, and the evil monster he slew for you. A beast with the torso of a man and the head of a bull. The Cretan crime against nature they called the Minotaur."

The little man played a couple of notes on his whistle, then sat back on his stool as he waited for the rumblings.

Sure enough, the crowd responded. "We know this one already, foreigner. Why would we want to hear it again, and from you?" The citizens of Athens, predominantly young, healthy-looking men in their prime, began to trickle away.

The bard allowed the tiniest of smiles to flicker across his face, and began to croon his tale. He started with the Cretan princess. Not the one who was giving evidence in the trial, but the older one, Ariadne of the beautiful hair. And many other beautiful places, he began to imply. Seduced by their very own king, Theseus, a man who'd never spoken a word to any of them, but who featured often enough in the bards' songs to make him as familiar as a regular drinking companion. The Cretan princess had barely begun to disrobe before Theseus before the crowd shuffled back again, sheepishly at first, then more exuberantly as the wine started flowing. By the time the promiscuous princess had bared her breasts, they were whooping.

☾

The story the bard sang wasn't the truth. He had no idea what the truth was. He wasn't from Athens, and he'd been passed on the song by another traveling minstrel in exchange for his last piece of bread. But as he sang, he observed the crowd jeer when he sang about the princess, and cheer when he mentioned Theseus's son, Hippolytus. He began to tailor his story to their liking. Tentatively at first, then more confidently, he shifted his story to topical news, the trial that was taking place in the palace the very next day. It was a risk, but he saw his crowd growing. He plumbed the depths of his memory for every shred of information he'd picked up about the trial, both on the road and in Athens. The princess was bewitched by Aphrodite. The prince was abandoned by Artemis. His audience lapped it all up. Because he was a more observant man than most, he noticed the shadowy figures on the edge of the assembly, cloths pulled over to disguise their faces, which would surely be female faces. Unlike the others, they were not whooping and cheering for the young prince and his heroic father. The bard noticed their disapproval, but he didn't care. He didn't sing for women. They couldn't pay for his songs.

He would inform other singers he met on the road of the Athenian preferences too, provided they weren't too stuck up to share food and information with him in return. But he might stay in Athens a little while yet. The trial was just beginning, and while Athens itself was a poor hole of a palace, men had come from far and wide to view it, bringing the smell of money with them, more than enough to attract a man who lived by his wits.

As the sun began to set, causing the newly built temple, higher on the hill than any of its predecessors, to glow like a beacon, the little man brought his tale to a close. He looked upon his audience, barely able to stand, hugging one another and shaking their fists at the Cretan princess. *A good day's work*. No one would run him out of the court now. He stood up and sauntered toward the kitchen to enquire about the dinner he had earned, and perhaps even a maid to accompany it.

ACT I

CRETE

The men of Athens are muttering to one another under their breaths, the normal boisterous shouts having given way to the silence reserved for a sacred ceremony. The room, the same one used for meals, has been cleared of tables. The long benches have been repurposed for the jurors, as they are being called. The maids have done their best, but there was little time between breakfast and the start of the trial. One man is sitting in a pool of meat juices. His clothes will reek of it later, but for now he hasn't noticed, and when he does, well, there's a maid for that too.

Some of them think to last night, when they saw the defendant cheering and drinking with the others, stretching out his legs at the table as if he had not a care in the world. And what should he have to fear from this court of men? There is only her word against his. What man has not witnessed the malice of a jealous woman?

And she is not a woman like other women. Daughter of a king, sister of a monster, a princess of Crete. All have heard stories of the women of Crete.

Outside there is a shuffling of feet. The men straighten in their seats, nudge their neighbors. Heads turn expectantly towards the door. She is coming.

It begins . . .

Phaedra

I was eight years old when I first heard about my mother's reputation, although I didn't understand what I was hearing then. We were outside the palace, and I was trailing behind Ariadne and Mother. Even at eleven or twelve, Ariadne was already as tall as most women, and I dawdled behind, watching their legs move in time, their long auburn hair swish back and forth, and I longed for the time when I would be as lithe and elegant as they were. That time never came.

I cannot recall now where we were going. I do remember that my father was away, and we were surrounded by soldiers and guards, men with long spears who wouldn't even look at me out here in the open, although when we were in the palace they would often smile at me, offer me a sweet if my mother wasn't looking, and tell me about the little girls they had left at home. They never told Ariadne such things, even though she was far prettier than me. Ariadne turned back and glared at me. "Keep up, Phaedra."

My mother paused and turned. It was uncanny how much they resembled one another, their hazel eyes shining in the sun, their skin tanned and glowing, as though my sister was not my mother's daughter, but her own self again, preserved in time. Perhaps that was the first time I realized that all the growing in the world was never going to turn pale, plump little me into a beauty like my mother and my sister.

"Phaedra, you are walking very slowly. Do you need one of the guards to carry you back to the palace?" I'm sure Mother said it out of concern, but even now I can feel the bolt of humiliation that shot through me at the thought of being carried through the palace gates like a sack of grain, bundled up in the arms of a guard. Ariadne snickered. I shook my head, resolute.

"No, Mama."

"Then do keep up, please."

She turned around again and began to walk once more. But the distraction had been enough to attract some peasants, working in a field, who came to stare at us, their jaws slack. I wasn't afraid. What could peasants do to us? We were surrounded by no less than eight armed men, every one of whom had placed his right hand on his sword or spear. We were royalty. Nothing could touch us.

And then one of the peasants called out something. I didn't understand what he'd said—I'd never heard the word before. My mother stumbled, her usually sure feet missing their mark. I frowned, bemused. From behind it seemed as though she had reacted to what he'd said, been hurt by it even, but surely that couldn't be possible. I ran to her side and saw her face, white, and Ariadne, clutching her other arm, stared back at me with confusion.

"Show some respect to your queen," one of the soldiers called, and slammed his spear into the ground, raising a cloud of dust that made me cough and splutter. My mother blinked a couple of times, then slowly drew herself back up to her full height.

"Leave them, please. We do not quarrel with peasants."

The soldier nodded curtly, and we moved on. Ariadne and I continued to stare at one another from our places flanking our mother, surprised by the note of fear in her voice. This was as shaken as we had ever seen her. And yet even then, I did not come to the proper conclusion, that even though we were royalty and were surrounded by men whose sole duty was to keep us safe, we could still be hurt.

That night my mother came by our room as we were preparing for bed. Ariadne, who had refused to talk to me all evening, was brushing her hair. I was staring into my basin, trying to squint so my blue eyes could appear hazel in the low light, with no success. My mother sat on my bed and, with no preface, launched straight into her message.

"Girls, you are getting older now, and you will be hearing rumors around the court. Rumors spread by our servants and even by our subjects. Words like the one the man shouted today. I want you to know that there is no truth in these rumors."

I turned to stare at her, mystified. Ariadne stopped brushing her hair and said, "What rumors, Mama? Do you mean any in particular?"

My mother inhaled sharply, then said, "There are rumors that I have been unfaithful to your father. These rumors follow every beautiful queen, as I am afraid you two will one day discover when you are married to a king, and they are very seldom true. In my case, they are certainly not. Do you understand me, Ariadne? I have never been unfaithful to your father, with no man, or"—she broke off and looked down at the floor, then continued—"or otherwise."

"I understand, Mama," Ariadne said. "I never believed it anyway."

I had no idea what they were talking about. I looked at them both, uncomprehending. I knew that there were courtiers who were starting to admire my sister; she had told me so herself, when she could bring herself to speak to me. Did courtiers admire my mother too? Not for the first time, I wished that I was not a girl, and a younger sister at that, but a boy, my world filled with possibilities. I wished my future offered more than growing up to become a queen, and a lesser one than either of the two women before me.

My mother left as abruptly as she had come. I wish she had shown some affection to me; patted me on the head, even. But she did nothing, and Ariadne got into bed and turned away from me, a sure sign that she had no interest in talking. So I was left to sit on my bed, turning the new word that I had heard over and over in my mind. *Kthenobate*. Was it something to do with animals? What could it possibly mean? There were two conclusions I could have drawn from that day, and I chose the wrong one. I had heard the fear in my mother's voice, the way that she had been embarrassed to speak to us, and I associated her words with her shame. Those peasants, with no weapons and no power, had been able to destabilize the queen of the palace, and I decided it was because of her own wrongdoing. If she had been true to the gods, the gods would have protected her. If she had been innocent, she would not have feared what anyone had to say about her.

It was not until ten summers later, when Theseus came to Crete, seeking power beyond what we could give him, that I learned the truth: that any man can throw words up into the air, and it is women who must pay when those words land.

☽

In the meantime, I banished the incident from my mind. Besides, there was enough to occupy me. Ariadne and I had a tutor who tried to school us in the basics of learning. It was a fancy of my father's, in which my mother humored him, even though she knew that there was no real reason for us to learn anything much, other than how to apply our face paint and how to ensure that a palace was well run, the honored guests taken care of, and the slaves properly directed.

But instead, my father, missing the son who had died before I was born, asked that we be taught matters of state-craft, of how to ensure that a kingdom was protected and how to make sure that peasants properly paid their dues to the court. We met all the slaves who worked so hard to keep Crete functioning, as well as the noblemen who advised my father and sometimes brought their children to court to meet us—hoping, especially if the child was a son, that we might just be tempted to fall in love, or at least in ill-timed lust, so their place at the palace would be elevated.

We learned basic accounting skills, although both of us balked at learning the notation that the counting slaves were expected to apply. We barely tolerated these lessons, and I'm afraid we were dreadful to our tutor, an elderly slave himself. For all her beauty, Ariadne longed to be out in the open air, firing arrows at targets. And me? I had a similarly unfeminine desire of my own: I wanted to paint.

Crete was famous for many things. Visitors who came to our palace, Knossos, were awed by so many features—our underground pools, our stately rooms, even our flowing water. Sometimes we suspected these visitors were just trying to flatter my father, and then we would see them holding their hands in the water fountains, exclaiming as the dirty water flushed itself away, and clean water flooded the fountains in its place. Knossos was the very center of civilization, and we knew we were lucky to live there. Or we thought we knew anyway; you can never know how lucky you are to have something until it's taken away.

But above all, Knossos was known for its murals. They decorated every spare wall, vast images so colorful and elaborately painted it was not unheard of to find visitors to the palace stroking the leaves to discover whether they felt soft, or even sticking their tongues against a dripping spoon of honey to try and taste the sweetness. The ingredients in the paints were a secret, known only to Knossos-born painters, who refused to share their recipes with outsiders.

Eventually, after much begging and crying, my father allowed me to paint one myself, on the wall outside the bedroom I shared with my sister. My mother was horrified. Painting was not an appropriate pastime for a young lady. But I loved my mosaic, the pinks and peaches I'd chosen showing off my unnaturally curved griffins. Every spare moment I had, I spent following the painters, longing to be allowed to work with them.

Most of the murals included that famous symbol of Crete, the Cretan bull. I didn't care for the bull myself, although I would never have dreamed of uttering that thought aloud. Because, as our tutor had drilled into us, we were the descendants of the Cretan bull, the form that the king of all gods Zeus had taken when he joined with our grandmother Europa, who went on to produce my father.

So, Minos was the son of the god Zeus; that was why we were the ruling family at Knossos. No one dared to challenge us, even though my father was getting older and had only daughters to secure his claim. Everyone knew that the gods looked after their own.

And we were doubly blessed. Because my mother, too, was the child of a god, this time the sun god Helios. I preferred this story because it was a gentler story, involving no deception or seduction. Helios had married a sea nymph, who gave birth to four children, of which my mother was one.

Ariadne preferred this story, too, for reasons of her own. When she had enough of lessons, she would slyly remark, "It's time for me to worship my grandfather," and she would stroll into the open courtyard and lie down on the grass, watching her brown limbs turn browner. And when we grew tired of being outside, there was the labyrinth and its hidden delights to tempt us, a second palace beneath our feet, with its own rules and its own ruler.

And so my days drifted by, a joyous mix of sun worship, escaping from lessons, and the heavy leaden smell of paint. The gods had blessed us, and I was faithful to them in return. Even though my mother tried to rein me in, to warn me that one day soon I would have to be married, to live the more restricted life of a queen, I didn't quite believe her, just as I had never quite believed in her innocence. I believed those days would carry on forever, not just for me but for Ariadne too, both of us living behind the veil of security that hid from us the true ugliness of the world. And maybe they would have done, were it not for the tributes arriving from Athens. And, in their midst, naturally, Theseus. The worst monster of all.

Xenethippe

We were the tributes, fourteen young men (if you could call Theseus young) and fourteen young women, crowded into the main hall in the Cretan palace. Knossos, it was called. And it was the most beautiful room I have ever been in. The ceiling was high, held up by magnificent columns and pillars so big I couldn't have placed my arms around them. And the walls were decorated with pictures, which someone told me later were called murals, depicting scenes from the tales of the gods.

I had grown up hearing those tales, about how Zeus defeated the Titans and how the gods visited special women to create the demigods, the kings that ruled over us all, but I'd never really felt them until now, seeing them daubed on a wall in sky blues and murky greens, yellows, bright blood reds and purples deep and dark as wine. Taking center stage was the founding of Crete itself, the white bull of Zeus visiting Europa, the mother of King Minos who was going to come and talk to us. And I'd never given it much thought before, even when I was tending to my father's bull and cattle, but looking at that picture now, that bull that was three times the size of me and at least double the size of the slender woman in the picture. Maybe it wasn't such a blessing to be visited by a god after all.

A lock of my hair fell into my eyes, and I pushed it out of the way. There were three of them, the queen and two princesses, sitting on the dais above us. The queen and the older princess lived up to the rumors we had heard about them. They were tall—far taller than me, taller than any of the men in our party, other than Theseus. They had thick, shiny hair that fell down their backs in elaborate braids. "Ariadne of the beautiful hair," I had heard the princess was called. A metallic brooch pinned it loosely back, in the shape of intricate curves and curls, mimicking the very curves of the palace itself. The women's hazel eyes glowed, and their teeth were white like marble. When they approached, every boy in our party stood a little straighter.

But what of the youngest princess, Phaedra? Not much was spoken of her back in Athens. She was reputed to be a beauty, too, but as part of a collective—"the beautiful women of Crete"—not in her own right.

I looked at her now, trailing behind her mother and sister. Begrudgingly, I had to admit that while she might not be as beautiful as her sister, there was something about her. An indefinable quality. Her hair was light, which we didn't see often in Athens, and her eyes were bright blue. Her mouth twitched as though she were laughing at a private joke. But if I had to say what that quality was? Well, innocence, I suppose.

My parents had been so pleased when we were informed that I'd been selected to represent Athens as a tribute. I was one of seven children, and worse, a girl. Our farm wouldn't have sustained all of us. Either I would have married another farmer, or, more likely, I would have been sent to the palace, to work as a maid. And everyone knew what work young maids at the palace really had to do, and the position they had to do it in.

In Crete, Athenian tributes were given food and quarters and work—*real* work. We'd always heard how their palace was so much more, well, palatial than ours. And now that I could see it for myself, it was true. When we arrived here, dirty, tired, and unkempt, we were shown into a room with a trough at the end and told to wash. We all looked at each other, no one wanting to be the first to desecrate that marble receptacle.

When the guards repeated the command, I kneeled and scrubbed my face in the water. The dirt swirled before me, a sound like a crashing wave was heard, and the grimy water disappeared, to be replaced by fresh. I fell back onto my haunches and the guards laughed, not unkindly. One of them even had an Athenian accent. He looked a little like my friend and neighbor Tritos, and I tried to remember if Tritos had a brother or a cousin who had been tribute in one of the previous calls. To think, it was possible to rise from Athenian tribute to Cretan palace guard. Crete was the land of opportunity in comparison to poor, wretched Athens.

But Theseus, the prince from nowhere, had spoken so convincingly in front of the crowd before we left Athens. Why should Athens send its best young people to Crete just because King Minos's son, Androgeus, had been killed by brigands during his Athenian travels years before? That hadn't even happened in my lifetime. What was his son to me? And besides, we were all so focused on the positions that awaited us after the test. But what about the test itself?

Before we could be assimilated into the Cretan court, we would have to spend the night in the labyrinth under the Cretan palace, built by the evil genius Daedalus. If we got lost in that labyrinth, it was reputed, we might die in there.

Just because the Cretans told us that no one had died in the labyrinth for a long time didn't mean they were telling the truth. And even the Cretans didn't deny that there was a monster at its center.

Theseus, the new prince, whom no one in Athens had even heard of before he turned up at the palace with Aegeus's cloak and sword, and a teenage son in tow, volunteered himself as tribute. He was going to kill the monster and put an end to the sacrifice of Athenian youths. There were mutterings about this, too, particularly in my parents' generation. As I said, it was seen as an honor when I was selected. So, wasn't this prince Theseus, a man twenty years too old to be described as an Athenian youth, stealing a place that could have gone to someone who had no other future in the worn-out kingdom he stood to inherit? I suppose we might have understood it a little better if Theseus's son had volunteered, but all he wanted to do was ride horses. While the tributes were being selected, he hopped from one foot to another as though he imagined himself on a horse. And he was back in the saddle almost before his father had finished his speech.

King Aegeus had blessed Theseus's plan, although his hand had clutched at his tunic briefly, as though afraid to lose a son he'd only recently discovered he had, and with that, we had boarded the ship to Athens, our entire mission changed. In previous years I had cheered and thrown flowers at the tributes leaving for Crete. This year the members of the crowd stared dully at one another, shouted a few muted cheers of "Good luck" and "See you soon, we hope," then melted away before we'd even lifted the anchor.

I kept watching the princesses. I was clean, for once, and yet their clean was cleaner than anyone I had ever seen, their faces glowing, while there was a deep tan on mine that wasn't going to wash off in a basin. I glanced towards the guards. They hadn't been unkind, true, but they also hadn't lowered their spears.

But if one of those guards was Athenian, that meant he'd faced the labyrinth and the monster at its center, and he'd survived.

That monster was the center of it all. Because if it were a real monster, a genuine, threatening monster, like the Scylla or the Charybdis, one that intended to kill us, then the Cretans were evil. If one or all of us could lose our lives tonight, then Theseus was right. Better to lose your virginity and keep your life. Although in the Athenian court, you could lose both.

I turned to look at him, and I realized that I was just following the gaze of that older princess, Ariadne. When she tossed her head and those chestnut braids rose and fell hypnotically, it was Theseus she was aiming her head at. They may as well have been the only two people in the room.

The Cretans shuffled and straightened, and we Athenians moved a little closer together, keeping Theseus at the center of our motley group. *Someone important is coming,* I thought, and sure enough, the king strode in a moment later. I remembered Aegeus back in Athens, bidding us farewell, an old, shuffling scarecrow of a man. Even the Cretans' king was of a higher caliber than ours. Minos stood tall, his hair golden like his youngest daughter's, his muscles still rippling, even though he must have been at least in his sixties. He held an axe in his hands, a special one with two heads, which I later learned was called a *labrys* and was yet another symbol of Crete.

The axe was only for ceremony, though; he almost immediately handed it to a guard, who carried it as carefully as if it were a baby to a special stand at the front of the dais. The guard bowed to Minos, who graciously inclined his head in response. I couldn't help it; I glanced at Theseus and saw a drop of longing in his eyes. Perhaps this was the type of king he hoped he would find his father to be, instead of the shaky—dare I say it?—drunkard who sent off his city's best youth to die with nothing more than a brief "Good luck."

Minos took his place at the center of the dais. The court was still, waiting for him to speak. He smiled and opened his arms wide.

"Young people of Athens, you are welcome here. You have traveled far to come to our court, and for that, we thank you." He paused. I glanced at his daughters. The younger one was transfixed, hanging on her father's every word, but the older only was clearly not concentrating. Her eyes were fixed the entire time on Theseus. "You may have already heard something about what we expect of you here. Let me put paid to rumors and gossip. To prove yourself worthy, we expect each of you to spend the night in our famous labyrinth, a maze built by the genius inventor Daedalus himself and named after the axe you have seen here before you. The labyrinth is dark and damp. I am told that there are strange echoes, perhaps the sounds of the ghosts that inhabit its very walls. This is not a task for the fainthearted. But everyone who succeeds will have proven their worth and will have Cretan citizenship in return."

I don't know if anyone would own up to making a sound, but a gasp went through us all. Citizenship? As a farm girl, as a woman, I could never have dreamed of such a thing in Athens. What we were being offered was a gift indeed. My parents had been right, for once.

"But what about the monster?" a clear voice called out. Theseus, although when I looked at him he didn't seem to have taken his eyes off Ariadne.

"The monster," Minos repeated thoughtfully. He licked his lips, and his jaws seemed larger and wolfish. "Yes, there is a monster in the labyrinth, I don't deny it. But if you are clever young people, you will stay out of its way."

☽

After Minos left, followed by his queen and daughters, we were taken to a smaller chamber with benches around the sides of the room. Serving women brought us wine, figs glistening with honey, bread dipped in olive oil. We lapped it up greedily. Only Theseus did not eat. He sat alone, the ghost of a smile playing on his lips.

I glanced at the murals that covered this chamber too. On the far wall, a picture I hadn't seen before, a man with a bull's head and a muscular human torso. The man seemed to rear out of the picture. The paint was still fresh. The picture worried me; I had heard of the gods taking human form, but not a form like this. A form so depraved. This could only be a depiction of—

"The monster," Pallas, a young shepherd boy I vaguely knew from back home, seemed to have read my mind. "What is he like?"

The guards exchanged glances, and the one who did not look like Tritos said, "Like a fearsome monster. The kind that would make your blood curdle."

We all looked around at each other, none the wiser. "But there are many kinds of monsters," Pallas. "Is he a giant, like the Cyclops, or a beautiful woman, like the siren, or—"

"Not a beautiful woman," the other guard said quickly, his Athenian accent stronger than ever. Now I was sure he was one of ours. "Definitely not that. Don't get your hopes up."

"You have actually seen the monster?" I asked; foolish, to stick my head above the parapet, especially when Pallas was probably about to ask the same question.

"Of course we have," the Cretan guard said a little too emphatically, and we all breathed a sigh of relief. Clearly they had not.

A new mood spread over our party. We were no longer willing tributes. Instead, we were revolutionaries, fighters, united behind the good Prince Theseus.

"We need someone to take the bowls back," the Cretan guard said suddenly. "Who . . .?" he looked at us. I didn't dare volunteer, but I leaned forward subtly and made eye contact when everyone else was looking away. It worked. "You, girl," he waved at me. I stood up, trying not to look too eager.

"Take these plates to the kitchen," he instructed me. I raised my eyebrows slightly.

"She has no idea where that is," the Athenian guard said, his tone light. "Down the corridor, turn right at the fountain, then right again at the mural of the bull—the white bull with silver horns," he said quickly before I could raise my eyebrows again. This place was full of murals of bulls. We had had a bull on our farm, but it was an old, decrepit beast that was good for nothing except fathering offspring on unwilling cows. "Once you get within spitting distance of the kitchen with the bowls, someone will pull you in anyway."

They stacked me up with bowls. I could have used a hand, but they didn't suggest it, and I didn't want a companion. This was my opportunity to explore the palace, after all.

I staggered down the corridor, peering around my bowls, looking for the fountain, then the mural of the bull. The fountain was huge and possibly the most beautiful man-made feature I had ever seen, incandescent drops of water shimmering in the sunlight. The guard had been right; I had no sooner taken a step around the corridor than a serving woman appeared to snatch the bowls away from me. My task was done here.

I should have headed straight back. The route was simple enough. But perhaps I could claim ignorance and explore a little further. I didn't plan on getting too lost. Instead of going back the way I had come, I turned right, then right again, and found myself facing yet another bull, the painted beast rearing above me. I turned to go back towards the chamber where my fellow tributes were waiting, and bumped into a solid mass of a man.

I knew as soon as he grabbed my arm that I wasn't going to get out of this easily. I cursed myself for letting my guard down. I would never have made such a mistake in the Athenian palace, but then, in a hovel, you assume that the men will be pigs. I'd allowed the ostensible sophistication of Knossos, with its running water and pretty painted walls, to fool me, but men were still men.

He pulled my arm up above my head and sneered at me. I opened my mouth to scream, but at that moment we were interrupted by a soft female voice.

"Let her go at once!"

My attacker and I both looked in the direction of the voice, and it is hard to say which of us was more surprised. He dropped my arm and bowed clumsily to the person running down the colonnade towards us.

"Your Highness," he said. Then he turned on his heel and left. I leaned against the wall and looked at my skin, a sour red mark encircling my upper arm.

"That looks painful," the girl said. "You should ask a physician about it." I looked at her. She was one of the princesses. The younger one. *The less pretty one,* I thought nastily.

"Yes, Your Highness," I said, raising myself off the wall, ready to go. She remained standing in front of me.

"Do you know that man?"

"No, Your Highness." Why, by Zeus and all the Olympians, would I know him?

"Well, are you going to tell someone about him?" she demanded, her tone imperious.

"Tell someone?" I tried not to laugh. "Tell whom? And what would I say?" We must have been about the same age, but her naivety made her sound like a child.

"He really hurt you. We don't allow behavior like that at Knossos!"

"I did not know, Your Highness. I have recently arrived from Athens." I tried to keep my voice level. It wouldn't do for her to realize I was laughing at her.

"Then you must know that we require a higher code of conduct here. He is one of my father's men. He should mind his manners."

"Your Highness, I must go. I am expected back with the other tributes." I gestured vaguely towards the direction I might have come from.

"I don't understand why you're not more upset about this," she burst out. "He really hurt you. Did you want him to do that?"

"No, Your Highness," I said, and this time I couldn't prevent my tone from sounding exasperated. It was one thing for me not to be more upset about a little grope that came to nothing. It was another thing entirely for her to imply that I had sought his attention.

"Then what is it that you are not telling me?" She was frowning, that pretty peach nose wrinkling in a fashion that I was sure all the courtiers found most charming. Perhaps they even composed poetry about it. But I wasn't a courtier myself. I was just a farm girl, and I told it the way I saw it.

"Your Highness, perhaps your father's men have a better code of conduct in public or when they are in the presence of women they deem their social equals. But behind closed doors, I can assure you that they are every bit as much animals as the men out there in those fields behind you. More so, because those are family men with their wives and children, and these so-called courtiers have left their wives behind to come to the palace for drinking and backslapping and whoring."

An ugly red flush appeared at her neck. "I could have you killed for speaking to me like that," she said slowly.

"You could. And then you would have done me more harm than the man you rescued me from." I raised my chin defiantly.

"What can I do?" she asked, her voice small and her shoulders slumping.

I shook my head, suddenly tired. "Nothing, Your Highness. Do not concern yourself."

There seemed to be nothing more to say. She watched me as I stepped around her to return to the other tributes. I made my way down the colonnade, then turned and looked back at her. She looked so sad, I wanted to say something to comfort her.

"Princess, you are . . . kind, and I'm sorry I was curt with you. Knossos is beautiful. I'm glad I came here."

She smiled, then said, "But that man . . ."

I laughed, a bitter sound with no mirth. "Knossos has its hidden secrets, its labyrinth below the surface. But Athens keeps nothing below the surface. Anger, greed, and lechery are all on display. And no one is safe."

I bit my tongue, afraid I'd said too much. She opened her mouth again, but then in the distance, we heard someone calling to her, and she whirled around and disappeared, leaving me alone in the corridor, my thoughts gyrating like dust motes in the sunlight.

Night Chorus

Crete, Crete, Crete. It looks so clean, it looks so bright. Its citizens are all honest, upright men. But we know what is beneath the surface. We don't mean the labyrinth.

They come to visit us, these upstanding citizens. They leave their wives on their farms and their estates, and they make use of the facilities of Knossos. They wash their hands in our fountains. They eat the king's fine food. They run those hands over our bodies. We are nothing more to them than another service, another amenity.

Then they go back to their wives, refreshed. Ready to serve Crete. To serve Minos. No thanks to us.

Xenethippe

I made my way back, this time being more alert to the hidden dangers that dwelt below the pretty murals. When I walked in, everyone stopped talking, then started again, relieved, no doubt, that it was only me. I could only make out one word from the babble: *Minotaur.*

"Stop." I held my hand up. "What are you all talking about?" I looked towards Theseus, but he remained silent, staring into space. I felt a twinge of annoyance. I don't know why it was that Theseus's magic never worked on me. Perhaps it was that wolfish set to his jaw.

So while Theseus continued to stare into space and presumably dream about the Cretan princess, Aias, a tall, gangly youth with a rash of pimples on his chin, told me about the Minotaur.

"They say he has the body of a man and the head of a bull," he said excitedly. I nodded; I could see that much from the painting on the wall behind him.

"But there's more than that. You'll never guess who his mother is."

I raised an eyebrow. "Some goddess, no doubt."

"Wrong! The queen of Crete, Queen Pasiphaë herself." He couldn't have looked more pleased if he'd impregnated her himself.

"Really? Then the father must be a god?" I was drawn in despite myself.

"Wrong again! The queen was besotted with a bull. An actual bull, in the field! Can you believe it? So she had Daedalus create a cow costume for her, and that's how she ended up giving birth to a monster."

I looked around. I could see that those of us who were farmers' children were looking more sceptical. This was not how we understood these matters to work.

"Perhaps she angered a god," Circe, a farmer's daughter from the far outskirts of Attica, ventured at last.

"Must have done," I agreed. The gods were known to be quick to anger. But why one woman had sex with Zeus in the form of a bull and gave birth to King Minos, while another did almost the same thing and gave birth to a monster, I had no idea. The others were making crude jokes about the palace murals with their preponderance of bulls, but I sank back and thought about that beautiful, elegant queen I had just seen, with her graceful daughters. To think that the same woman could have birthed those girls and the bull-headed monster. And how did she birth it, anyway? I'd seen cows giving birth. A human woman would have been torn in half. I shivered and tried to imagine something else. I noticed Theseus watching me. His cool gaze from cold grey eyes didn't make me feel any better. I slipped off the bench and casually approached the guards.

"Yes?" the Cretan guard asked; I wished it had been the other one.

"I was just wondering. Do you know Tritos?" I smiled, just making chit-chat, even though the guard had a spear and I was unarmed.

"Yes, I do," the Athenian guard said. "He's my cousin. How do you know him? Did he ask after me?"

"Not exactly," I acknowledged. "He's my neighbor. You resemble him."

"Ah, little Tritos. I'm amazed he isn't here, actually. This would be his year, wouldn't it?"

I thought of Tritos, his chest still pudgy with puppy fat. It was possible that in a different year he might have been selected—his archery skills weren't bad—but this year, he hadn't even bothered applying. I tried to answer tactfully. "I think his family needed more help with the harvest than expected this year."

"Help with the harvest" was always the excuse given, implying as it did that the family had had such a bumper crop that they didn't need to send one of their children away to make a living.

The guard understood the code, because he nodded and didn't ask any further. Instead, he said, "I'm Kitos, and this is Palos."

"We're not supposed to fraternize with the tributes," Palos objected, but half-heartedly.

"Ah, this one's a neighbor of my cousin. That makes her my neighbor." I could feel him looking me up and down, but unlike in the encounter outside, I didn't mind. After all, I'd been doing the same to him.

"So if you're from Athens, that means you survived this night?" I asked. He laughed.

"Everyone survives. Don't listen to the nonsense that lot are talking about a monster." He jerked a thumb at the others, whose conversation had left behind the sexual encounters of the queen and returned again to the beast we were to face.

"So there's no monster?" I asked.

Kitos looked at Palos.

Palos shrugged. "I think there's a monster. The kitchens send meat and other delicacies to the labyrinth every night. But . . ."

"Yes?" I prompted.

"No one's seen this monster for a long time. I mean, a really long time. So maybe it's an old monster now. Maybe it's just not that interested in us."

Kitos nodded. "We're not supposed to tell you this—"

"So don't," Palos interrupted, but again, his tone was languid, and he made no effort to stop the Athenian.

"Just stay close to the entrance to the labyrinth," Kitos continued. I focused my eyes on his chiseled face, which was not exactly a hardship. The resemblance to Tritos was lessening with every word he said. "The real danger isn't a monster—it's the labyrinth itself. If you get lost in there, it can take days before they find you."

"People have been known to go mad," Palos chipped in.

"Why are you telling me this?"

Kitos grinned. "Maybe I'd like to see you come out again."

I could feel a matching grin spreading over my face. It vanished again when I remembered that Theseus was taking us all home to Athens again, where the only possible employment was serving the drunk lords at the court their wine, then smelling it on their breath later.

☽

At twilight, we were taken to the entrance to the labyrinth. It was in the very center of the palace, which I hadn't expected. With a shiver, I realized that the labyrinth and its monster must have been under our feet the whole time.

We were led down the steps and into the cavern that opened out into the labyrinth. The rules were simple. We were each to walk, one by one, into the darkness. While we were not to wait for one another, we were permitted to join forces should we meet inside the winding paths. We were reminded that there was a monster, and we should not remain in one place. We were to stay inside the labyrinth until daybreak, when a horn would be sounded, and we could make our way back to the entrance. A light would be shone into the cavern to help us find our way.

If we came back any earlier, the guards would ensure that we returned into the darkness. That was it, simple enough. It was what wasn't said that was more chilling to me: What happened if we didn't make it out? Clearly no one was coming to find us. I wasn't worried about the monster. I was more worried about dying alone in the dark.

For that reason, I disregarded the advice about staying in one spot. Instead, I remembered what Kitos had told me. I walked into the labyrinth in my turn, shivering as the cavern grew darker and danker. I turned left, then left again, then left once more. I could no longer see the entrance, but I knew exactly where it was. Then I found a little alcove and snuggled down into it. I considered sleeping, but it was too cold for that. Instead, I pulled my cloak about me and waited for the daybreak.

My eyes gradually adjusted to the dark, but not perfectly, so I could see only about two meters in front of me, after which the darkness seemed to stretch out forever. After a while it seemed as though water had crept into my bones, chilling me from the inside out. This was the cost of that running water up above, I realized suddenly. It had to come from somewhere. But it also had to go somewhere, and here it smelled, a sour stench that perforated my nostrils and overwhelmed my brain. I would never be able to rid my skin of that smell, not even with the magical Cretan water basins.

And then there were the noises, sounds that in daylight I'm sure I could have correctly interpreted as winds rushing through the tunnels. But in the dark, it sounded as though the ghosts of the Cretan ancestors were wailing through the tunnels. In addition to those cries were the cries of the living: my fellow tributes, wandering the passages, sobbing in fear.

I stayed still, and then I realized that I had another problem: With no access to sunlight, I had no way of knowing how much time had passed. It was probably less time than it felt, but how would I know when I should return to the surface? I was close enough to the entrance that I should hear the other tributes returning, but what if they got it wrong? There were so many questions I should have asked Kitos. I huddled into my alcove and tried to banish the mural from my mind: that terrible deformed figure with horns sprouting like short swords from its head.

I needn't have worried. Because as it turned out, sleep came to me. I dozed, dimly aware of the jagged edge of wet rock pressing into my lower back. After what could have been minutes or hours, I was woken by a horrific scream the likes of which I had never heard before and hope never to hear again. It was the sound of a creature in pain—terrible, soul-destroying pain. I'd never heard anything like it on the farm, but I told myself it had to have been an animal, a beast. It certainly couldn't have been human, even if it did sound at first as though it were calling for its mother. The tunnels, playing tricks on me again.

I forgot the injunction not to look for one another, and I raced towards the source of the noise, sure that one of my fellow tributes was being gored by the monster with the body of a man, the head of a bull, and the heart of a demon.

I didn't get very far before, to my surprise, I was overtaken by guards racing past me, spears and swords at the ready. I was so shocked I stumbled to a standstill. The guards weren't supposed to come to our aid; that defeated the very purpose of this test.

And yet here they were, thundering down the passages. I dropped out of sight into another alcove, not wanting to be run down where I stood. After they had passed, I started to follow them, more slowly now as I didn't want to lose my bearings, and besides, what could I do that an armed flank couldn't? And so, because I was walking slowly, I was one of the first to see him after he gave the slip to the guards and made his way to the entrance to the cavern.

My heart seemed to stop in my chest. I didn't understand what I was seeing. It had human legs, long and wiry, but where a man's body should be I could see horns, bigger than my own torso, drooping down and swinging back and forth. It was this erratic motion that confused me; it did not seem to follow any sort of direction, and I thought that the monster must be mad and about to charge for me.

I put my hands behind my back and felt for the wall. I had no weapons. No princess was going to save me this time. But the beast blundered on past, those legs focused even while the head bobbed about crazily, and I took a deep breath and began to follow it, thinking that if I kept it in my sights, I knew it wasn't behind me.

As we came closer to the entrance to the labyrinth and the light, the puzzle ahead seemed to resolve itself, and I saw I was not seeing one malformed monster, but a man carrying the head of a beast and the body of a man, somehow balancing his twin loads so that the head of the beast hung down to one side and the legs of the man to the other. And as I continued to follow, letting go of the wall now, I finally saw that the object being carried was both a man and a monster, the body of a man with the head and horns of a bull. What was more, it was dead, its head bouncing from side to side. And finally, as they stepped out into the final passage, with a crowd of people waiting for them at the other side, I saw that the man was Theseus, and he was carrying the Minotaur.

Phaedra

No one ever slept much the night the tributes went into the labyrinth. There was too much excitement in the air. Some people even threw "labyrinth parties," and it was well known that certain members of court could be relied upon to take wagers as to which of the tributes would be the first to emerge. Ariadne and I were always warned that it would be most unseemly for us to be found at one of those parties, which was why I was surprised when I retired to our room to find her bed untouched. Surprised, but not shocked. Ariadne always pushed a little harder at boundaries than I did.

I hadn't even removed my chiton when I heard the shouting. At first I froze. Were we under attack? My first instinct was to barricade my door, but then I heard footsteps rushing past and heard someone call, "The Minotaur!" Swiftly I pulled my peplos over my clothes and joined the throngs of people hurrying towards the entrance to the labyrinth. When I reached it, I noted without thought that my mother and father were already standing at the entrance, my mother's long hair unbraided and flowing over her shoulders. But then I saw the man who had emerged from that bitter cold entrance, and I had eyes for nothing else.

One of the tributes, the tall, severe-looking one, was bowed under the weight of a giant beast. Blood was dripping off his arms and splashing onto the floor, a hot,

metallic smell rising to my nose, completely annihilating
the smell of the cavern. It could have been his blood, I suppose, but I never really thought so.

The tribute walked to the front of the cave and paused
for a moment, silhouetted in the light. Then he raised his
burden high above his head, every muscle rippling, and
dropped it to the ground with a thud so loud it reverberated in my ears. He remained standing there, his chest
heaving.

I looked around at my own people, the Cretans. No one
moved. No one even spoke. It would be usual to smell wine
on the breath of most of those there, after a night of revelry,
but it was as though everyone had sobered in an instant. My
father was fully dressed, his robes resplendent in the early
morning light. And my mother's face was impassive and
still. She hadn't seen me, but I knew what she would expect.
I, too, remained still. Then I saw the entrails that slipped
and slithered across the tribute's hands, and I covered my
face with my hands.

Still no one spoke. The stench of blood continued to rise
from the body as the tribute stared directly at my father, as
though challenging him. My father hunched a little. He
opened his mouth and closed it again—a mistake.

It was the tribute who finally broke the silence. "No longer will Athenian youths be sent as tributes to Crete, Minos.
I am Theseus, prince of Athens, and I declare it to be so."
Although his voice caught where he hadn't quite got his
breath back, his words were firm.

My father's mouth tightened. "Your Highness." He
looked as though he were struggling for words, but eventually he said, "I had heard that King Aegeus had been joined

by a son. But I would have expected him to announce his visit, not sneak in like a thief in the night."

Theseus remained standing tall despite the rebuke. "I have come to rescue my people. I will take all the tributes back with me, past and present."

There was a little murmur through the guards at this, not entirely a positive one.

My father said, "Any Athenian"—and he stressed the word *Athenian*—"will be welcome to leave with you. As indeed, they are all free to do at any time. We do not keep our citizens prisoner here."

Theseus looked satisfied at this but then added, "And what if there are any Cretans who wish to leave? Do you keep them prisoner?"

I had expected my father to rage at that. Instead, he looked sadly at the viscous mess oozing from Theseus's hands and said, "If any Cretans wish to leave with you, they are *not* Cretans."

He turned and walked away, his walk almost a shuffle. He had aged in the last twelve hours, while Theseus seemed to have taken on more of his mantle. Theseus stood tall over the corpse. I wondered if my mother would go to the body now, but she turned and followed my father, her head held high.

Slowly, my fellow Cretans also drifted away. Theseus stepped down and dipped his finger in the blood, then touched it to his forehead. He had marked his kill now, and he, too, stepped away, wincing slightly as he did, as though he didn't want to be associated with such a vile event.

He detached something from his waist, a golden ball of twine, and then I felt my heart truly would stop. Theseus's shoulders sagged as he walked away, presumably in the direction of his boat. Again, the resemblance to my father struck me, and in that instant, I knew that Theseus was who he said he was. There was something majestic about him. I was the granddaughter of a god. I recognised my own kind.

Everyone had gone now. Quietly, I stepped towards the bloody mess Theseus had left behind, then knelt down and placed my hand gently on those once-fearsome horns. I wanted to cry, but I knew I was taking enough liberties. Soon my parents would be looking for me, and not only me. Ariadne had not gone to a party after all.

I would have stayed there forever, but I heard the soft noise of someone clearing her throat. I looked up and saw one of the tributes, the girl I had spoken to earlier. For a few moments, I just stared at her, unsure what she was doing there, or if she even was there at all. She looked back at me, perhaps wondering the same thing. Finally, I spoke. "You've come out of the labyrinth, haven't you? Have you seen my sister?"

"Your sister, Your Highness? No, why do you ask?" Then, as my meaning dawned on her, "You think your sister is in the labyrinth? Should someone not be sent to find her?"

Her words puzzled me still further. Nothing about this morning was making sense, except for that gold ball of twine attached to Theseus's waist. But I answered the girl anyway. "Oh no, she won't need anyone to help her out of there. If she wants to stay in there, she will stay forever."

"Why do you think she went in there?" the girl asked. She was being overly familiar, but perhaps she, too, was affected by the strangeness of the situation. I answered her anyway.

"I shouldn't say."

"Was it because of Theseus?" she asked.

"I really shouldn't say," I said again, and then, "But I never expected this." I stroked one of the once mighty horns and shivered.

She frowned, then took another tack. "Your Highness, the other tributes—they may be lost in the labyrinth."

I hadn't expected that response. "Hasn't anyone brought them out?" The sun had moved a quarter of the way across the sky. *They should all be out by now*, I thought. But everyone had left them behind.

"No, Your Highness. They are still inside. Would you be able to find someone who can fetch them out? Could you instruct one of the slaves or the guards?"

"Slaves or guards? What good would they be? I'd better go and find them."

"*You*, Your Highness?" she asked.

"Yes, me. No one knows this labyrinth better than me, after all. Well, no one except Ariadne, but she's not here." *Oh, Ariadne, what have you done?*

I no longer cared what this unknown girl thought of me. I brought my lips down to the broad forehead in front of me, then whispered a few words to the gods. I stroked the horns, symbol of Crete and all it stood for, and I asked the gods to wreak their vengeance and to let me witness it. That would have to do. I could make proper libations later, but for now, I had to usher those poor Athenians out of the labyrinth. Most of them were little more than children, and they would be terrified. I strode towards the entrance to the labyrinth, then turned and looked back at the girl. "Are you coming?"

She muttered, "I suppose so."

"Then we will need equipment. Wait here."

I went to my own room to find an old peplos for her, and a portion of bread that had been left for my breakfast. I couldn't have eaten then anyway. I also lit a torch; I wouldn't need it, but it might make the tributes feel safer. I returned to the labyrinth and passed the peplos and bread to the girl. The eagerness with which she received them both shamed me. She probably hadn't eaten all night.

To calm her further, as we walked through the labyrinth I pointed out the various features which I knew so well. The light danced on the ceiling. I had never taken anyone through before, and in other circumstances, I might have enjoyed it.

One by one, her fellow tributes emerged from the shadows, blinking in the unexpected light like moles emerging into the sunlight. They all spoke very little after expressing their initial, mumbled thanks.

"What people don't realize is that it's a labyrinth, not a maze," I said carelessly, finishing my tour as we rounded up the last tribute.

"Are they different?" the girl asked hesitantly.

"Oh yes. Very different. A labyrinth has only one path to the center. A maze has many. So if you keep your wits about you, you can't go wrong."

"Where is the center?" she asked. "Can we see it?"

"I . . . I'd rather not take you there," I said, sadness overwhelming me as the reasons for our impromptu tour flooded back to me. "Not today. Besides, these people would rather have some food and a bath."

I could hear the snickers behind me. I supposed no one was going to draw them a bath, but I had done as much as I could.

Soon we came to the opening and walked out. Although there was nobody waiting to greet us, I saw that the Minotaur's remains had been cleaned away. Like everything in Knossos, the floor was once again gleaming and immaculate. I pointed the tributes in the direction of their ship and left for my own room, needing sleep before I confronted my parents and told them about the ball of gold twine I knew would be missing from the dresser I shared with Ariadne.

Xenethippe

The princess slipped away, and I updated everyone. Outwardly, we all rejoiced, but inwardly, I suspect I wasn't the only one who would have preferred Theseus kept his savior complex to himself.

Seemingly forgotten by everyone, we roamed Knossos in a pack. There was tension everywhere we went, people skulking in corners and whispering behind pillars. We bumped into Kitos, who glared at me.

"You could have warned me. Who is this Prince Theseus anyway? Aegeus didn't have a son."

"He does now," I said wearily. Minos had said he had heard of the new prince, but obviously that knowledge hadn't trickled down to the troops. "Aegeus fathered him on a peasant woman, forty years ago. He left his sword and cloak and told the woman to instruct the prince to come to Athens to claim his birthright."

Kitos raised his eyebrows. "And it took him forty years to do so?"

"Apparently," I said. "Is there somewhere we can get some food? Most of us haven't eaten."

He looked at the row of ducklings following behind me. "By rights, I should send you all down to the shore, to Prince Theseus's boat. Goodness knows, enough people have told me to go down there this morning—people I thought were

my friends." I didn't say anything. He sighed. "Come on.
We can get some food in the guards' quarters."

Gratefully we accompanied him to an airy room,
much like soldiers' quarters anywhere. There were long
benches pulled up to rough tables, and men shouted
and called to one another while women bustled about
with plates of food. I devoured my share and didn't mention that I'd already had some bread.

"So why do you think Theseus has turned up now?"
Kitos asked. He seemed unwilling to leave, although
whether that was because he preferred our company or
because no one else wanted to sit with him, I didn't know.

"Just between us?" I asked, using a hunk of bread to
wipe my bowl clean. "Aegeus is old, and he has no other
heir. There's a kingdom going spare there."

"Yes, but . . ." Kitos paused, perhaps trying not to be rude.
"The kingdom is Athens. It's a bit of a joke, isn't it? There's
utter lawlessness in the palace. None of the surrounding peasants ever pay their dues. You know why Aegeus continues to
send the tributes? Because Minos pays him for them."

I hadn't known, but somehow the knowledge didn't surprise me. I wondered if Theseus knew, though.

"Yes, but . . ." I thought of Theseus, of his cold gray eyes.
"I suspect Theseus has bigger plans for Athens."

Kitos threw back his head and roared with laughter.
"Big plans for Athens? Good luck to him."

"Are you going to go back?" I asked, although I already
knew the answer.

"No, I am not. Go back to a king who sold me like chat-
tel? My parents who have eight children younger than me

and could barely remember my name? Marry some Athenian girl who has spread her legs for half the court before me? Look, Xenethippe, here I am a Cretan guard. That means something. I've been given opportunities. I've been encouraged and allowed to grow. Here I can take a wife and support her and children too. And look at the palace!" He threw an arm out, not caring now who heard us. "It's always clean! The geniuses who designed this place made the river flow through the palace itself. And that's not just for the king and his closest advisers. Everyone here can access it. What does Athens have to offer that can rival Knossos?"

"You make me wish I could stay myself," I joked, feeling awkward in the face of so much passion. His chest heaved and his dark brown eyes were clear and earnest.

"So stay. No one is stopping you."

"But King Minos said—"

"Minos didn't say you have to go. He just said Theseus could take with him anyone who wanted to go. And he will find there are fewer of those than he thinks."

"He might not," I realized suddenly. "There's not that much room in the boat."

Kitos laughed, then looked serious again. "I do not trust this Prince Theseus. I wish you would stay, Xenethippe."

"And do what? Crete is very progressive, but I don't think Minos is looking for a female guard."

"You haven't seen the bull leapers," he said. "Those girls are fearless. I'd rather have them watching over me than half the men in here."

I raised an eyebrow. Around us, men were clearing their plates and getting up to go back to work. The other tributes had eaten their fill and were waiting for me to tell them what to do next. Under the noise and clatter, I could just make out what Kitos was saying.

"You could be my wife. It might not be what you came to Knossos for, but it would be an adventure. And you seem like a girl who is up for adventure."

I flushed red. I could feel the blood lighting up my face, belying any denial I might make about the effect Kitos's words had on me. He stood up.

"Just something to think about. Now if I were you, I would take your little ducklings back to the boat. If there really are limited spaces, I wouldn't count on Theseus waiting for you."

I took his advice and we meandered back to the boat, unsure what to do with ourselves again. One or two tried to talk to me about Kitos, but I brushed them off. I'd rather spend time with my own thoughts, processing what he had said. Did he really mean it? Or had he said it knowing that I was going back to Athens, and it was an offer he'd never have to make good on?

☽

When we reached the boat, Theseus was sitting in the stern with the captain, Pirithous. Those two were cut from the same cloth, tall, lean men with gray eyes and strong jaws. Men you wouldn't like to cross. They had been conferring quietly, but they looked up when we approached.

"Here you all are. You took your time," Theseus called. I wanted to object; he had left everyone in a labyrinth. But that cool, assessing gaze made me hold my tongue. I'd stood out from the crowd enough already.

Theseus scanned us while we stood silently, waiting to be allowed to board the boat again.

"Pirithous, they are all the current crop of tributes. We haven't been joined by more than a handful of Athenians from the previous years."

"Yes, sire," Pirithous said; clearly, a man of few words.

"Do you think this is a problem? Will it weaken our position with Minos?" Theseus sucked in air, concern showing on his face.

"Perhaps, sire, but it resolves another problem for us. There wouldn't have been room in the boat to take them back."

Theseus laughed and clapped the man on the shoulder. "A good point, Pirithous. And we can always come back to recover them, once we have made the changes in Athens we are planning. They will all want to join us then."

Changes in Athens? I wondered what he was talking about. But his next words were to send a shiver down my back.

"And besides, Pirithous, we may not have a boatful of Athenians, but we have something better in the hold. Something closer to Minos's heart." And Theseus grinned, the wolfish smile that mirrored the bloodthirsty gaze of the bull king.

I stepped onto the gangplank to board the boat, worried about what I might see in the hold.

Phaedra

I sat upright in the chair, avoiding the temptation to fidget, to slouch, and to kick my legs. This had been Ariadne's chair, and I didn't want to give my parents any reason to believe I wasn't ready to take her place. She'd been missing for an entire week now, and although she'd left us no message, we all assumed she'd been on Theseus's ship the day it set sail for Athens. Except now it was back again. I couldn't bear the thought of not seeing my sister, so I'd begged my parents to allow me to be present here when Theseus returned.

I looked across at my mother, but she wasn't paying me any attention. She was crossing and uncrossing her hands in her lap. I could see a tiny spot of blood by the cuticle of her left index finger. The sight shocked me and took my mind off my discomfort temporarily. For a woman like my mother, that little drop of red blood was as scandalous as if she had stripped naked in front of the entire court.

I looked around that court now, wondering whether I could see what was making my mother so nervous. All the great lords were assembled below the dais, and it seemed that, like me, they'd all decided to be on their best behavior.

For a full seven days, I had been the only royal daughter at court. It had been almost unbearable. They had stationed three extra guards outside my room. I protested, saying that I was perfectly safe, but they had not listened to me, and after I'd almost made myself hoarse with arguing, I realized that the guards were not there to keep intruders out—after all, had Theseus not already left with the greatest prize of all?—but to keep me in. I understood this instinct a little better, because I, too, had thought I knew Ariadne, and yet I could not comprehend her actions, so I ceased complaining.

My parents had also tried to question me several times about Ariadne, her motives and her movements. But I had had no more idea of what she was planning than they did. If it weren't for that ball of twine, and Theseus's unerring path to the center of the labyrinth, I'd believe it was as likely she had slipped into the ocean as run away with Theseus. She had not discussed with me her plan to assist Theseus through the labyrinth. I did not know where they had gone.

There was no question that she had assisted him. I had seen him emerge myself, glittering ball of thread tucked into his tunic. There were very few people who could help him to move through the labyrinth so easily anyway; Ariadne was one, I was another, and the third was dead. Besides, I had also seen that ball of thread perched on Ariadne's dresser for a full moon of days, a gift from an admirer she had not known what to do with.

I could not explain Ariadne's actions, but my heart broke just as much as my parents' every time I remembered the consequences, and so I tried to be as tolerant as possible of the questioning.

I sought my own answers in the small shrine at the back of the court. Knossos has shrines and temples every way you might look, but I decided the best god to pray to was not a Cretan favorite but an Athenian one. I prayed constantly to Poseidon, Theseus's father. It seemed counterintuitive, and yet all the gods understood the need for vengeance. I could have prayed to my own grandfathers, Zeus and Helios, but they would already favor my suit. I wanted to ensure that the entire pantheon was ready to inflict the punishment that Theseus deserved.

A scuffling of feet brought my attention back to the scene in front of me. The lords were exceedingly dull, and as this was a state occasion, the ladies were not present, so I could not admire or condemn their hairstyles. Instead, I stared at the frescoes, willing them to move. I had always disliked the frescoes in the Great Hall. They were gloomy, maroon and burgundy, punctuated with the occasional white bull, and they mostly depicted scenes of gore: bulls gouging men, bulls trampling men, bulls and men in a battle. Bulls were the symbol of Crete, and you couldn't escape them, but right now they just reminded me of what Theseus had destroyed.

I looked at my father in his horned helmet. He smiled at me. Weakly, I brought myself to smile back. I knew we had an image to uphold. I had been told enough times in the last week alone, never mind the lifetime that preceded it.

I watched as he leaned towards my mother, but before he could say anything, the doors to the Great Hall swung open and the Athenians strode in. There was a murmur from the people below us, which was quickly extinguished. I sat forward, straining for a glimpse of her. There were more muffled whispers from the crowd below, and from the corner of my eye, I saw my mother reach out her hand, pale and trembling, and my father grasp it in his own. Something was wrong.

The Athenians parted to allow Theseus to step to the front. Theseus. Taller than I had remembered, with a craggy face that never broke into a smile. I felt again the hot fervor of rage that boiled up from within me at the sight of him, and not just because he had taken my sister from me. I had promised my parents that if I were allowed to join this meeting, I would not allow that rage to show. I gritted my teeth and pushed my body down into my chair, determined not to spring to my feet and denounce him as a murderer and a violator of the principles of the gods. The gods would punish him, my mother had said. And I believed her, because anything else would make living unbearable. But where was my sister?

As if in mockery of my thoughts, Theseus began to speak.

"Your majesties, King Minos and Queen Pasiphaë, I bring you news. Good news for you, although not so for me."

He paused and looked about him. He didn't look particularly upset, I thought sourly. The same idea must have occurred to him, because he dropped his head. Like a flock of geese, the Athenians copied him. Most of them were unknown to me, the young men and women who had come to Crete with Theseus, but a few had worked in our court for years. There was Ajax, for instance, one of our cooks, and Alexandra, who had been a handmaid to our mother. They had known Ariadne and me since we were children, and yet they dropped their heads with the rest of them. And then there were the other Athenians, the warriors who had come in the second ship that was currently docked in our harbor. They hadn't accompanied Theseus on his first visit, when we hadn't known who he was.

"Your majesties, we left your kingdom only a week ago and have been beset by storms ever since. We were forced to dock at a small island not far from here." Theseus paused again, then looked directly at my father. "While on that island we were blessed with a visit from the god Dionysos himself, together with his loyal followers. And who could be surprised that Dionysos, showing the good taste for which he is renowned, fell in love with your daughter, the beautiful Ariadne, who was to have been my bride when we reached Athens."

I heard my mother gasp beside me and looked over to see her grip her hands together tightly. Her mouth was working but no words came out. I had no words myself. Where did Dionysos live? I wondered. On Olympus, of course. When Hades had taken a similar liking to Persephone, he took her to the Underworld. Would the same thing happen to my sister? Athens had already seemed a world away. Was I ever going to see her again?

Finally, my father spoke. His voice was much deeper than Theseus's, and yet he sounded less sure of himself. "Theseus, thank you for coming back to us with this news. Ariadne's mother and I thank you for thinking of us in this way and for"—he looked down at his chest briefly, then back to Theseus—"for letting our daughter go to join the great god Dionysos, one of the twelve Olympians. As you know, I myself am descended from the great god Zeus, and therefore it is not surprising that another god should have fallen in love with my daughter."

I was surprised; his words seemed innocuous enough, but his hand twirled around the hilt of his sword. He meant to send Theseus a message, but I was not sure what that message was.

Theseus dropped his head. "You are most welcome, King Minos."

It was as though the entire court breathed a sigh of relief. I could see the noblemen below relaxing in their seats, loosening their grip on their swords.

"Will you stay and rest before your journey back to Athens? We can offer you more provisions," my father said, leaning forward. I supposed he could afford to be generous now. My sister was going to marry a god.

"Provisions, yes, but there is something else I will need." Theseus looked around the court and smiled, but his eyes didn't crinkle. "I intended for Ariadne and me to be the start of a beautiful alliance between Athens and Crete, a symbol of the new order. I'm happy for you, King Minos, that your daughter has been so honored, but it does leave me without a bride."

My mother let slip a small cry, and my father hushed her with a glare.

"Prince Theseus," he said, holding up his arms. "We do not grow brides on the vine here in Crete."

It was then Theseus turned that cold stare to me, as if bartering for meat in a market. "You have a younger daughter, do you not? The Princess Phaedra?"

It took everything I had not to leap and run from my chair. This was a state of affairs I had not expected. I looked more closely at Theseus.

"Phaedra is still young," my father said.

"Old enough, I understand. Come, Minos, do you suppose I will not look after your daughter? She will be a queen, the Queen of Athens."

"When your father dies," my father taunted, and Theseus scowled.

"Yes, *when* my father dies," he said curtly, and I saw my father toy with a smile, proud of a small victory. "But in the meantime, she will be a princess, and I can assure you, she will be treated with as much reverence in Athens as she is in Crete."

Was I treated with reverence here in Crete? My mother still spoke to me as though I were a child, and so did various old servants and maids. I had the run of the palace, true, but that was more because everyone was happy to ignore me and I was used to entertaining myself. Ariadne had been treated with reverence, and until she had run away with Theseus, there had been much discussion about which of the young nobles she might marry. I'd never heard anyone wonder who I might marry.

Theseus. I could marry Theseus.

The last time I had seen Theseus he was standing tall above a pile of steaming entrails. I felt ill, then I felt again the cold rage gripping my heart. No one could expect me to marry Theseus. My family had seen more than its fair share of outrages lately, culminating in Theseus spiriting away Ariadne. We were a devout family; the gods would see justice done, not another barbarity on our family. And marrying Theseus, after all he'd done, would be an outrage.

Theseus and my father bartered facts back and forth like a game; my father seemed to be trying to point out the downfalls of Theseus's plan. My mother had blanched to a sickly white. She was the only Cretan woman in the room, aside from me, and utterly silent. As these two men debated my future as if I were a piece of marble or a bar of gold, the full implications of their negotiations hit me with nauseating force. I would be married to Theseus. I would have to leave Crete, which I knew so well, every beach and inlet. I would have to leave the palace. I loved my home, with its beautiful shimmering frescoes and mosaics. And there was the labyrinth, the place where I had spent so many happy hours. I remembered the first time I had been able to slip away from my brother and sister, the undisputed king and queen of those winding passages. I had roamed by myself, touching every damp wall, feeling every cool drip of water, confident in the knowledge that I was exactly where I wanted to be. And best of all, I remembered the childish glee I had felt when I finally walked into the center, just in time to hear an unusually worried Ariadne say, "Am I going to have to tell Father I have lost her?"

I had skipped out in front of her, laughing and dancing as she tried to swat me in exasperation. After that day, the labyrinth was my home just as much as the upper level of Knossos was.

"Phaedra," my mother said sternly, and I whipped my head towards her. At the same time Theseus looked at me, his eyebrows raised. I heard one of the Athenians mutter, "This one is just a child," and I flushed.

"Yes, Mother?" I asked, because it didn't seem that she was just recalling me from my thoughts. For once, a response was expected from me, in the Great Hall, in front of everyone.

"Your father and Theseus were asking whether you wished to go to Athens with Theseus. To be his bride," she said. Her words were pointed. My father looked at me pleadingly.

"Will there—will there be olive groves?" I asked, trying to buy myself time.

Theseus laughed, and a chorus of laughter rippled through the Athenians in response. "Indeed, Athens is famous for its olive groves, planted by the patron goddess Athene herself. If olives are what you wish for, Princess, we can supply them in abundance."

Theseus wanted me to agree to go to Athens. But what did my father want? He looked on me kindly, but his expression gave no clue. If he didn't want me to go, wouldn't he say something? Remind me about the olive groves we had here in Crete? We had talked beforehand about the things we could not say, but we had not anticipated an offer of marriage. My mind was racing, my hands were trembling.

"Phaedra," my mother said again. "Phaedra, you must answer Prince Theseus."

The gods would give me a sign. But Theseus had already called on the gods, mentioning the goddess Athene. Was that my sign? I knew that the gods would seek vengeance on Theseus for the crimes he had committed. But what was my part in that punishment? Was I needed to bear witness? Perhaps a god had spirited Ariadne away precisely so I could fulfill my own task of accompanying Theseus.

An answer was needed. I had to do what the gods wanted, even if it was not what I wanted. The scales in my mind's eye tipped in favor of the marriage.

"Yes," I said, the words tumbling out now. "Yes, I would like to go to Athens. I would like to marry Theseus."

The Athenians gave up a great cheer, and after a few seconds, the Cretans joined in, banging swords on shields and spears on the ground so that the entire Great Hall reverberated with noise and chaos. For a moment, I felt proud: Ariadne had slipped away like a thief in the night. She hadn't received this send-off. But then I remembered that Ariadne had been chosen by a god and was perhaps already living on Mount Olympus.

"Prince Theseus, you will forgive us, but we had not planned on Phaedra leaving us so soon. There are many preparations we must make for her wedding. Allow us to host you for two nights, and you can leave straight after the wedding." My mother's voice was as calm as ever, although I noticed that her hand trembled a little.

"Thank you, Your Majesty. We will accept your kind offer of hospitality and allow you to prepare for your daughter's departure." Theseus, too, sounded calm, but I noticed that although his words appeared to reflect my mother's words back to her, he'd made a couple of small changes. First, he'd used the word *xenia*, or "hospitality," the more sacred term which implied that guests were under the gods' protection. No stabbing them while they slept. But second, and more important to me, he'd not talked of my wedding, but my departure. I wondered if my mother had also noticed the changes and what they might signify.

I followed my mother and father out of the Great Hall, all the court standing in wait for us to leave. As soon as we were back in our own chambers, my mother burst into tears. I stepped back, stunned. I had never seen my mother cry.

"What are we to do, Minos?" she asked. My father embraced her, his arms stiff and awkward.

"I'm not sure there is anything we can do. He won't hurt Phaedra."

"You have no way of knowing that," she protested, and he nodded, but his eyes had the faraway look that meant we were not to disturb him, for he was thinking of kingly matters.

"Those foul Athenians!" my mother continued, and my father's eyes came back into focus. "They have already killed three of my children. Must they take a fourth? Must they take my baby?" My heart twisted. My mother never talked about Androgeus, my oldest brother, killed while traveling in Athens. If he hadn't been killed, I thought suddenly, we would never have agreed to the tribute system. And then Theseus would never have come here and wrought this damage. But her words still confused me. Ariadne wasn't dead, after all.

She pulled away from my father, but he held her tight. "They have taken three of mine, also, Pasiphaë." She looked up at him, her face red and blotchy, and then she drew him tight against her so I could not see her face. I think, although I cannot be sure, that she uttered the words *thank you*.

Helia

There are many sayings about what Cretans like. Specifically, "You can't be a Cretan unless . . ."

"You can't be a Cretan unless you like honey cakes."

"You can't be a Cretan unless you like mazes." (Not true. I was born in Crete, and I've lived in Crete all my life, and I hate the labyrinth.)

But the real saying, the one that rings truest of all: "You can't be a Cretan unless you like bulls."

I love bulls.

I love leaping over them. I am a Cretan bull leaper, and I am really very good at what I do.

I first started training to leap over bulls when I was five years old. People who are not Cretans think that is awfully young to start bull leaping, but if you leave it until any later than five, you may as well not bother. You become scared, you see. Timid. You imagine the worst will happen, and then it does. There was a girl who trained with us for a while when we were all eight or nine. She was a nice girl, and she'd been identified as a possible bull leaper because of the athletic prowess she showed in the field, working with cattle.

Cattle are not bulls.

Needless to say, it ended badly for her. She saw the bull's horns before she saw the empty space beyond, and she leaped straight onto them.

Even if you do start leaping at five years old, you don't start on a fully grown bull. That would be madness. You start with the calves, babies leaping babies, and you work your way up. It's unusual for anyone to be good enough to leap on the massive bulls, the ones with shoulders as wide as hallways and as high as the palace roof, until your late teens. And if you've managed to stay the distance for that length of time without getting gored or trampled, you perform for the king and the court. You do that only for a short length of time—a year or so at most. Because when you get older, your eyesight is no longer as precise and your limbs are no longer as nimble. And while Minos's guests might be keen to see the bull draw blood when the famed Cretan bull leapers miss the mark, Minos himself doesn't want to lose status like that. So you jump for a year or so, and then you are paid a large sum of money, large enough to buy a farm, if you like, or to drink and gamble your way through the court for a couple of years, which is definitely the more common route, and you stop leaping and bear youngsters with your stories of leaping instead.

And after only ten years of leaping, at the very tender age of fifteen, my dream was coming true. I was going to leap in front of the court. The youngest leaper to do so in about twenty years, I should add. I had never seen anyone my age leap for the king. But at the next autumn festival, I was going to do so. I was that good.

I may sound arrogant. If so, I will just say that arrogance is another characteristic that goes along with being a bull leaper. And also, I really was that good.

So that was why I was so upset when I was told that I was not going to be leaping in the autumn festival because

I wasn't going to be in Crete for the autumn festival. I may as well have been in Hades by then, because I was going to be sent to Athens. A place with no bulls and no leaping. A place I had only vaguely heard of before I was told I was going to go there.

It was felt that as a status symbol, the princess should be accompanied by one of the famed Cretan bull leapers. And anyone could have been chosen, but only one of the famed Cretan bull leapers performing at a high level this time round was female. Me. So I was going to have to go.

I screamed and yelled, and when I got very desperate, I cried, but it was no good. I still had to go. And then our tutor, Proctus, took pity on me, and appealed on my behalf. Because while I was still going to have to go to Athens, I was at least to be allowed to leap before the court first, as part of the princess's wedding ceremony. And if I did that, and did it really well, then King Minos would realize that he couldn't possibly lose me to the Athenians, who did not even have bulls, and I would be allowed to stay in Crete and leap over bulls until I reached a ripe old age.

And because I was going to be accompanying the princess, it was decided that I should move to the princess's quarters that night and stay with her retinue. I was no happier about this than I was about any of the other developments. Yes, as bull leapers, we have always known that our life is not our own. But there is a polite fiction around it that suggests we are citizens of the court.

My crucial objection to moving in with the princess was the effect it would have on my training. This may sound like a lie, but believe me, it wasn't. We got up before the rosy fingers of dawn in order to train. As Proctus always said, the bull is training all the time he is awake, just being a bull, a creature who can kill you with a toss of his head. So you have to get up before him in order to beat him. I couldn't be slipping out of the royal quarters before Helios had appeared in the sky, to practice leaping over inanimate objects. (We did not practice on a bull before dawn. That would be a sure way to antagonize him into killing you.) But Proctus pointed out that I had been practicing for ten years now, and two days of rest were not going to make a difference. Some of the leapers swore by a couple of days of rest before a court appearance.

I agreed in the end, but I didn't feel good about it. Mostly, I agreed because I wanted to meet this princess. I was too busy feeling sorry for myself to really feel sorry for her, but deep down, I knew that she was getting as poor a bargain as I was. We both had only two days before we would be taken away from our homes, our positions, from everything we ever knew.

I had never even seen the princess before. Oh, from a distance, in a parade, perhaps, but not up close. We kept to ourselves, with our vigorous training program, and the same could be said about the royal family. And you can be sure none of them wanted to be seen too close to the bulls. I assumed this princess was very beautiful because the Athenian prince wanted to take her back to his palace, so when I did meet her—or rather, I should say, was presented to her—I was a little surprised by how ordinary she looked. She had pretty blue eyes, true, and very unusual, but her hair was a dingy sort of pale brown, and her face was still pudgy, like a child's. At least I wasn't pudgy. There's no chance to get pudgy when you jump over a bull several times a day.

"Your Highness," I said, dipping my head.

"You leap bulls?" she asked. Afterwards I wondered if perhaps I should have been offended, that she asked about the bulls before she asked my name, but at the time, all I thought was that she cared about the thing I cared most about.

"Yes," I answered. "I have since I was a little girl, Your Highness."

"What is it like?" she asked.

She had leaned forward slightly, and I didn't think she was just being polite or making small talk. She genuinely wanted to know, which made me feel bad because I didn't know how to tell her. Could the wind describe what it felt like to blow, or the sun to burn down heat? Jumping bulls was all I knew and all I wanted to know, the only thing that made me feel like all my limbs were where they should be, and my heart was beating at the correct pace.

"It feels like freedom," I managed, stumbling over my words. Behind me, someone snickered, and I felt my face redden. But the princess just nodded.

"I thought it might," she said.

☽

King Minos came into the room some hours later, and we all sprang hastily to our feet and then fell to our knees. I had never seen the king up close before. The resemblance between father and daughter was uncanny, the same bright blue eyes, and while his hair was flecked with gray now, he, too, would once have been fair. But it was more than that. It was the way they held themselves, the surety that they carried with them. The knowledge that they would always be first in any situation in which they found themselves, always be in the right in any argument, always justified in any decision. I had thought Phaedra was not regal because she was not interested in weddings and clothes, but now that I looked at her, I realized I hadn't understood what being regal meant. I saw that the king carried a small labrys, an icon of Crete I didn't much care for.

"Father," Phaedra said, then, "Abba," the childish form. Her lip trembled.

"Please dismiss your staff, Phaedra. We have much to talk about." Her father's voice was firm, and it contained a hidden warning: *We are royalty. We do not cry in front of the staff.*

We didn't wait to be dismissed. First the maidservants trooped out, then I followed. I was at the door when I heard the king say to me, "You are our latest leaper, are you not?"

I turned and dipped my head. "Yes, Your Majesty. My name is Helia." I wasn't sure why I said that. Would he care what my name was? I was surprised enough that he had recognized me as a leaper.

"Helia. How very fitting that you should perform at Phaedra's wedding. Her grandfather on her mother's side is the god Helios."

"Yes, sire," I said, dipping my head again.

"Let us hope you jump well. It will be a good omen for Phaedra's wedding and for her life in Athens." He turned back to Phaedra. I waited for half a beat before realizing that I had been dismissed, then tiptoed out of the room.

☽

The next morning I rose early. I wanted to see the bull before leaping. We can be superstitious, and it is a common belief among leapers that if you do not speak to the bull, ask him to work with you and not against you, he will take offense and make your leaping all the harder. But a royal ceremony, even for one as much on the periphery as me, was a massive undertaking that required much preparation. Even the princess was dragged reluctantly from her paints, and the last I saw of her was being squeezed into a new chiton while no fewer than six maids curled her hair around hot coals.

Fortunately, I did not need that level of attention. I was given a new tunic, which sat a little uneasily on me. It didn't stretch and move the way my well-worn tunic did. If this ceremony hadn't come about in such a rush, I would have been breaking this tunic in for the last couple of weeks. But there was no time for that now. No time for a proper warm-up either, although I tried to limber up by hopping from one foot to another.

"Why aren't you in the warm-up yard?" a familiar voice called out as I skulked at the back of the dining hall.

"Proctus." I turned in relief. "I need to greet the bull. Please tell these people to excuse me."

He nodded and made his way over to the tall, silent man who ran the royal household and, by extension, was managing the staff during the wedding. I couldn't hear what he was saying, but I could see him gesturing towards me, and I expected he would come back soon triumphant. I had never seen Proctus lose an argument, especially where the bulls were concerned. It was just Cretan culture. Cretans respect bulls and bull leapers, and the bull leapers' tutor above all. And besides, the chief of staff was tall and thin, but Proctus was a meaty man, one who carried power in his thick fore-arms and his hefty fists. He never needed to use that power, but it was there all the same.

But instead, he listened quietly as the other man explained something to him, his lip curling superciliously. Proctus's shoulders sagged, and as he shuffled back to me, I could see he hadn't won after all.

"I'm sorry, Helia," he said. "It's not that fellow's decision. He's just interpreting the orders he's received from higher up."

"How high?" I asked, but I already knew. There was only one man who would leave Proctus this accepting of a decision that was so contrary to our usual practice.

"The highest. The king himself wants the entirety of the princess's entourage to accompany her into the temple. No exceptions." The furrowed look on his brow betrayed him; he was as concerned about this as I was, if not more so. So I tried to perk up a bit and put his mind at rest. He couldn't help this any more than I could.

"It will be fine. The bulls all know me. I've leaped all of them before. And besides, this isn't even a major leap, is it? More of a ceremonial demonstration."

Proctus did indeed seem to look more comfortable as I spoke. "Good point, Helia. I will go and have a look for you, see which bull you are jumping. As it is in honor of a young princess, there is no reason we couldn't choose one of the younger bulls." A younger bull would be less aggressive. It could also be smaller. "And I can greet the bull on your behalf."

I was inclined to scoff at the latter offer. We both knew that the bulls would not accept a proxy supplication. But he was trying, and it wasn't his fault, as I kept saying to myself.

"Thanks, Proctus. That should do the trick."

He nodded and scurried away on his errand, leaving me alone. I didn't have long to sit and brood before I was hustled into the ceremonial line and provided with a veil. None of us could be allowed to outshine the princess on her special day.

I didn't pay much attention to the ceremony itself. It took place on the seashore, next to Theseus's boat, as though he had already packed and was waiting to leave, and we were just slowing him down. Even the rituals seemed rushed. The priest sacrificed a small goat that was wandering in the fields, a fire was built on the sands, and Theseus and the princess, instead of bathing in goat's milk, were washed quickly in the sea. Everyone seemed jittery and on edge. Finally, it was time for me to jump.

"The tides," Theseus said vaguely, waving towards his ship, but Minos was having none of it.

"Phaedra is a Cretan princess. She will leave in accordance with Cretan custom."

I stripped off the veil and the fancy clothing. I couldn't do anything about my hair, trussed and tangled as it had become in the sea air, but I had a small strip of leather that I used to pull it back, out of my face. I walked as calmly as I could to the arena and eyed up the bull waiting for me there. Proctus had chosen well. It was a young bull, one that had always been surprisingly docile. One that we used for the youngsters to practice on.

I looked at the crowd. Even Theseus was taking an interest now, watching me closely. His eyes were a dark shade of gray, and it had a sinister effect, making it seem as though there was nothing behind them. Proctus was in the front row, and he nodded to me firmly, no doubt intending to remind me of my training. The crowd did not exist; they were nothing to me. Nothing existed except me and the bull.

I took a deep breath, spat on my hands, and ran. The new tunic crackled on my body, not as supple as I would have liked. I felt the wind blow through my hair, ripping away the tie so my hair exploded in a mass of salty curls, but it was irrelevant. Nothing mattered except me and the bull. Me and the bull, the bull who was standing there, waiting for me, its eyes dark gray and soulless, its head tossing up in the air as if to say, "Who are you? We have not been introduced. How dare you cross my boundaries?"

I bit my lip and threw myself into the air. It was no good. I could feel the parabolic arc that I was taking, weightless and then heavy again, and I could see the bull's horns, and I knew that I had miscalculated. I wanted to cry out, to call for the mother I hadn't seen since I was five years old and whom I'd thought I no longer cared for or about, but that would have been to betray my fear, and as strong as my fear was, it was no match for ten years of training. So instead, I closed my eyes, and I prayed to Zeus that while I knew the landing was not going to be a soft one, perhaps it could at least be a quick one.

Phaedra

With the death of the bull leaper, a blanket of silence fell over the entire crowd. I felt sick. I knew it could happen, but I hadn't seen it, not in my lifetime. I looked at her small body, seeming so much slighter than it had the day before, impaled on the bull's left horn. A red rivulet of blood from the gash in her side began to trickle down into the bull's eyes. Frustrated, it tossed its head in the air, and the girl's head whipped back and forth on her neck like a child's ball.

No one moved. No one seemed to know what to do, not even the bull, who stamped its foot into the ground and brought up a cloud of dust. I remembered another slim body, a pile of gore tangled up in the horns of a bull, and I wanted to cry. This was barbaric, I wanted to shout, but I didn't. After what seemed like a lifetime, several men ran out with sticks to chase the bull back into its pen and to retrieve the corpse from those deadly horns.

My father's face was as white as a passing cloud. This was a terrible omen. For my wedding and my marriage, for the journey ahead of me and my life in Athens, but somehow, I couldn't think of that. I had seen her only the day before. She had been so passionate about bull leaping. So sure of her place in the world. She had been alive.

We sleepwalked our way through the final rituals. Even Theseus looked a little shaken, although his eyes remained as cold as ever. When the rituals were complete, I looked to my parents. I half ran towards my father, but my mother got in the way. I expected her to chastise me one final time for running like a child, or to give me one more lecture on appropriate behavior as a princess in a foreign court, but she did neither. She pulled me into her chest and held me there. I listened to her heart beating. Finally she drew back, kissed me drily on the forehead, and swept away.

After my mother's farewell, my father came and pulled me close, so close that I could smell the oils he used to keep his beard smooth. He hadn't held me this tightly since I was a small girl, and I wanted to cling to him, to make the embrace last longer. But he put his mouth to my ear. Everyone around us would have thought that he was whispering endearments or telling me how much he would miss me. I would have expected the same. But he whispered something very different.

"Phaedra, I know you are angry, but you must contain yourself while you are in Athens."

I tried to pull back, but he held me tight. "I will," I whispered in return. "Don't I always?"

He continued as though I had not spoken. "You know you cannot challenge Theseus without exposing Crete. Without exposing your mother. Do you understand me, Phaedra?"

I wanted to cry. I was my father's favorite child. Ariadne and I had joked about it; she, my mother's duplicate, but me, the golden girl who could do no wrong. I hadn't done any wrong now, but he was speaking as though I had.

"Remember you are a princess of Crete first," he finished, his breath hot on my neck.

"Yes, Father," I muttered, hoping that he would release me. He did, and then he looked at me, his face clouded with worry, every year of his life etched on his forehead in a way I didn't remember from a couple of weeks ago.

"I hope you will stay safe," he said. I remembered the gift he had placed in my trunk, the small double-headed axe wrapped in cloth. I had smiled, thinking back to those long-ago training sessions we had done as children, twirling axes with blunt heads and more often than not dropping them on our toes. But he had looked as serious as he did now, and had said, "I hope you will never need to use this, daughter of Crete."

☽

The rituals complete, or as complete as they were going to be, I was finally assisted into Theseus's boat and shown to a bench to sit on. I was shivering, my arms and legs sticky with seawater, and someone threw a rug over me. I looked back towards the shore; I so seldom left the palace complex, and I had never left Crete, but now I was departing in a boat. I stared at the palace, trying to burn it onto my eyes so I would never forget, but seeing it from the outside only served to remind me that I was now an outsider. I had considered it a single entity, but looking at it from this viewpoint, it was a structured set of buildings leading seamlessly into one another. It was neat, I thought, almost against my will, but it was not elegant. It was not beautiful the way I knew the murals and frescoes inside were beautiful. Had it really seemed so regimented, so well proportioned, when I was weaving my way through the corridors? Where would our room, mine and Ariadne's, have been? I tried counting windows, but my sense of direction was confused, and after I assumed I had found our room and was staring at it wistfully, I realized the windows were too large.

We had planned for several members of my retinue to join me, including the unfortunate bull leaper, but I saw Theseus speaking to my father, and I heard the words *no room*. My father nodded, his chest deflated and all his fight gone.

"Her retinue can follow. But she must be accompanied by at least one maid, Theseus. It's not seemly otherwise."

Theseus frowned, as though he were going to object, and then he shrugged and agreed. I saw my most trusted and long-serving maid, Aenea, approaching the boat, but my mother suddenly reappeared from her quarters, her skin dewy and her face freshly painted. She plucked at Aenea's arm. Another conversation took place that I could not hear, and then Aenea turned and walked away, and my mother's own, oldest servant, Kandake, approached.

My heart sank. Kandake had never had children of her own. She was only a couple of years older than my mother, and she had always served her exclusively. She'd never been given the care of any of us, which seemed strange to me now. Instead, I'd shared various nursemaids with my sister, none of whom had ever been able to control Ariadne. I wouldn't have wanted to take any of them either, but I would have liked someone closer to my own age, like Aenea. I couldn't imagine myself sharing my impressions of the Athenian court with old Kandake. Sour Face, as Ariadne had called her, but never around her or within my mother's hearing.

Kandake was hoisted over the side of the boat and sat down beside me. She stared wordlessly at my mother, recrimination obvious in her eyes. Our bags were hoisted into the hold, and then we cast anchor and set sail. My new life was about to begin.

☽

It was cold at the back of the boat, so somewhat reluctantly, Kandake and I huddled together for warmth. She smelt of goat's cheese and olives; I still reeked of the salty sea. Neither of us spoke. As I began to dry off, I shared my blanket with her, and she took it without a word.

☽

The boat was very busy, with men manning the sails and the oars, and no one paid any attention to us. I looked about for the girl I had spoken to when the tributes first arrived, the one that had made her own way out of the labyrinth. I thought, foolishly, perhaps, that we could be friends, or better still, she might be my lady's maid, but I could not see her. One of the other tributes passed close to me, and I grabbed at his sleeve.

"Where is the girl?" He looked blank, and with annoyance, I realized that I didn't know her name. "The one who came with me when I led you out of the labyrinth."

His eyes darkened as he tried to pull away from me. "I don't know," he muttered.

"I think you do know," I said, my tone as regal as I could make it, summoning my mother. He shook his head frantically.

"No, I don't. Except . . ." I nodded at him to go on. "Except that she angered Theseus, somehow. I don't know how. And no one has seen her since we left Crete."

I wanted to ask more, but he scurried away, and after that nobody ventured close to us. At first I watched the water, the blue lights dazzling and jumping in the sun, and the frothy splashes of water on the side of the boat, but even that became tiring.

I must have fallen asleep, because the next thing I knew, there weren't two women sitting on the bench. There were three.

I looked closely at the third woman, and I could barely believe my eyes. She looked happier and healthier than I did, her flesh tanned and her face freckled.

"Ariadne? What are you doing here?" I hoped that I sounded delighted. But I was starting to have that sick feeling in my stomach, the sense that now that Ariadne was here, my presence was no longer required. Theseus needed one bride, not two, and here was his first choice.

"I came to see you, naturally. Good grief, is that Kandake? She snores like an ox." And Ariadne smiled and grabbed my arm in a way that was very real, and physical, and not at all dreamlike. I looked at Kandake; she was indeed snoring away, her breath coming out in little puffs of bad air. "Don't worry, Phaedra, I'm not here to steal your handsome prince. I've already made that mistake once. Now he's all yours, as much as he's any woman's."

"What do you mean? Why was it a mistake? You left with Dionysos."

She laughed, throwing her head back and not caring who heard her. There was something a little malicious in the sound, as if she were laughing at me.

"Oh, little one, don't believe everything you are told." And she tossed her head back again, and this time I saw it—the handprints across her brown throat.

"Ariadne, what happened to you? Are you . . .?" But I couldn't ask it. Not when she was sitting next to me, her thighs squashed against mine. Not when her hair was longer and more lustrous than mine, and her skin browner and healthier. Not when she looked so alive. Maybe I was dead.

"Don't worry about me. It's time to worry about you." She smiled, the sly, mischievous smile I knew so well.

"I need to be careful in the Athenian court, I know. Everyone says that."

Ariadne sniffed. "Fine, if you want to be a know-it-all, suit yourself. But I'm not here to warn you about the Athenian court. I never got there, remember? I'm here to warn you about Theseus."

"Theseus? What about Theseus?" I looked at her, but she stared straight ahead.

"Just be careful, little one."

Kandake snorted beside me. I looked over at her, but she was still asleep. When I looked back to my right, Ariadne was gone, and what I had thought was the pressure of her thighs was actually a pile of ropes.

I blinked. By rights, I should be waking up now, but I didn't feel as though I had been sleeping. Ariadne was the consort of a god now. Had I had a vision? I remembered those blistering prints across her throat and bile rose in my mouth. A dream, surely; a dream.

I wrapped my arms around my shivering torso and listened to the sounds about me, the gulls in the air, the splashing sea, and Kandake's regular breathing. I closed my eyes, in my mind still seeing Ariadne's throat, and I heard footsteps.

Instinctively, I kept my eyes closed and just listened. Two men were speaking, their voices low.

"We have the white sails, my lord. They're below the deck."

"Indeed. And we did promise, didn't we, that we would change the sails should our mission prove successful?"

"That we did."

I froze. I didn't recognize the first speaker, but I knew the second one, the person addressed as "my lord." That was Theseus, my new husband.

"There are many tasks that need to be attended to at sea. Our priority must be keeping the ship afloat. Getting everyone back to land safely. Do you understand me, Pirithous?"

Pirithous, the captain of the ship. The only man on board almost as tall and lean as Theseus himself.

"I understand you, my lord. Minor details sometimes get forgotten when men are at work. If no one has been tasked with changing the sails, the sails may not be changed." Pirithous's voice was quiet and confident, but I did not understand his meaning. Why were they planning not to do something they had promised to do? And to whom had they made the promise? Who cared what color the sails were? Although black was an odd color to choose; the ship had looked quite funereal in our harbor. Perhaps it would look equally out of place in the Athenian dock.

"Then we understand one another. Thank you, Pirithous, you have always been my most loyal aide, and I will see that you are properly rewarded when the time is right." I heard the footsteps coming closer and was startled by Theseus's cry. "What is this? Why are these women here?"

I looked up at him, blinking, trying to pretend I had been asleep. Next to me, Kandake was doing the same thing, but naturally, without pretense.

"Did you hear anything I just said? Did you?" he asked. He leaned over us. He hadn't raised his voice, but there was a steel to it that was more threatening than blustering and blowing would have been. Slowly, I shook my head.

"Really? You heard nothing?" I shook my head again, more vigorously this time. I remembered Ariadne telling me to be careful, and the Athenian boy telling me the girl hadn't been seen since Crete. I felt Kandake clutching at my arm, and we huddled together again, this time out of fear.

Theseus sighed and leaned back, apparently convinced. Kandake didn't relax her grip on my arm, though. I was going to have a dreadful bruise in the morning.

"Would you look at them, Pirithous? Not a word to say between them. Like a pair of mutes."

Pirithous crossed over to us, his long legs making short work of the deck. He picked up the pile of ropes next to me, as easily as if they were a pile of feathers, although they must have weighed more than I did.

"You should be thankful, Theseus. No man suffers more than the man with a nagging wife, isn't that what the poets say?"

Theseus laughed, that strange barking sound with no real humor in it. "Do they, now? Well, perhaps they have a point. Come on, Pirithous, we have work to do. We can leave these scared chickens to their nap."

The two men walked off, and as they left, I heard Theseus say, "One wouldn't stop talking, and now one won't say a word. No such thing as a happy medium." Pirithous laughed, a more melodious laugh than his friend's. As I watched them go, I thought that Theseus might be the better built of the two, with the more princely looks, but a woman might still be happier to be Pirithous's wife, even if he did dislike a nag. And then I remembered all over again that I was Theseus's wife, as impossible as it might seem to me right now.

The rest of the journey passed without event. Kandake whimpered a little once the men left, but she soon fell asleep again and went back to snoring beside me.

I had no further visitations from anyone, and unlike Kandake, and despite the soothing motion of the boat, my thoughts were too troubled to sleep, so I sat awake and watched the sparkling of the sea until I felt I might go blind from it.

After about half a day, we reached the Athenian coast. The crew shouted and jumped for joy, while Kandake and I stared mutely at our new home. Even the reclaimed Athenians, those who had seemed so happy in our court, were hugging each other, laughing and smiling.

The delight was only short lived, though, because soon the crew returned to preparing the boat to bring her in to land. No one came near us to change the sails, and so they remained, proud and black, unfurled by the strong wind against the pale blue sky. They must have stood out for miles.

My eye was constantly drawn to them, and yet I didn't dare look up for fear that Theseus would see me and know I had overheard their conversation.

As the ship came closer to the land, the sailors took up oars. They hadn't needed to use them for most of the journey because of the strong wind, but now more delicate skill was needed to navigate the rocks. The sea crashed loudly against the shoreline, a more aggressive sea than the gentle one we were used to in Crete. Of course, Poseidon was reputed to be Theseus's father. His godly father, because he had a real father, as well: Aegeus, the king of Athens. Theseus was doubly blessed.

If I may be considered naive in matters like these, I can only offer in my defense that I was brought up in the Cretan court, where we spoke of them daily. I knew, without a shadow of a doubt, that my maternal grandfather was Helios, the sun god, and my paternal grandfather was Zeus, king of all the gods. I didn't need to be told these things; the evidence was all around me, in the garments we wore, in the way I was addressed by courtier and commoner alike. And even though I had never met either of my grandfathers, I also hadn't met any false claimants.

Why would Helios come and visit his daughter and granddaughters when he had to pull the sun around the world every day? And Zeus had many sons, so it was no surprise that he didn't pay special attention to Minos, his son by Europa. (And I had met Europa, my grandmother, many a time before she died. I never dared raise my father's conception with her, though. My grandmother even terrified my mother.)

More to the point, we knew that we were descended from gods because we were rulers. My father had a divine right to rule Crete because his father was the god of the whole world. And when Theseus had arrived in Athens, bearing his mortal father's sword and his godly father's stature, he was immediately accepted as both the son of Aegeus and the son of Poseidon. And the heir to the throne.

As we neared the Athenian coastline, I saw a long horseman on the cliff, watching us. He was tiny in the distance, but I have good eyesight, so I saw him raise an arm when he saw the ship. Then the horse reared up, and they took off, racing as though the gods of the winds were chasing it. Theseus saw me watching and smiled.

"That will be my son, Hippolytus."

"You can tell from this distance?" I asked. I was surprised. No one had mentioned a son to me, let alone one old enough to ride a horse.

"I can tell by the way he drives that poor horse, although the horse will love him despite it. Or perhaps because of it."

He looked as though he were about to turn away, and I wanted to keep his attention, so I searched for something else to say. "How old is he? Your son, I mean. Not his horse."

"He must be about sixteen now. Or, no, seventeen. It has been eighteen years since the battle with the Amazons."

"So, his mother was . . ." I barely dared finish the sentence.

"Antiope, queen of the Amazons. Ah, well, we all did stupid things in our youth, and I certainly have no regrets where Hippolytus is concerned. He's a fine boy."

I did not want to hear any more. How many foreign queens and princesses had Theseus carried off, exactly? But then eighteen years ago, he must have been about Hippolytus's age. About my age.

"Land ahoy," the sailor in front of me called, making me jump. And then Kandake and I were very much in the way, no matter where were went, as the crew worked together to bring the boat onto shore. It was an arduous process, and by the time we had finished, it was nearly nightfall.

"Should we camp here tonight and head to the palace tomorrow?" Theseus asked Pirithous. Pirithous looked as though he was about to answer, but we were interrupted by a shout from shore.

"Alas! Alas! Pirithous, have you returned to us?"

A horse rider down below was waving frantically. It wasn't the same rider we'd seen earlier. I could tell from the way he was handling the horse. That earlier horseman might have been a centaur. This one was wishing he was back on his own two feet.

Pirithous and Theseus exchanged a quick look, and then Pirithous called out, "We have returned, yes. But why do you say 'alas'?" His voice was strained, and he pulled nervously at his clothes. There was little sign of the confident captain who'd seen us home here.

"I say 'alas' because you have returned without the prince." The man on the beach below was still trying to reign his horse in. He didn't look up at the boat to see Theseus himself standing there, nodding at Pirithous to continue.

"I do not understand, friend," Pirithous croaked out. "The prince is here."

"The prince is here? Then I have even more reason to say 'alas'!" The man gave up and slid down off his horse. It was a bumpy landing, and the horse looked at him with disdain.

"Do you have news, man?" Theseus had given up on Pirithous, clearly. He pushed past him to the front of the ship. "Speak clearly."

The man fell to his knees. In doing so, he lost hold of the reins. The horse cantered off. The man looked after it with a mix of longing and exasperation, but only for a second. He gazed up at Theseus.

"All hail, Theseus, King of Athens. Your Majesty, your father is dead."

ACT II

ATHENS

*T*he room has alcoves in the corners. Cutouts where statues of gods would have been intended to sit, before the occupants of the room realized it was too dark, too unbefitting for the gods they should be honoring. These alcoves cast shadows within themselves, and a superstitious man might imagine even on a sunny day that there was a small creature twitching inside, watching them. Few of the men here could squeeze into one, not since they were boys. It makes sense, then, that the figure concealed in the alcove in the far right corner is no man.

Medea—the witch, as she is known—is not as young as she used to be, and her back aches from being folded into this space. She's Phaedra's cousin, but she's old enough to be her mother, she thinks wryly.

From where she hides she cannot see the princess, but she can picture her. She remembers the conversations they have had, the secrets Phaedra confided to her, and she wonders what she is feeling now. This solitary girl in a room of men. So vulnerable. Or so it would seem.

Medea does not know the truth. Phaedra calls Hippolytus a rapist, and Medea believes her. But that doesn't mean every word Phaedra says is true. After all, women are capable of far more than lies when they need to be. Medea knows that better than anyone.

Medea

I listened to the seagulls screaming on the breeze and sighed. The day had begun with so much promise, perhaps the best day I'd had since I fled Colchis and my husband, Jason, with only the clothes on my back and the arcane knowledge in my head.

Aegeus had invited me to breakfast with him in his private chambers. Oh, I knew what people were saying, but they were fools. If there had been any of that going on, he wouldn't have needed to invite me to breakfast, would he?

I conducted myself as though I were the goddess Aphrodite stepping down from Mount Olympus to visit the king. I sucked honey off the end of my finger like a young girl, laughed at the predictable jokes, and idly wondered what I would say were he ever to ask me to stay the night. I was not too precious about the act, which would surely be over as quickly as a sneeze, with a man Aegeus's age. And my reputation, frankly, could not descend any lower. But if I were to take that step, I wanted to maximize all possible benefits. Did I want to be a queen of Athens?

As we finished our breakfast, we were disturbed by a knock at the door. I looked up in surprise, expecting Aegeus to be furious. The last messenger to interrupted our private time together had been banished from the city. But today, the old king, his hand trembling, put down the fig he had just raised to his mouth, and called, "Come in," as though he had been expecting this interruption.

A messenger, one I had seen before loitering about the court and drinking cheap wine, came in. His face was pale, and he stuttered with false starts before saying, "Sire, the ship has returned."

"Medea, leave us," Aegeus said. His voice was quiet, but firm. It was the most kingly I had ever heard him sound, so I obeyed. That was a mistake. I got up and left the room, pulling the heavy door behind me. Once outside, I straightened my chiton and walked back to my own suite of rooms with my head held high.

I barely had time to sink down onto my couch, so much more comfortable than those in the king's chambers, and remove my veil, when I heard the commotion from outdoors. I sprang up and stared at my maid, Agneta. Her look of horror mirrored mine. We had both heard such outbreaks before, and they had never boded well for us.

"Should I investigate?" she asked me, her lips dry.

I shook my head. "Send Cassandra." It sounds cold-blooded, as though I had favorites among my maids, women I was prepared to sacrifice (certainly I did). But Agneta was from the north, not even a Greek, more of a foreigner than even me. Cassandra was an Athenian, known to everyone, with a dull Athenian husband and at least two Athenian children I had never met. She also had several high-ranking Athenian lovers. No woman was safe if a city was being ransacked, but at least there might be men who would take care of Cassandra.

Once Cassandra had been sent out, her excitement betraying her own lack of experience, Agneta and I moved towards the large open window that looked onto the sea. The gentle breeze ruffled our hair, and the air smelt salty and clean, creating the illusion that all was right in the world, but we were not fooled. In the distance, we could see a ship slowly making its way into the harbor. A crowd was clustering beneath the cliff before the waterfront, and a cold hand seized my heart. Cassandra scurried back into the room.

"It is Aegeus," she announced. I nodded at her to continue. "He has leaped from the cliff and killed himself."

I stared at her. I felt nothing for the man himself, or at least I told myself that, but I could see all my hard work since arriving in Athens slipping through my fingers. "But why?" I managed. It was that message. I should have stayed.

"It is his son, Theseus," Cassandra said, her chest puffed up with the importance of her message. "Theseus is dead."

She babbled some nonsense about a ship with white sails meaning the prince was safe, while a ship with black sails meant he had been killed. We all turned to watch the ship's slow progress, black sails fluttering in the breeze.

"But," I said aloud, although I was really talking to myself, "the ship hasn't even docked. Didn't Aegeus even want to wait and hear the story?" I remembered Prince Theseus, his cold, gray eyes assessing me and finding me wanting. They say there is no fool like an old fool, and while Aegeus had prided himself on bedding many women, and losing his head over none of them, Theseus, his supposed heir, had him as giddy as a boy in the throes of his first romance. Theseus and I were the same age, and yet Aegeus had always referred to him as "the boy." Theseus's son, Hippolytus, an actual boy, or at least a young man, he called "my grandson." I found both of them to be unsavory, but I had been careful not to let Aegeus know. I'd seen him dismiss his oldest advisers in favor of "the boy."

Neither of my maids answered my question, which was perfectly correct, as I had not addressed it to them, and their answer could not have shed any further light on the situation. Instead, we stood in silence and watched the ship dock and the passengers emerge. I pressed my hands to the pillar before me, but Agneta was the first to speak.

Her voice shaking, she said, "Cassandra, I thought you said he was dead."

"They said he was," Cassandra said, then added, uselessly, "The sails are black."

We couldn't argue with her, and yet none of us was in any doubt that the tall, lean man striding across the beach was anyone other than Prince Theseus. Returned from Crete and, it appeared, from the dead.

The bedraggled young peasants that Theseus had taken with him to Crete began to emerge from the ship, little mice blinking in the sunlight. I moved away, losing interest, but turned back again when Cassandra cried, "But who is that?" We watched as a young woman, not Athenian by the look of her elaborately styled hair, stepped gingerly out of the boat and onto the shore. An older woman tried to assist her, but the young woman shook her hand off.

"A bride for Theseus," I said disdainfully.

"No," Agneta objected. "She's young enough to be his daughter. Perhaps he has brought her back for Hippolytus."

Cassandra giggled. "I doubt that very much," she said archly. "Or if he did, he wasted his money." I allowed myself to smile. The first time I was introduced to Hippolytus, he made a point of telling me, going so far as to point his finger at my chest in emphasis, that he was a follower of Artemis, and as such, impervious to my wiles. As though I would ever waste my wiles on a colt like him when there was power to be found elsewhere.

"I still say she is a bride for Theseus," I said firmly. I studied the girl, her skin pale, and her hair a bright color not often seen this far south. "And what is more, I can tell you who she is. She's my cousin, Phaedra. A princess of Crete."

Even Cassandra was awed into silence. As a granddaughter of the sun god, I have many "cousins." Usually, the children or grandchildren of women who would like a little more distinction than to claim to be another conquest of Zeus, or even Poseidon. In this case, though, Phaedra really is my cousin. Our mothers were sisters, and our grandmother was one and the same woman.

My curiosity piqued again, we watched the procession straggling back to the palace. Theseus, now informed of his father's death, led the way, baring his breast and howling the requisite cries of anguish. It may have been genuine grief; I had no way of knowing. I had thought I knew Aegeus, and yet I had left him to leap to his death.

The tributes surrounded Theseus, those eager young faces looking tired and drained and in need of a hot bath. And in the middle, looking paler and more shocked than any of them, the Cretan princess, Theseus's new bride.

Even though she was my cousin, we looked nothing alike. She was small and fair, with plump skin that looked as though it would bruise easily. I'm tall with dark hair and skin the color of a burnished olive. Her blue eyes gave her an air of innocence. I had heard that her mother closely resembled my mother, and there was an older sister, reputed to take after her and to be a beauty, but this child must take after her father. One normally feels sorry for girls who resemble their fathers, with their strong jaws and mannish chins. But in this instance, this girl's face was soft and feminine. She looked like a startled bird, the type of girl a man, or at least a certain type of man, longs to take care of and make a little nest for. She would never be famed for her beauty, though.

They made their weary way back towards the palace, not realizing that I was watching every step they took. Theseus paid no attention to the new bride. And she paid little attention to anything around her, her focus seeming to be on her own feet. I wondered if it were just Crete that she missed, or if she had learned something on the journey about that so-called heroic husband of hers. The number of women he had kidnapped, perhaps, or the son whose mother he had raped, the son who must be of an age with her.

I agonized in my room that night, trying to decide whether it was better to throw myself upon Theseus's mercy or to avoid him completely and hope that I could live here undetected until I could make my escape. It wouldn't have been possible in many courts, but Athens was so disorganized. I had a private suite of rooms off the main corridors, with my own exit to a small courtyard I could use for my ablutions. I had only two maids, Agneta and Cassandra, and it would be easy to spin a story about how they were restoring my rooms ready for the next guest. The general chaos that pervaded the kitchens meant that they would easily be able to fetch me food without anyone noticing. The risk was that Theseus, with his piercing gray eyes, would prove to be sharper than his lackadaisical father, and I would be found out. And Theseus could have me put to death as a fugitive and a thief or return me to Corinth in chains.

Not for the first time, I wished that I had someone with whom I could discuss these matters, but there had never been anyone. Even my beloved Jason, when he was my beloved, had been—not to mince words—no match for me in terms of intellectual capacity. Pure brawn was a different matter. Perhaps if that other sister had arrived, the one with her mother's face, and mine, I might have tried to reach out to her. But this girl with her round cheeks and her sweaty forehead was only a child. I could not seek counsel from her.

I tossed and turned, probably keeping Agneta awake too. If I knew Theseus would honor his father's wishes and respect xenia, I would throw myself on his mercy. But if he were likely to hold the popular opinion, that I was a witch who had beguiled his father, I should stay hidden. I briefly considered beguiling Theseus, but I knew that the tricks that would work with a seventy-year-old man were unlikely to work with his son.

I hated being indecisive. And I hated waiting. I am a woman of action, not a philosopher. I know that history will judge me, but history is written by men. I did not want to be at any man's mercy, not again. By morning, I had made up my mind. I would keep to my rooms, and I would make my preparations to leave. My maids could spread the rumor that I had sneaked out of the palace in fear of

Theseus, and they would be able to bring me the food and other supplies I needed. I just needed to stay out of Theseus's way. After all I had been through, I told myself that I didn't care whether I lived or died. And yet, I had to admit, Theseus still frightened me. There are worse things than death.

Phaedra

I don't know what I had expected. I hadn't expected Knossos. The Cretan palace is one of the marvels of the modern world, after all. But the Athenian palace . . . it would be an exaggeration to say that we would have used it to shelter goats, but not to say that we would have used it to shelter the goatherd.

The walls were primitive, slapped together, without any paint. The floor was muck, with no covering. The furniture could best be described as rustic. No one had spent any time lovingly carving decorations and embellishments, the way the master craftsmen had in Knossos. The smell evoked those goats only too well. Theseus must have seen me recoil.

"I know it's not what you're used to, Princess. I'm not going to pretend otherwise. And I'm also not going to say it's something I'm especially proud of. But believe me, by the time my reign is done, it will be more than a rival for Knossos."

From another man, this might be considered boasting—saving face in front of the unhappy young bride. But Theseus's tone was so matter of fact, and his lack of concern for me so apparent, that I just took it as a statement of intent.

"This will be your quarters," he said abruptly, stopping in front of a low door. "Now if you will excuse me, I must go and see to my father's remains. I will see you tomorrow."

"Will you not be back here later, sir?" I asked, startled. My parents never spent a night apart.

"No, my quarters are on the other side of the complex. Sleep well, Princess," he said.

"Queen," I said, stunning myself with my audacity.

"I beg your pardon?" Theseus turned around, and for the first time, I felt as though he looked at me, actually saw me, Phaedra, a woman and an equal, not just a young girl he'd dragged halfway across the world to satisfy his own ego.

"I'm a queen now, not a princess. Your father is dead, which makes you the king. And I am your wife, which makes me—"

"—a queen." He finished the sentence for me. "Well, well. Perhaps the little dog has some bite in her after all. Good night, Your Majesty." He gave me a low, sweeping bow, then turned and left, chuckling a little. When he reached the end of the corridor, I watched him straighten himself, then hunch over again a little before he rejoined the Athenians. The model of a grieving son and heir.

Left alone, I opened the door and looked into my rooms. I had hoped that they would be better decorated than the rest of the palace, but I was wrong. There was a main room with two small adjoining rooms. I opened and closed the doors, then sank down onto a small chair in horror. There was no lavatory.

A hesitant tap on the door. "Come in," I called.

"Madam?" Kandake stood in front of me wringing her hands.

"There's no toilet," I said miserably. "What are we to do?"

"We will have to go outdoors," she answered. "Same as any peasant."

"But I am not a peasant," I said. "I'm the queen."

"Queen of what, though?" she asked, and for a moment, it was like having my mother there. Then she flushed. "I'm sorry, Your Majesty—I overstepped. I can't do much tonight, but I can try to track down some facilities for you."

"Facilities?" I asked, my eyebrow raised. I wasn't sure what she meant. She couldn't install running water.

She wrung her hands some more. Finally, she gave up. "A bucket, madam. Then at least you will have some privacy."

I stared at her, trying to make sense of what she'd said. Then the sheer ridiculousness of the situation hit me, and I started to laugh. I was slightly hysterical. If she had joined me in laughing, we might never have stopped. But she didn't. She folded her arms and watched me, her expression patient, as though it were not the situation that was laughable, but that I was an overexcited child who must be indulged. And so my laughter hiccupped out, and I felt more ridiculous than ever.

"Where shall we sleep?" I asked. We inspected the rooms and found a medium-sized bed in one of the adjoining rooms, and a small bed in the other. The room with the smaller bed had a window that looked out onto the sea, though.

"You could take that one," I pointed at the larger bed, but she shook her head.

"I will take this one, Madam. It is more fitting. And besides . . ." She started to say something, and then her words tailed off.

"Besides?" I prompted.

"You may not always sleep alone now."

For one strange moment my thoughts flashed back to my sister, with whom I'd shared a room all my life. But then I realized what she meant, and I blushed. "Oh." I turned away. I hadn't expected it would be like this, in this small, dirty little set of rooms with grubby walls, and with Kandake only a flimsy partition away, able to hear everything.

The next knock on the door, more forceful, was the men delivering our trunks. Kandake took out the bare necessities that I needed to sleep, then ushered me into the larger bedroom and closed the door on me. I was so tired I collapsed into bed. My last thought before drifting into sleep was that I would have to build a shrine in my room the next day. We prayed to the same gods and goddesses, but I did not want the Athenian priests hearing my prayers.

Trypho

The king is dead, long live the king. So we said, and we should mean it, too. And I did, I did, if only because Hippolytus was a far worse prospect than Theseus.

Old Aegeus had not been a clever man, nor a wise king. He had ruled with the bare minimum of effort. He'd allowed himself to be captivated by that witch, Medea (and *witch* was a polite term for the woman). We all saw her, simpering and making huge eyes at him, even though he was old enough to be her father. And I saw her rolling those same eyes when she thought no one was looking. Aegeus had been a fool to take her in. He'd been a terrible king, too. It could not be said that Athens prospered under his rule.

And yet . . . and yet, you knew where you were with Aegeus. He could be managed. He could be led. He was a straightforward man with straightforward lusts and desires. He wasn't kind, but his innate laziness meant he wasn't cruel either. We didn't prosper, but we survived. And, let me be honest, some of us *did* prosper.

I knew we had a problem as soon as I saw Theseus. If you want my opinion, although it is treason now to say it, I don't believe he was Aegeus's son. If his mother told him he was, she was a liar. Aegeus was entering his dotage. He'd never had an heir, but there were women all across Attica who'd been told if they bore a son nine months after his visit, he should come to the palace. For forty years, none came.

It was child's play for Theseus to present himself as a long-lost son and an heir to the throne. And better than that, an heir with an heir already assured. We keep ourselves to ourselves in Athens, and we hadn't heard all the stories about Theseus, although we knew that he was a friend of Herakles, and the boy, Hippolytus, that came with him was the son of an Amazon queen, obtained in murky circumstances. I tried to give Hippolytus the benefit of the doubt. He certainly wasn't to blame for his father's dealings. He was a tall, surly boy, but I still reached out to him once or twice, let him know about the debates that had been organized for the youth, that sort of thing. He soon made it clear to me that he was only happy when he was off riding his horse, and as my riding days are behind me, that was an end to that.

I don't know how Theseus explained to Aegeus that he'd been roaming the earth for forty years before he came to present himself at court as Aegeus's son. I wasn't in Aegeus's confidence by that stage. My fault—I hadn't been delicate enough with him about Theseus. I'd challenged him too directly. Perhaps Aegeus wasn't the only one becoming foolish in his old age.

So Theseus had been acknowledged by Aegeus. And Theseus decided that, as prince, the first change he would make was to revise the tribute system, a decision I took rather personally as it was I who had thrashed the details out with Minos many years before. Minos—now *there* was a king. Minos's advisers were not given the wide mandates that Aegeus gave me. And yet, despite having fathered at least three children and probably four on his wife, Minos found himself in a similar position to old Aegeus's. He was without an heir unless he adopted that cuckoo Theseus, who was married to Minos's last surviving daughter. How the world turns and turns about.

But that was still to come. As I said, Theseus decided that he would abolish the tribute system, and Aegeus was all for the plan, having forgotten that cold winter's day many years before, when Athenians were dying because of a lack of food and fuel. He and I bundled up in furs that were almost threadbare, and we sailed to Crete to negotiate a settlement. Minos would provide us with money while, in return, we would provide him with fourteen fine young men and women, none of whom would be able to find employment in Athens, and all of whom would be capable of starting their own revolution if we kept them here. I had liked Minos, and before we left, he had pulled me aside.

"Look here, Trypho," he had said, smiling in what I suspect he believed was a friendly manner, but which still came across as more of a snarl. "There's room in my court for ambitious young men like you." It was sheer flattery; even then I had not been a young man.

"Thank you, sire," I had replied, "But I owe loyalty to my king"—or some such nonsense as that. Truth was, I had far finer clothes than the ones I was wearing hidden back in Athens, where Aegeus couldn't see them. I didn't think there was anywhere in Crete that Minos's more clear-sighted eyes didn't penetrate.

In any event, Aegeus mentioned none of this when Theseus volunteered himself as the oldest of the tributes, and he stood out like a sore thumb, although we were all under pains not to mention it. I would have managed the plan better myself, but I had no interest in doing so. I would have sent the young calf, Hippolytus, instead. He might lack Theseus's steady hand and experience, but he was a good fighter. And if he hadn't returned, Theseus would have the chance to father a new heir, one that didn't have the—to put it politely—character flaws of his current son. But I was not involved. Theseus went himself.

And here I made my second mistake. I was not dependent on the ship returning to hear news of how events transpired in Crete. I had my own sources. And so I heard how Theseus had defeated the Minotaur and had run rings around Minos, and now he was coming home with a Cretan princess in tow (although my sources were a little confused here, and for a while I thought he had managed to secure not one but two princesses, which would not have damaged his good standing with his father). But I did not want Aegeus to know how deep my sources in Crete ran, and so I kept the information to myself. As a result, I heard along with the rest of the palace when Aegeus threw himself over the cliff and dashed his body on the rocks below, mistakenly believing his son Theseus to be dead.

They say that old men come to resemble old women, while old women just become crones. It was certainly true in my case. I found myself actually shedding tears for that rascal Aegeus, although Zeus knows he would never have shed any tears for me. At least someone shed tears for him, mind. I didn't imagine the witch lost any sleep, and Theseus and Hippolytus certainly didn't.

☽

Theseus was respectful enough. He explained to me and to the other viziers his plans for Athens in painstaking detail. However, he would not be swayed, no matter what our opinions were. And we were all set against this "democracy" he wished to introduce. Rule by the people? Had Theseus never met his fellow man? Most of them are pig ignorant, interested only in themselves and their base desires. They wish to be led, to be told what to believe, to be told what taxes to pay and what little treats those taxes will be spent on. Handing over power to the people is tantamount to handing it over to the priests. I warned Theseus of this in those early days when I thought he was genuinely seeking my opinion. Later I knew better, and I smiled and nodded politely. We were very polite to one another, Theseus and I.

I was daydreaming about leaving the court, about retreating to my farm out of the city, with its sunsets over the hills, that morning when I first met the Cretan princess. I stirred my spoon in my honey and listened to the cacophonous roar of Hippolytus and his friends behind me, playing some game that involved their knives and the table. The blades sliced into the wood, again and again and again, while the boys cheered and jeered, and my head throbbed. I would have liked to believe they would have showed more decorum if Aegeus were still alive, but it wasn't true. This court had become a bear pit, with Hippolytus the chief bear. His friends were chanting his name and beating either their breasts or the table when they came to an abrupt halt. I looked up in interest; I knew that Theseus must have entered the room, because he was the only one that could curb those young cubs. But until I saw the princess, I didn't know why he would have bothered.

The princess. She was very pretty, with her big blue eyes and her pale skin. She looked around, blinking, fright obvious on her face. She was the only woman in the room. Theseus stood nearby, a small smile playing on his lips. She could expect no support from that quarter. I didn't know why he'd even brought her in here. Aegeus had had the sense to keep Medea in his chambers, and she wasn't even his wife.

"Hippolytus," Theseus called. "I want to introduce you to my son," he said to the princess.

The volume in the room dropped. I looked around and tried to see the dining hall, so familiar to me, through the eyes of a newcomer. There were at least fifty men, lined up on benches, with their plates in front of them, in various states of dress, from simple woven shirts to full battle armor, all staring openly at the new arrival. Their knives were poised in mid-air, great chunks of meat speared onto the blades to be torn off with their teeth. Two men who had finished their meal were paused, mid-arm-wrestling, unsure whether to drop their hands or not.

That was the corner of the room that Theseus led the poor princess to, although at least it was not one of the arm-wrestling lads to whom he was presenting her. Hippolytus, tall and slim, leaned against the wall. He shared Theseus's pronounced cheekbones and wry mouth, although his bright blue eyes added an appeal to his face that his father's was lacking, and his bearing was more elegant.

"Madam, may I present my son, Hippolytus."

Phaedra dipped her head. "I am pleased to meet you, Hippolytus."

Hippolytus sneered, raising his upper lip in a parody of disgust, although it was not enough to completely mar that beautiful face. "Madam," he drawled. "The honor is mine . . ."

Theseus just rested his hand on his son's shoulder and said gently, "Hippolytus, Phaedra is my wife now."

"Then you are the unlucky one," Hippolytus said. Phaedra gasped, and a few of the young men chuckled. One of the arm-wrestlers outright guffawed. "Oh, I don't mean anything about you, personally, Madam," Hippolytus said, opening those big blue eyes wide and bowing to her in an exaggerated display of courtly manners. "I am sure that you are most charming. But marriage is not an institution that I support."

"Indeed?" Phaedra said, her voice shaking a little.

"I am afraid that it has been Hippolytus and I alone for too long, since his mother died," Theseus said, not removing his hand from the boy's shoulder. "And we are only recently come to court, as you know. Perhaps his manners are still a little rough."

Phaedra was silent, and no one present came to her aid. Finally, she choked out, "What is your objection to marriage, Hippolytus? Surely you will soon be of marrying age yourself."

"Like my mother before me, I am promised only to the goddess Artemis," he proclaimed grandly.

"The virgin goddess?" she asked.

"Yes, indeed, and more than that: the goddess of the hunt, the goddess of nature. The goddess of all things good and pure and beautiful in this world."

The atmosphere was oddly charged. It was as though, despite the room of people, and Theseus's hand on his son's shoulder, the only two people in the room were Phaedra and Hippolytus. "That may change as you grow older," she said, although her face suggested she had not attained many years herself. "You may find that there is room for Aphrodite, too."

"Aphrodite? The goddess of the bed chambers? Pah!" And he slammed his hand down on the table. Around him, the young men gave their own cries of approval.

"We live for the hunt, don't we, gentlemen?" he shouted.

"The hunt!" They all took up the cry and then repeated it at different intervals, so the room shook with their calls.

"That's enough," Theseus said finally. "The hunt is all very well, but Phaedra is right in reminding you that there are other goddesses to serve. Such as Athene, patron of this wonderful city. No, Hippolytus." Theseus lifted a finger as he saw Hippolytus open his mouth to object. "I will not hear a word against Athene. We will need her wisdom and her magnitude if we are to make Athens as great as it deserves to become. You didn't see Crete; otherwise, you would know how far behind we are.

"Perhaps one day Queen Phaedra will let you know how magnificent her city-state is. But in the meantime, I see her breakfast has arrived, and I have matters of state to attend to." Theseus bowed, and in perhaps his most unchivalrous gesture since kidnapping Hippolytus's mother, left the room.

Phaedra stood looking about her as a servant held up a small bowl of yoghurt. The normal place to sit would be next to the prince, her stepson, but she didn't move.

I had thought it preposterous that anyone would bring a young woman here to introduce her to that boor but something in Hippolytus's demeanor made me stop. His eyes were wide, and his skin looked clammy. If I hadn't known better, I would have believed that he was captivated by her. A strange turn of affairs, indeed.

With reluctance, he turned his back on the princess. He returned to punching his fellows on the arm and boasting about kills. The princess shrank back, her manner one of disgust. I saw my opportunity. I nudged the open chair next to me with my foot. Sensing a friendly face, the girl came and sat down, and the servant followed with her yoghurt.

At first, we talked of small matters: her voyage to Athens and the sunshine that Athens had enjoyed since she arrived. But eventually I led the conversation round to Aegeus.

"You served him as an adviser, didn't you?" she asked. "Was he a good leader?"

"Ah, my lady, there was never another leader like him," I said, leaning forward. That part was true, at least. I extolled all Aegeus's virtues, the battles he had won, the kindnesses that he had bestowed on the people, the wisdom he had shown in judgements.

I allowed my eyes to become a little wet as I spoke, and I know that she noticed.

"You spoke well of Aegeus, good sir. You make me sad that I never met him."

"Thank you, Your Majesty. He was a good king—perhaps not as ambitious as some, but a good king to us, his people."

"I would hope that the elders would say as much of my father, King Minos," she said seriously, and I was pleased to see that her own eyes were welling up with tears. I put my hand over hers briefly, my rough old skin looking incongruous against her pale plump hand, and then took it away quickly. The intention was to look fatherly, not like an amorous old man.

We returned to the small talk. I tried to draw her out to discuss her home, Crete, and the new king of Athens, but she was too well bred. I did notice something interesting when we spoke of Theseus, though. She was absolutely brimming with anger. I doubted Theseus realized, not least because of her milky skin and her downcast eyes. But nevertheless, there it was, below the surface, a real hatred.

When I spoke of Theseus, her eyes narrowed by a bare margin, her nostrils flared ever so slightly, the color in her cheeks deepened a shade. But why was she so upset? Was it his treatment of her, taking her from her family? Was it the fact that he had installed her in the palace but had not given her the proper respect his wife should be accorded? I thought there was something deeper there as well, something that had happened in Crete. I would make enquiries of my sources, but I also resolved to win the princess's confidence. After all, my enemy's enemy is my friend.

Phaedra

For the first ten nights, all I wanted to do in the Athenian court was cry. I missed Crete—and not just my mother and father and my sister; I missed the palace. No matter how much I scrubbed myself, I could never feel clean in the Athenian court, and I could never rid my nostrils of the smell of rot and decay that permeated the place.

I knew that Kandake felt the same. She spent all her time in our rooms on her hands and knees with a brush, torturing the floors to give up their dirt. Every night she would give a sigh of satisfaction. But every morning, a thin layer of dust would lie over everything again, and she would have to start afresh.

I never saw Theseus. He may have heard rumors about how much weeping I did. I don't expect I would have wanted to spend time with me either. But I did not weep for Theseus because I did not want to waste my tears on a monster.

"Why did you help him, Ariadne?" The question was always on my lips, and I wished she would appear to me again so I could ask her.

I'd joined Theseus for breakfast that morning because I had no choice. He'd told me he wanted to introduce me to his son. I had no idea that he intended to leave me with him. Afterwards, I was to sit in my room and try to decide what the worst of it had been. In the Cretan court, women would join the men for breakfast. Here, that was clearly not the case.

I'd been the only woman there, and I'd felt exposed and raw. But it was Hippolytus who left me feeling as though every cell in my body was suddenly flooded with a powerful charge—Hippolytus's bright blue eyes that seemed to hover before me, tormenting me; Hippolytus's words that wove their way round my head and wouldn't let me go. That night, I went to sleep and dreamed of Hippolytus, not as a man, but as a centaur, his torso fused to the horse he rode so well.

"He is your stepson," I reminded myself when I awoke. "He is Theseus's son, his pride and joy." And yet I remembered the way he had stared at me, those azure eyes challenging me, angry and furious; he was like and yet not like his father, a true son of the sea. He was my son now, too, and yet he was only a couple of years younger than me.

At some point I must have fallen asleep, because I heard voices down below, a chorus of women calling to one another, but when I looked out the window, all I could see was the empty courtyard, bathed in moonlight. I sat down on my bed, expecting that the noise would stop, but it continued. I focused my mind, trying to pick one voice out of the cacophony, and the longer I listened, the more the noises began to make sense.

"Don't go alone to Adrastos's room. Always in pairs, always, always in pairs."

"Dardanos is a pervert and a bully. He beat me for making his bed badly, but I swear there was nothing wrong with the bed, and his eyes shone brighter with every stroke."

"Mryto is a pervert, but he won't hurt you. He will ask you to beat him, as though he were a horse. He pretends you have all the control."

That last one made me sit straight up. There were men who would do such things? I pulled my sheets around me and listened to the voices calling. And some women who couldn't even call, but only wept.

I pulled my knees up under my chin and thought, for the first time since I had come to Athens, of the tribute I had spoken to, the one I had later helped out of the labyrinth. This was what she had been trying to tell me. This was the lot of the common woman, the serving maid. Forced to go into men's rooms and do unspeakable things. I sat alone on my bed and listened, and heard that there were others worse off than me. I was thankful that Theseus seemed to have decided that I was his wife in name only, even as I wondered why he had brought me all the way from my home if he did not intend to use me in the way that men do. I cast my mind back to those burly men in the dining room. Which one liked to beat, and which to be beaten? And in the end, was either better? Perhaps you had no bruises if you held the stick, but the woman who had spoken was right.

You had no control.

I pulled the covers around my head, but I could not drown out those voices. This information must be useful to them, or at least a release of their pain. But I felt it burden my shoulders, weigh me down. I could not carry so much grief. I had my own grief to bear.

I lay listening to the voices until sunrise, when they faded away. And as my hand brushed my cheek, just before

I fell asleep, I realized that my face was wet with tears. I didn't know these women, but I felt that we were sisters. I had shared their darkest nights and would wake a wiser woman.

꒩

The next morning, I arose and dressed. My maid was still sleeping, so I left by myself, slipped out of the palace, and returned to the shoreline. I wanted to see if I could see Crete, a distant dot on the horizon, but all I could see were waves crashing onto the beach.

"Treacherous waters. I hope you weren't thinking of bathing."

I started, then turned to see no other than Hippolytus behind me, his mouth upturned in a smirk. His tunic was tied loosely around his waist, and I could see through to his muscular torso. The skin below was glowing gold, as though he were the son of the sun god. I had never seen so much male flesh outside of a painting. I remembered my dream—that would be the place where his skin fused with that of the horse, and I swallowed suddenly. I had been thinking of entering the water and letting the salty waves brush the dirt from my skin, but I would never admit to it now.

"Is it not treacherous of you to refer to them as such? I thought you were descended from the god Poseidon?" I asked, wanting to gently remind him of his religious duties and to redirect my own mind to the importance of the gods. He was my stepson, even if the relationship felt ill-fitting and ill-suited, like a man's tunic tossed casually over a small woman.

"I told you, I worship Artemis." He tossed his head into the air, his nostrils flaring. I closed my eyes briefly.

"I worship all the gods," I said quietly, "but particularly those from whom I am descended, as is right. The sun god Helios, and—"

"I do not care which gods you are descended from." He cut me off and laughed at what must have been a most shocked expression on my face.

"Sir, if you continue to defy the gods like this, they will punish you," I tried, not wanting to give up too soon.

"Is that what you believe?" he asked, twirling something in his hand. Looking closer, I saw it was a riding crop.

"Of course," I said, firmly, ignoring the fire in my lower abdomen. But he was already striding away with long loping steps.

"There is only one goddess worth obeying, and that is Artemis," he called back over his shoulder. "Mark my words: she will protect me from all others."

I shivered at his unassailable arrogance, and as I did, a cloud passed over the sun. It seemed my grandfather, the sun god, wished to tell him otherwise.

Night Chorus

We are the women of Athens,
although we could be from anywhere.

Listen to us. Just listen.

Beware. Here are the men who have hurt us.
We don't want it to happen to you.

Alcestis forced me when I was only fifteen.

I am old enough to be his mother, but . . .

Never, never, never be alone with Dioscouros.

Won't someone listen? I just want to be heard.
I just want to be believed.

I had no choice.

I didn't want to.

It happened to me.

And me.

And me.

Me, too.

Phaedra

And yet, even after a moon phase had passed, there was still no sign of the gods visiting punishment on Theseus. I saw little of him. I didn't go back to the shore, not because I was avoiding Hippolytus, but because the weather had turned, and it was more pleasant to keep to my rooms, eat the food that Kandake prepared for me, and sleep, dreaming of vengeance.

As I lay on my bed or knelt in front of my shrine, I would wonder about what form the gods' punishment would take. I wanted to know how I would foresee that it was about to happen, so I could ensure I was there to witness it, just as I'd been there to witness Theseus's transgression. I even speculated whether I might have a small part to play in it. I would imagine leaving a rope coiled in the corridor for Theseus to trip on and break his neck, or else leaving a piece of food out which would turn rancid and cause him to choke and die. But I would always follow these thoughts by muttering, "As the gods wish." The revenge the gods would wreak would be enough for me.

I needed to paint, I realized. I couldn't go on like this, feeling unsettled and out of place. I needed to make my mark and show I belonged here. I knelt at my trunk and pulled out my paints. My hand brushed against the small labrys, but I pretended I hadn't felt it. A shudder ran through me as I passed my hand over the colorful paints instead and then grasped the brush. Why would any woman want to sew, I wondered, when she could have all these joys in her palm?

I stood, brush in one hand, chin in the other, poised before the wall. I didn't intend to apply any colors at this stage—just a preparatory whitewash. And yet I hesitated, not so worried that I might get caught as I was that I might get it wrong. This wall was rougher than the ones in our palace in Crete, less finished. I didn't really know what I was doing. Perhaps I needed to—

I stopped myself. All I was going to do was put a whitewash on the wall. Even a labourer could do that. Tentatively, I lifted my brush and made the first stroke.

And then, so fast that I wasn't sure what had happened, the paint was controlling me. I was smoothing paint across the wall as though I were a mother caressing her baby's skin. Enjoying the feel of the brush under my fingers, the wall under the brush, like a musician bringing his composition to life. Subjecting the wall to my will, my vision, like a god giving birth to the world. It may have just been a pale white coating, the dull surface of the wall still shining through, but to me, it felt like a masterpiece.

Soon I realized that there was a reason why labourers were given this task: the brush size. My delicate little brush, so perfect for sketching people or Cretan bulls, was terrible at coverage. A man with a broad brush and big arms could have covered this in a quarter of the time I was taking. But I didn't care. I persevered, my wrist aching, until the thin white strokes in the centre of the wall spread out and around to fill the space. I crouched down to cover the lower end of the wall, and I pulled up a chair to reach its top. The fumes in my nose made me dizzy, but I gripped onto the top of the chair for balance and hung on, determined to make that wall mine.

Finally, the wall was covered. I stumbled back to the floor and looked at it. The wall was patchy. The paint was uneven. I could see clear brush strokes throughout. But it was my wall. I'd decided I was going to paint it, and I'd painted it. And that could only ever be a victory.

Now I had to decide how I was going to decorate that wall. This part of the endeavor I had given less consideration to. I could have started with a Cretan bull, accustomed as I was to sketching them, but I couldn't picture a bull without remembering that slim body impaled on the horns, a sight that haunted me still. I needed something fresh—a sign that I had adopted my new home. I wondered about the symbol of Athens, the wise old owl, evoking the goddess Athena, but I had never seen one up close, and I wasn't sure I could get the eyes right. Poseidon was Theseus's father, and he carried a trident, but it felt too obvious.

After much deliberation, I decided on the sea, blue waves slapping onto a coastline, with golden sunshine up above. That would be a fitting symbol: Poseidon, the father of Theseus, in partnership with Helios, the grandfather of Phaedra. Husband and wife bringing gods together. My mouth twitched a little as I remembered a lecture that Alessandro, our master fresco maker, had given his apprentices, not realizing that I was sitting in.

"Remember that while you may be the artist, the great lord who has commissioned your work—he is the patron. And what, above all, does the patron want? Why, to be flattered. To watch the artist disappear and the subject come to the fore. And how do we do that? We make them feel important. They say they are descended from the gods. Then we make them the gods. Flattery is everything. Flattery pays for your dinner."

I'd looked around the Great Hall at that point, my least favorite of all the rooms in our palace, yet beloved of my father, and noted the strength and power of the Cretan bull. Flattery, indeed. And who would be remembered longer? Alessandro, the genius who painted those murals? Or King Minos, son of Zeus, the Cretan bull personified?

Bearing this in mind, I decided to put the emphasis on the sea below, and not on the sun in the sky. Perhaps it would be more flattering to remind my new husband that his father was the king of the ocean.

I enjoyed painting the colors even more than I'd enjoyed the whitewashing. Here was opportunity, a chance to dapple the ocean with different shades of blue, to distinguish the waves with slivers of white and black. Was it the artwork I dreamed of in my head? No, of course it wasn't. There was a huge gaping chasm between the two; even in my enchanted state I had to admit that. But I was still enjoying the process, throwing myself into it completely, until there was no distinction between me and my work. No doubt anyone else would envision me as naive and foolish, a spoilt princess playing at being an artist. And later, when I looked on my wall, with its splotches of blue and white paint applied seemingly at random, that was what I would think, too. But at that time, paintbrush in hand, I wasn't playing. I thought I *was* an artist.

I could have carried on all day. The sun was low in the sky by the time I finished the water to my satisfaction, and the sudden chill made me realize that Kandake would be back soon with a hearty stew. At least this time I had a surprise for her, even if I knew she wouldn't approve.

Kandake

The Athenian palace scared me. I was glad I wasn't a younger woman. All around me tiptoed serving women and maids, silent like cats. They wore flat slippers to avoid drawing attention, and long sleeves to hide the bruises on their arms. Before I knew it, I was doing it as well. What was worse, when Phaedra finally did leave her room, she tiptoed, too. No one treated her like a queen. Everyone just ignored her. I continued to fetch her food and water, and we mostly kept to ourselves in our own rooms.

We never saw Theseus. Phaedra seemed unaware of how her value was falling every day, spending all her time either working on her picture—her "mural", as she called it—or on her knees in front of the little shrine she'd set up in our rooms. A baby could have changed everything, but there was no chance of that. I heard the girls crying in the night, and I thought Phaedra must be the only woman who was sleeping alone, other than me. But I was an old woman. She was supposed to be the queen.

I was fetching food from the shared kitchens one day when I heard one of the serving women mention Phaedra's name. My head lifted, but then I dropped it again, not wanting to be seen.

"Did you hear the queen has been flitting about the prince again?"

"Prince," another woman replied. "Overgrown boy who prays too much, if you ask me."

"As long as he's just praying," a younger woman said, and despite myself, my heart went out to her.

"But you should see the way he looks at the queen," the first woman said, laughing now. "I think he prays for forgiveness, for betraying his precious Artemis."

Several women hissed at her now, and I made my departure. It was bad luck to criticize any of the gods, everyone knew that, and especially one of the Olympians. It wasn't as though they would ever interfere in our lives—they were too busy with the city rulers. But they could blind us just by thinking about it. I had better offer something at our little shrine myself.

☽

On my way back to our rooms, I saw a group of young men, circled around something on the floor. My heart stopped and I thought I saw a pile of bloody meat, but when I looked down, it was only one of the men, wearing a red tunic and crouched over a pair of dice.

"You lose again, Otreus," he called gaily. "The luck of the goddess remains mine!" I couldn't see him clearly, past all those hefty backs and shoulders, but I knew who it was. And then I saw someone else, standing across from the circle, also watching them. Phaedra. My heart sank, and I watched as Hippolytus straightened up and crossed over to her while the young men parted silently.

"If it isn't our newest princess," he said, chucking her under the chin.

"Queen," she retorted, and stepped back, away from his reaching hand. It was a mistake; the crowd of men had reformed around them. She must have stepped on one of their feet, because I heard a yelp. I looked about wildly, having no idea what to do or whom to turn to.

"Queen," Hippolytus said, and scowled. "Queen or fool. Perhaps they are synonymous. The last royal woman who visited us wasn't that bright either."

"You mean Medea?" Phaedra asked.

He nodded. "Awful woman. You know what she did?"

Even I knew what she had done, although the rulers usually kept their gossip away from people like me. To seek revenge on her husband, she had killed her own children. She should have been punished, but her grandfather, Helios, the sun god, had spirited her away here. The old king Aegeus had taken her in, and it was generally considered that she had both kingly and godly protection. Earned under his bedsheets, no doubt.

"Make no mistake, my father will not be smitten in the same way my grandfather was," Hippolytus said, his tone harsh and grating again.

"Smitten?" Phaedra asked, surprised. "I thought he showed her forgiveness and hospitality."

Hippolytus laughed, a short barking laugh that made him sound like his father. "The hospitality of his bed, you mean? No one was going to slit her throat in the night while she slept in the royal bedchamber."

Phaedra blushed, and with her pale skin, soon her entire chest was glowing.

"Did I say something to upset you, Princess?" he sneered, and the men around him stamped their feet and whistled. This was turning nasty fast, and again I looked about wildly.

"What's going on?" I heard a voice roar, and my heart lifted with hope. "Hippolytus, I had better not find you gambling again.

"Hippolytus! Where is your father?" The crowd fell apart. A man pushed me aside as easily as if I were a tiny bird. He was a giant of a man, with a lion's skin stretched casually across his shoulders. The young men flocked to him, and both Phaedra and I took advantage of the confusion to slip away.

We didn't talk about the incident, though. I didn't even tell her I'd seen her.

☽

That night, for the first time since I was a young girl, I stayed awake listening to the night chorus. This time, though, it wasn't just Theseus's name I was listening for. I was intrigued to hear whether Hippolytus was mentioned. Whether his devotion to the virgin goddess was as strong as he made out.

By the morning, I had to admit defeat. While every one of Hippolytus's friends were called out by name, as bullies, abusers, and rapists, I never heard Hippolytus's name. But I'd seen the way he'd looked at Phaedra. Desire that strong would have to be quenched somewhere, and I felt sorry for whichever maid might find herself blocking his path.

Medea

We continued with our plans to leave Athens. Agneta was most concerned about our lack of a destination. She began to make discreet inquiries in the kitchens and other places where women gathered. I could not muster as much interest. Was this to be my life, throwing myself upon the mercy of one amorous king after another? I did not care whether I lived or died, but I could not say that to Agneta. So she carried out her investigations, and I carried out mine, sending Cassandra to gather information about how the little princess was faring in the court.

The first indication of trouble in Olympus was when she told me that the princess was not sharing a room with Theseus.

"Perhaps it is a sign of respect," Cassandra suggested.

"Perhaps," I said in a tone that sounded like it had been doused in vinegar, "it is a sign that Theseus has brought back a hostage rather than a bride."

Her face fell. For someone who hated her own husband, Cassandra was a romantic at times.

I decided that I couldn't rely on spies anymore. I had Cassandra make a robe for me, a long black one with a hood in which I could swoop through the corridors at night without drawing too much attention to myself. It made me appear something like a bat, which appealed to me.

A bat was a creature of the night.

I began to creep about the palace when it was dark and
quiet. I spied at doors and listened at windows, and what I
saw made me despair. Old and young men alike, regardless of
their politics, used and abused women as though they were
mere tools for their pleasure. No so-called decent women
lived in the palace. Unlike in other palaces, there was no
queen with her retinue, which would include the wealthy
women married to the advisers of the king. Any married man
took care to ensure his wife stayed at home, to provide for her
safety. And to ensure that she didn't know what he got up to,
naturally.

This was the poisonous atmosphere into which little
Phaedra was introduced, like a precious flower on a bar-
ren mountain top. I watched, interested, to see what she
would do.

But for a time, it seemed she would survive. Theseus was
too busy to pay her much attention. I could not resist drawing parallels with my own situation. While Theseus was
battling with every member of the court, he was not looking for me. And thank the gods (assuming there were any)
because I was in no doubt that he would have me killed if
he did find me.

☽

It didn't take long for the news to reach me. Of all the
heroes to turn up in Athens, Herakles was perhaps the one I
least wanted to see. Apart from Jason.

It is a funny thing about Greece. We use this word *hero* in
a way that is completely divorced from its true meaning. Save
a child from drowning, and you will be called a fine man, a
savior, a man everyone wants to know. But be the child of a

god, with big muscles or a cunning mind, who does nothing for anyone other than yourself, and you are a hero.

This logic applies only to men, obviously. A woman descended from a god still has to be either a good woman or a witch. What would it take to be called a heroine?

Herakles is such a lump of a man. No subtlety. No brains. It is impossible to see what he and Theseus have in common, until you realize that isn't why they are friends. No, they are friends because Theseus is able to lead Herakles around by the nose, like a prize bull, and Herakles is too stupid to see what is happening. What's more, Herakles' boisterous reputation and his much-sung daring exploits provide Theseus with a convenient disguise for his worst impulses and schemes. It wasn't Theseus—oh no, Herakles led him astray. Those two buffoons once kidnapped one of the princesses of Sparta, who is still only a child. Uproarious fun for all, except Theseus managed to take a pretty ransom for it, something the bards don't sing about.

But all that aside, Theseus did not want Herakles in Athens. On one of my nightly jaunts around the palace, I happened to stray near to the chambers Herakles was staying in, and I overheard them speaking.

"Anyone would think you didn't want me here," called a large booming voice. Herakles, indubitably.

"Now why would you say that, Herakles? You know I am always happy to see you. I just happen to be busy at the moment." The cool dry, tones of Theseus, too refined to ever be raised.

"A scheme?" Herakles interrupted. "I love a scheme."

I pressed myself against the wall and listened, amused. If Herakles shouted any louder about the proposed scheme,

I might as well have stayed in my own chambers to listen to this conversation.

"Not exactly a scheme. A political . . . endeavor. Look, old friend, it isn't your sort of thing. It won't take me too long to establish. Why don't you go on a quest in the meantime, and I will send for you when it is done?"

"Is this the 'democracy' I keep hearing whispers about? Giving the rule to the people? Sounds like a load of nonsense to me."

I bit my lip to stop myself from laughing. When even Herakles criticizes your political plan, perhaps it is time to reconsider.

"It's not nonsense. Kings and queens descended from gods—that's nonsense. No offense meant, old friend." Theseus added the last part hastily, and I could only imagine Herakles weighing that hefty club in his hand. He was reputed to take his parentage very seriously indeed. It was the bane of his life, if the bards were to be believed, as the goddess Hera continued to torture him for being the illegitimate and best-loved son of her husband Zeus. His scrapes and torments had nothing to do with the mortal men and husbands Herakles had offended over the years, in one way or another.

"Isn't that how you rule, Theseus? No offense meant here either, friend," Herakles asked, displaying a degree of intelligence I hadn't thought possible.

"At the moment. But my plan—'democracy,' as you call it—will still need men to be in charge. Strong men. Intelligent men. Competent men."

Herakles guffawed. "Strong, intelligent men who just happen to be descended from gods. Your plan is too subtle for me, Theseus, and I believe you will still be in charge when you have finished putting it in place. But there is something else I wish to take up with you. I hear you have a couple of royal captives in the palace who might be descended from the gods themselves."

"You mean the Cretan princess?"

"I think I do. I only caught a glimpse of her with Hippolytus. Why didn't she join us at dinner? I hear she's your new wife, after all."

"Don't be ridiculous, Herakles. She's just a child. She's here to make sure Minos doesn't launch any stupid endeavors before I have my troops in order." There was an irritable edge to Theseus's voice.

"But you did marry her." Herakles seemed unbothered by his friend's rising temper. No doubt he was used to it, or perhaps Herakles was just used in general to others getting irritable in his presence.

"I suppose so."

"Then why are you not bedding her? She's not actually a child."

"I have a lot to plan at the moment. I don't have time for distractions."

I could almost see Herakles shaking that large head of his, his shaggy hair making him look more of a lion than the dead animal draped round his shoulders. "You've changed, Theseus. Well, if you haven't time to bed her, I take it you don't object to me doing the deed?"

There was a splutter from Theseus, and I stuffed my fingers in my mouth to stop myself laughing. "Are you absolutely mad, Herakles? I'm trying to *avoid* war with Crete, not start one."

There was a pause, and then I imagined that leonine man shrugging philosophically. "Very well. You have enough maids here to do the job. Some of them are even quite willing."

"I am aware," Theseus said curtly.

"Is someone out there?" Herakles said suddenly, and I froze. I'd let my guard down. We all paused for a moment while I didn't dare breathe.

"Must have been a draft," Theseus said. "But Herakles, you said captives. Did you have someone else in mind? The older Cretan girl isn't here."

"What older Cretan girl? I would hope one is enough." And Herakles paused a moment to guffaw again; the man took his own entertainment with him everywhere he went. "No," he continued when he'd finished laughing, "the witch from Colchis." My heart stopped beating in my chest. How did he know I was here?

"What are you talking about?" Theseus asked. "Medea isn't here anymore. I know she had my father under her spell, but she hasn't been seen since he died."

There was silence from the two men before Herakles said slowly, "And yet she hasn't been seen anywhere else. Or seen leaving, for that matter."

"What are you implying?"

"I'm implying nothing. I'm telling you what everyone is saying outside Athens. First she took the father, then the son. I came here expecting to find her sitting in pride of place, but I haven't seen her."

"By Zeus." Theseus whistled. "I assumed she had the good sense to leave. I haven't seen her. I certainly haven't bedded her."

"No?" Herakles asked slyly. "I thought perhaps that was why you weren't bedding the Cretan girl. You prefer them a little more mature?"

"And homicidal? No, thank you. Besides, Corinth was about to declare war on Athens for sheltering her."

I wished I could sit down, but I needed to stand. I couldn't bear what was about to come next, and yet I would have to.

"Ah, yes, I heard Jason is still out for her blood. Can't say I blame him. What right did she have to kill his children?"

These men. Worse gossips than the kitchen maids.

"Perhaps she thought they were her children, too," Theseus said drily, and Herakles almost killed himself with laughter, accompanied by the sound of a hand slapping against another body part. His meaty thigh, I presumed. He began to choke, he was so delighted by the joke, and I took the opportunity to sneak away, even though I wanted to hear if they would say anything more about my ex-husband. Everyone always focused on the killing of the children. No one ever asked why.

☽

The next night, I stayed far away from Theseus's chambers. I had drawn enough attention to myself. And yet, sense would have dictated that I stay in my own room. Send my maids out if I needed gossip. Better yet, send my maids out to negotiate our passage away from Athens.

I did none of these things. If I had to justify it, I would say I needed human contact. Perhaps that was even true.

I slipped out of my room. As always, the smell of the Athenian court accosted my nose. The rancid stench of a place that didn't see enough daylight or soap. The corridors were dark and quiet as the inhabitants of the court either slept or conducted their affairs under darkness.

My cloak covering my head, I followed the directions that Cassandra had given me, down the winding hallways. I hadn't known that the court extended this far, the corridors reaching back like tentacles. Now the smell was more the dry smell of a place that was never used. I wiped cobwebs out of my eyes. My own rooms had been placed conveniently beside Aegeus's, but Theseus had shown no such courtesy for his wife. If she hadn't been so young, she would never have allowed this state of affairs to pass. Her father commanded an army.

When I reached the rooms, I took a deep breath. There was no point in listening at the door. The rooms were quiet, and no torchlight shone from beneath the door. The queen had gone to bed. *She may not even answer,* I thought. And still, instead of creeping in to see her mural, I raised my hand and knocked at the door.

There was a little scuffle behind the door, and then it opened. Two frightened pairs of eyes peered out at me. She hadn't even believed that she had the privilege of ignoring my knock. I was disappointed. I had expected more from this princess. I had expected an equal.

I pushed the women aside and strolled into the room. I turned back towards them and pushed the cloak from my forehead. I would not be judged by the likes of them, I wished my posture to say. The response I got was not what I expected, though.

"Ariadne?" The princess stepped towards me, raising her arms, and then dropping them again in disappointment. "I'm sorry, madam. I mistook you for someone else."

"My name is Medea," I said, trying to keep my voice haughty. "You may have heard of me."

The older woman shuffled, but the princess put her hand on her arm.

"Yes, of course. We are cousins, is that not so? No wonder you appear so like my sister. Why have you come here, and at this hour? Do you bring a message from Theseus? Or from"— she paused and seemed to struggle with her words—"anyone else in the court?"

"I came because I wished to see you," I said. My reply sounded foolish in my own ears, but it seemed to satisfy her. A little too late, it occurred to me that I could be handing her the bargaining tool she sought, a chance to tell Theseus where the witch Medea was hiding. And yet, perhaps in the darkest part of my soul, I knew that was what I was doing. Perhaps I wanted to give her an advantage.

"Go back to bed, Kandake," she said. "I will speak with my cousin"—she looked about the rooms and wrinkled her nose—"in private, if that is possible."

The maid's already short upper lip curled under, but she nodded her head and disappeared into the smaller of the two bedchambers. Phaedra sat down at the table in the main room and motioned me to do the same. I sat and we looked at one another, neither of us wanting to break the silence. But my age gave me greater patience.

"Why did you want to see me?" she asked.

"You are my cousin, and the new queen of this court. Are these not reasons enough?" I prevaricated.

"Certainly." She smiled, the polite smile of a well-brought-up young lady. Perhaps I could smile like that once.

"Besides"—my tone as airy and light as a bird released from its cage—"I trust you not to say anything to Theseus. About seeing me. We are family, after all."

Anger flashed over her face. "I do not speak to Theseus." Inwardly, I smiled. I had not really known why I had come to see her. It certainly had nothing to do with family. But that sudden, intriguing loss of control, in one brought up to be so restrained, had fulfilled my desires. There was a story here, and I was bored and in need of entertainment.

"Why are you here?" I asked, trying to provoke a return of that spark. "Surely you could have taken your pick of the kings of Greece. Why come to this backwater?"

For a moment she looked flustered, looking down at her hands in her lap. Then she raised her head, eyes blazing. "Isn't the better question, why are you here? What if I were to tell him?"

What indeed? But I smiled and replied, "You won't."

"What makes you so confident?"

I waved my hand at her chambers. "My rooms are nicer than these, and I am not the queen. Perhaps the king might reward you for giving him the information. But we both know better."

She was silent again. This time, I didn't think that she would speak first, so I did it for her, saying as I rose to my feet, "It is late, and you must be tired. I wanted to see you, and perhaps you did, me, too. We are family, after all. But I will not return unless you want me to."

I gathered up my cloak and stepped to the door, holding my breath in my mouth. A small voice came from behind me.

"Thank you. No one visits me. I never get to speak to anyone. I'm—" And she broke off here, although I was sure she was about to say that she was lonely. Her naivety was astounding. She finished quickly, "Please do come back."

I nodded in acknowledgement and swept out of the door.

Phaedra

I'd had more human interaction in one day than I'd had in all my time at Athens.

After my altercation with Hippolytus, I veered between indignation and fear. How dare Hippolytus speak to me like that? I was the queen. I was his stepmother. I should speak to Theseus and have him disciplined. But then I would remember the pride in Theseus's eyes when we saw the horse-riding boy on the shore. And then there was the late-night visit from my cousin. Was she a friend? I did not feel so, and yet something stopped me from running straight to Theseus and telling him all about her. She was a murderer, wasn't she? Why should I hide her? But then, so was Theseus.

Let the gods punish Medea—that was nothing to do with me. I continued to offer my sacrifices to every god I could name and to those that were nameless. The vengeance I had come to witness would be revealed soon.

I didn't spend a lot of time thinking about my rescuer. After all, he hadn't really rescued me, just distracted the boys and allowed me to escape. But that evening, I was waiting for Kandake to return from the kitchens with my evening meal when instead a servant I hadn't seen before knocked on the door.

"Madam, your presence is requested in the dining room," she said, her voice little more than a whisper.

"When?" I asked, panicked. I wasn't dressed for company, and I didn't know when Kandake would return.

"Now," she said, and then she leaned forward. "Herakles has requested it specially."

At that point Kandake bustled back in. I rocked on my heels while Kandake sent the other woman back with the message that the queen would be with them shortly.

I had never met Herakles, but I had heard all about his exploits. Everyone had. Before Theseus had arrived in Crete, Ariadne had told me that she intended to find him and marry him one day.

"But how do you know he will want to marry you?" I asked. This seemed a grandiose declaration even for Ariadne.

"I will make him want to marry me," she announced, tossing her long auburn curls haughtily. "I will be the woman who tamed the lion killer."

Lion killer. Wild-horse tamer. Most beloved son of Zeus. The epithets that accompanied Herakles were many.

"We must be related to Herakles," I remember saying to Ariadne, who turned and stared at me in disbelief. "He is the son of Zeus, and we are the granddaughters. Doesn't that make him our uncle?"

"I don't think it works that way with gods," she said firmly. I had nodded, although no one was ever sure how it worked with gods, and certainly many heroes seeking favor with my father had presented themselves to him as his "cousin."

"Gods are very confusing." I had sighed, vowing to spend more time devoting myself to their shrines in the hope that understanding might be revealed to me. But now

Ariadne was married to a god, and I was alone in the Athenian palace with the son of Poseidon, and no one seemed to care whom I was descended from.

Kandake busied herself tying my chiton and arranging my hair, and I let my mind wander. Unfortunately, these days when I did that, it tended to wander towards Hippolytus. I remembered Ariadne's words about taming the lion killer. Perhaps I could be the woman to tame the centaur. But no, I shook myself. I had forgotten that I was Hippolytus's stepmother. He was not mine to tame, and I should not be thinking this way. I hated his father. But the son, the son was younger, more malleable. He hadn't yet committed the egregious sins of the father.

I wished Ariadne were here now. However, if she were, I'd be back in Crete, but I wanted . . . not her advice, exactly, but her view. I wanted to know what the wildest, boldest course of action would be in this situation, so I could react against it with a more reasonable plan. Without her as a touchstone, all my plans seemed equally unreasonable. I remembered again my cousin tossing her head, the long auburn hair that looked so much like my sister's, cascading down her back. She was a lot older than Ariadne—closer to my mother's age—but perhaps I could speak to her.

I let out a small cry as Kandake stuck a pin into my head instead of my hair, and she nodded, looking satisfied, before murmuring an apology.

☽

My hands shook a little as I walked down the hallway, and I pulled anxiously at first the neck, then the hem of my chiton. I had never shared a meal with the Athenian court before—not properly. My mother had naturally spent hours ensuring that my table manners were immaculate. But the Athenian court was such a different place to what I was used to. For all I knew, they speared their meat on their swords or were required to use bows and arrows to shoot animals before eating them raw.

It was obvious when I walked in the room which man was Herakles. I had thought Theseus tall, but this giant towered over him. I had thought Hippolytus muscular, but Herakles' arm was as thick as my waist. And I had thought the men noisy before, but with Herakles laughing uproariously in the middle of the group, I almost needed to cover my ears. The large group of men parted as I entered, and I stepped towards the giant in the middle.

"Sir," I said, nodding to him. He had curious hair, I reflected, the color of the lion's pelt slung around his shoulders, and I wondered if that was intentional.

"Madam," he said in return, bowing his head courteously, before he turned back to Theseus and guffawed again. "See, Theseus? I told you dinner would be improved by a lady being present. Keeps us all on our toes."

I couldn't see the humor, but I smiled anyway. I also realized that he was my savior from earlier in the day, when Hippolytus had been tormenting me in the corridor.

"She's no lady," I heard a voice behind me call out, but not as loud as he might have done any other time.

"That's enough, Hippolytus." It wasn't Herakles who spoke; he was too busy laughing and spluttering wine. It was Theseus, his face as frosty as ever. Herakles was supposed to be a great friend of his, and yet, from his expression, he would rather his friend were anywhere other than in his court.

I was shown to my seat, and we proceeded to eat one of the strangest meals of my life. I was seated next to Theseus on those uncomfortable wooden benches. Strangely, Theseus took his meat with his left hand, not his right, which meant that our elbows jostled awkwardly. It was the most physical contact I'd ever had with the man who was supposed to be my husband, and I suspected from the way he pulled his arm closer and closer to his body that he found it as repulsive as I did.

On my other side sat Herakles, his muscular thighs so large that he took up more than his fair share of the bench. As a result, I was pushed from one side to the other, now moving towards Herakles to avoid Theseus's elbows, now back towards Theseus to avoid being knocked off my seat by Herakles' arms. I was going to have a lot of bruises when I got back to my room, I thought grimly to myself. And opposite me, seeing my dilemma and snickering to himself whenever his father looked the other way, was Hippolytus.

"So tell me, Hippolytus, how do you like the court now that your father is king?" Herakles asked, leaning over the table. I breathed out a little into the space he left behind.

"I do not like it," Hippolytus said insolently. "My father had more time and more interests before he became king. He has not been riding with me once since he returned from Crete."

"Your grandfather has only just died," I exclaimed before I could stop myself. All three men turned and stared at me, Hippolytus outraged, Herakles stunned, and Theseus merely looking intrigued, as though a mute had spoken.

"I did not know him well," Hippolytus retorted. "I did not know until very recently that he was my grandfather. I have completed the necessary mourning rituals." And he scooped up a large helping of bread and thrust it into his mouth, chewing furiously, no doubt to avoid further conversation.

"Yes, yes, people need to mourn," Herakles said, waving a chicken leg in the air as if to show his dismissal of the concept. "But men need to ride as well. You will lose your knack, Theseus, if you do not practice." He winked, an overly grotesque demonstration in case we had missed his deeper meaning, and I flushed and looked away, although not before I noticed Hippolytus doing the same thing.

"Surely either I have a knack, or I need to practice," Theseus said irritably, but the subtlety was lost on Herakles. "As I have told you many times, Hippolytus, and you only this afternoon, Herakles, I have more important matters to attend to at present."

"More important than riding?"

"What could be more important than riding?" Herakles and Hippolytus spoke at almost the same moment, causing Herakles to burst into laughter once more. He leaned back in his chair, and I sucked my breath in again.

"Governing the city, for one. Creating a new system, one in which every man can serve his city, and the city serves every man." His words were clipped, and he paused in his eating to look, not at Herakles, but at his son.

"Not women, eh, Phaedra?" Herakles asked, nudging me in the ribs and laughing again at his own perceived wit. I smiled weakly.

"Herakles, it is one thing for you to jest, but Hippolytus needs to take this more seriously. If my system succeeds, the city-state will be governed on merit. Hippolytus cannot rely on inheriting a crown the way I did. He will have to earn it."

I don't know what sort of reaction Theseus expected to his outburst, but encouraged by the yawns that Herakles was giving, Hippolytus merely rolled his eyes.

"I don't want to inherit a crown or govern a city. I have told you before. I want to serve Artemis and ride my horse. And before you say anything," he said to me, "the two are synonymous. There is no disrespect to the goddess here."

I tossed my head and stared him straight in the eyes. "I wasn't going to say anything. What you do is of no interest to me." Hippolytus flushed and looked away, and next to me, I heard Herakles whistle.

"She's certainly got you shown, Hippolytus. I suggest you stop now, before you're the one wearing a bridle. And Theseus," he added, leaning across me so that I had to lean so far back I almost fell off the bench, "I'd suggest you keep an eye on your pretty young wife."

I heard stomps and wolf-whistles from the rest of the tables and realized that all other conversation had stopped.

"Perhaps I should be excused," I muttered, looking down at my hands. I was suddenly very conscious of being the only woman in the room other than the serving women who came in and out infrequently. I twisted my hands in my lap, remembering the night chorus. There were still flecks of paint under my nails, and that made me feel better somehow.

"You will sit there and finish your dinner," Theseus said, and his voice was so firm that even Hippolytus looked up in surprise.

"Sir, I do not think you should scold your wife," he objected. "She is not your child."

"No, but you are," Theseus said. "I have had it with the lot of you. Herakles, you bring nothing but chaos in your wake. Tell us of this quest you need aid with, and let's be done with it."

Now Herakles, too, looked disgruntled, and we all ate in silence for a while, our chewing sounds the only noises that anyone could hear. But clearly the quest was close to Herakles' heart, because before long he started to describe it.

He was not a good orator. The quest involved some sort of a mermaid, or perhaps a siren, and the death and destruction that was to be visited on the unfortunate creature at Herakles' hands. I couldn't entirely understand why either; although a princess I'd never heard of was mentioned, the better answer seemed to be "Because it is there." I pictured the poor creature, its entrails dripping from the hands of a so-called hero, and I could not prevent myself from saying, "Can you not let the poor creature rest in peace?"

I didn't realize until I spoke that there were tears welling up in my eyes, and I hastily brushed them away, but not before one stray drop fell down my cheek. Herakles stared at me in disbelief, the great hero overcome by a woman's tears.

"That's enough, Phaedra," Theseus said. I stared at him, his image growing wavy as the tears came fast and thick now.

"But you . . . you speak as though this creature was a monster," I blurted out. I could have bitten my tongue off. I had gone against every warning, every admonition of my parents. There were things we did not speak of. My father's last words before I left Crete echoed in my head. I had to protect my parents' reputation. I should never have spoken.

Support came from an unexpected source. "Let her go," Hippolytus said. I looked at him in disbelief, so surprised I stopped crying. "Really, Father, just let her go. She's stayed for the entire meal. Let her go to bed."

"Then you must walk her back to her chambers. She can't walk back by herself like that."

Hippolytus nodded and pushed back the bench. Everyone else was forced to scramble for balance. I was able to slip out more easily, as the bench on my side of the table had been pushed back much farther already, to accommodate Herakles' meaty thighs.

"Sir," I said, bowing my head to Herakles, the guest at the table. My parents would be aghast by the meal I had partaken of, and my own breaches of etiquette, but I could at least finish on a better note.

He nodded back, still clearly uncomfortable, and his large bulk relaxed and slid closer to Theseus. They began discussing the provisions that Herakles could expect from Athens for his journey. I was clearly dismissed, from the table and from the very mind of my husband. Hippolytus took my elbow and we left the room.

Neither of us spoke as we proceeded down the corridor, Hippolytus still gingerly holding my elbow.

"Thank you," I said when I had control of my voice again. "I lost my way there. It was kind of you to assist me."

He flushed. "I care nothing of women," he muttered, although he did not drop my elbow. "Nothing to do with me. I shouldn't have interfered."

"But you are the son of a woman," I said, "and a woman who did not live with men, at that."

"What are you saying about my mother?" he said, dropping my elbow as his face glowered with instant anger. "She was devoted to the goddess Artemis, as am I."

I winced as I heard his single-mindedness once again. Mortals had been punished by gods for less. "It is good that you are devoted to the goddess Artemis. But there are other gods and goddesses. Your father knows that. Why do you not offer libations to all the pantheon?" I suggested.

"Be quiet. You're no queen. You call yourself a queen, but you are nothing. My mother was a real queen. She ruled her people by herself."

"Hippolytus," I protested. I placed my hand on my stomach, winded.

He looked down my body, his eyes widening as he took in my breasts, my stomach, my legs. I felt naked in front of him. "I worship only Artemis. If you wish to worship adulteresses like Aphrodite, be my guest. Just stay out of my way," he snarled, and he strode off.

I stared after him. I'd never met an Amazon. They weren't welcome in the Cretan court. But I'd heard the stories of them, those unwomanly women. They took one of their breasts off in puberty, believing it was better to be able to shoot an arrow than to feed a baby. They raided neighboring villages and stole baby girls. If they did, by some foul set of circumstances, fall pregnant, they kept the girls and dropped the boys off at those same villages, for the mothers of the girls they'd stolen to raise as their own. They were wild and free, and I could understand that Antiope, their queen, would have raged against being captured and impregnated by Theseus. But Theseus had never even tried to come to my room. I would hardly describe myself as an ardent follower of Aphrodite.

I opened my door, holding my head high. Hippolytus was just a boy, I reminded myself, although a small voice in the back of my head said that in that case, I was just a girl. But I was a married woman, and I had seen death and destruction he could only imagine as he trotted about on his horse. What could he possibly know about the world and the way it worked? *Nothing* was the answer. He knew nothing at all. I walked with the gods. The gods would punish Theseus for his actions, and they wanted me here to bear witness. That was all.

I went straight to my room when I got back and eased my sandal off my foot. A loose strap had given me an awful blister, and to my horror, as I pulled the sandal away, strips of my skin came with it. I limped to my bed and fell asleep.

Night Chorus

No woman is safe when the hero Herakles is in town. Visit your mother, draw kitchen duty, stab yourself with a carving knife, do what you must to get out of his way.

But someone must serve him. Someone must stay.

Once it was me . . . I thought I wouldn't walk for a week.

He left me a handful of coins on the pillow, and I didn't want to take them, but I had to because my son was unwell.

I cried. I cried until my heart would break, and he flipped me over as though I was a ragdoll and carried on. Herakles hates to see women cry.

It's funny, though, how he's always been so close to Hippolytus. Like an uncle, and yet Hippolytus avoids women.

Is it really that strange? Hippolytus may not bed women; he may spend all his time on his knees in front of the altar, but his eyes will still follow the queen across the room. His pupils dilate, and his breathing gets a little faster, just like when he sees a hind to kill. He's still young; there is time.

So is she. Fool Theseus, marrying a woman young enough to bed his son. So you think they have . . .?

Not yet.

Maybe.

Soon.

In the meantime, there is Herakles to worry about.

Herakles. He never stays long. There is that, at least. He never stays long.

Medea

Like a hive of poisonous bees, the entire palace was buzz-ing with talk about Hippolytus and Phaedra. Under-standable, in a way; a palace is such a contained environment, and it thrives on drama. Why do you think there are so many stories about the gods on Olympus? If you believe that sort of nonsense, which certainly I do not.

Hippolytus was a handsome young man, and Phaedra was a pretty enough girl, and Theseus certainly wasn't pay-ing her any attention. The rumors were an inevitability. I wondered what they would have been like if Theseus had brought his original intended, the beautiful elder sister. I suspect he would not have neglected her in the same way. Cassandra told me that she had been selected by Dionysos to be his bride. That is as likely as my grandfather Helios sending a chariot of fire to rescue me and bring me to Ath-ens. It makes for a convenient story, but it does rather make one question the truth it is standing in for. Presumably she ran off with a fisherman. Or a drunk.

Perhaps the stories about Hippolytus and Phaedra would have remained just that: stories. Except that Theseus announced that he was going away on another trip, this time to tour Attica, the region surrounding Athens.

It was left to the women to consider what this plan meant, to weep quietly and hope that the ensuing lawless-ness would be like a fever in a teething child, ferocious but brief. For Theseus, showing the most spectacular error of judgement possible, did not put one of the graybeards in charge, or even one of his own contemporaries. He left Athens at the mercy of Hippolytus, chief of the wild youth.

His devotion to Artemis irked me. Another goddess. One cannot move without stumbling over a god or goddess in Greece. I supposed I was lucky, in that I had caught the attention of a hero, not a god. My husband, Jason, was the great-grandson of the god Hermes, a relationship that was so distant it was hardly worth bragging about. Not that this stopped him.

No one could talk Theseus out of his hare-brained scheme, although many tried, and so it was that I watched from my window as the entire palace, aside from my handmaidens and me, traipsed down to the beach to watch him set sail.

What a ragtag motley crew they were. The Athenians. The city named for the greatest goddess of all, and yet its inhabitants looked more like stray dogs. Everyone's clothes were a little shabby and, worse, a little dirty. Even the supposed aristocrats looked as if their servants had given up drawing hot water for their baths and had started giving them cold seawater instead. The animals that ranged about the crowd's feet were mangy, and the children looked as though they might have fleas. There was no unity in the march to the beach, and stragglers would try and catch up, then give up and saunter easily, chatting to their neighbors as though they were going on a daily stroll instead of a parade required by the king.

"If Theseus wants to turn these peasants into a worthy nation, he has his work cut out for him," I remarked to Cassandra.

"Really? I heard he intends to turn Athens into a nation to rival Crete," she said.

"How did you hear that—I mean, who told you?" I amended my words hastily. Despite her long-suffering husband, Cassandra loved to regale us with stories of assignations with powerful men.

But this time she just arched her eyebrows and said, "I hear things." I let her have it. It didn't do to push her too much; she would clam up completely.

Looking down instead, from the window I saw the Cretan princess picking her way through the crowd. She looked unperturbed by the bright sun that had so many others blinking, a detail that disturbed me somewhat. I, too, can stare into the sun without feeling any pain. A family trait, and if so, was it one inherited from our shared maternal grandfather? And what did that make of my belief, or lack thereof, in the gods? I shook my head and focused again on the princess.

We watched in silence as the Athenian prince shouldered his way towards her, little caring about the people he pushed out of his way. I wished I could hear their conversation. She looked up towards him and smiled, while he threw his head back and roared with laughter. To my more mature eyes, he looked a buffoon.

"Do you think she has stolen a lock of his hair to keep under her pillow while she sleeps?" Cassandra asked, her tone dripping poison.

"She's married to the king," I reminded her mildly. "And what's it to you?"

She scowled and said nothing.

"What's Andros doing today?" I asked her. As always, the mention of her husband caused her face to curdle.

"He's visiting his mother," she said briefly, and slouched down in her seat. I wondered why I had felt the need to deflate her so. Was it some sort of blood loyalty to my cousin? Was it the sight of her, so pretty and defenseless? Hippolytus was leaning over her now, although I stiffened to see that she seemed to lean in towards him and open her mouth as he spoke.

"When are we going to leave Athens?" Agneta asked suddenly. I looked at her, surprised. It wasn't like her to interject, and it wasn't like her to criticize me, even by implication. The first time I'd seen her, she had been a small child, engulfed in clothes that were too warm for our balmier weather, a souvenir Jason had brought home with him from his voyage further north than anyone had ever been. And my first indication that my husband was not the hero everyone thought he was. I had insisted, in front of as many people as I could gather, including several priests, that she become my personal maid, a request he found impossible to refuse. If I were half as kind as she thought I was, I would have released her by now, made arrangements for her to travel back to the family she hadn't seen in over ten years. But her gratitude made her an excellent maid.

"In good time. Why are you in such a hurry?" I asked.

She sniffed. "The atmosphere is not good here. Something bad is going to happen. I can sense it."

I laughed. "So what are you now, some sort of soothsayer? There is nothing wrong with the atmosphere."

"The king is leaving, and a boy is in charge. Everyone is unsettled. You can't feel it?" she retorted.

"You're lucky I don't have you whipped," I said, my tone light but the warning clear. She muttered the following words under her breath. I still heard her though.

"You can feel it. That's why we're still here. You love the chaos."

I frowned and decided to pretend I hadn't heard her. After all, there was some truth in her words. I looked down again at the prince of Athens and the princess of Crete. Was there something between them? I wasn't sure.

☽

That night, I made my way to Phaedra's bedchamber again. I pulled my cloak tightly about me. I was glad that Agneta was safely stowed away in our chambers. If Cassandra chose to venture out on a night like tonight, she was a fool.

This time, Phaedra was ready for me. She opened the door herself. We arranged ourselves again on either side of the table, and she poured wine for us both. I sipped the wine carefully after waiting for her to do so first. It wasn't poisoned, but it also smelled and tasted of fish scales, so I pushed mine away as soon as I was able to do so.

"Tell me, Phaedra," I asked, my words as quick as the bull leapers her city was famed for. "The court is saying that you and Hippolytus are having an affair. Is this true? The gods will not be pleased." I waved my hand towards the makeshift shrine that took up half the table, as there was no room on the floor for it.

She flushed red, the type of blush that only the thin skin of a very young woman can reveal. I could have warmed my hands on her chest. I was envious. I had not blushed in a very long time.

I waited for her answer, but she countered me with another question. "Is it true that you killed your own children?"

"So they say," I replied, glad to hear my voice sounded steady in my ears despite the inevitable racing of my heart that always happened when someone mentioned my children. "But I do not see what that has to do with you and the young prince."

"Why?" she asked.

"Why do you ask?" I was thrown. Only yesterday I had been silently furious because no one ever asked me this question. If I believed in gods, this would be a clear example of them granting a wish that should never have been made. I looked over at Phaedra. Despite that fiery color that deepened her face and chest, her expression was stony. I did not think prurience motivated her, but I still was not minded to answer.

"Because I do not understand. They were your children."

No one understood, and yet I wanted to make her understand. "I heard a story recently," I said slowly, choosing my words carefully, "about a king from the East, a wise king, who was brought a baby by two women. Both claimed to be the mother. They asked him to settle the dispute."

Her face had lit up. She was so young, I thought, she still wanted to listen to stories.

"What did he do?" she asked.

"He told the two women that he would cut the child in half, and they could carry away a half of a baby each," I stated baldly, offering no gloss.

"But that is barbaric!" Her voice rose, and then she remembered the time of night and quieted again. "I had heard that they are not civilized in the East. So what did the women say? Did the king kill the child?"

I smiled despite myself. Her enthusiasm was surprisingly sweet. "One of the mothers told him to do as he suggested, and they would each return home with half a child. It was fair, after all. The other said no, give the baby to the first woman. Don't kill the child."

"Ah, so it was not barbarism on the king's part," she replied, smiling as she saw, or thought she saw, the purpose to my story. "The real mother would rather the other woman took the child, even if she missed out herself. The imposter wanted her half of a child."

She was so pleased with her cleverness that she spontaneously clapped her hands, and I felt my heart seize within my chest as I remembered my own little daughter performing that same gesture when she first touched her nose or first pulled herself to her feet. I shook my head and concentrated on the story instead.

"That is what the bards are saying the king intended," I agreed. "He gave the child to the woman who would rather have given the baby away."

"But you do not agree," she said, leaning forward.

"Was the other woman stupid? What use is half a dead child to her? Why would she want to take home a mutilated corpse out of a desire to have her fair share?"

"Then what is the true meaning of the story? Perhaps she believed the gods would intervene and save the child before it died?"

I laughed, a short, humorless laugh. "I do not believe in the gods. Do you mean to say you do?" This was not the diversion I had had in mind when I came to these dirty little rooms. I had meant to tease her a little, find out some gossip, perhaps gain a nugget of information to treasure to myself. I imagined us playing a game, perhaps one of the strategy games that old men play. Each moving a counter until one player was destroyed.

"Of course I do." Her voice was higher than mine, the pitch lighter. I was reminded again that I was of the age of Theseus, while she was of the age of his son. "If I didn't believe in the gods," she added, "I wouldn't be here."

"I don't understand," I said, my brow furrowing. "You are here because you married Theseus. What does your belief in the gods have to do with it?"

She paused. "I cannot say," she said.

"You've said enough already," I said. "But keep your secrets, if it suits you." I pretended to take another sip of the foul wine.

"Theseus is a monster," she said, her words falling out, as though a stopper that had been preventing her from speaking was suddenly loosened. "I am part of the gods' plan to visit suitable punishment down on him."

"This night is taking a very strange turn," I remarked, more to the air than to my companion. Her wine cup was empty, I noted. Perhaps the blush had not been entirely motivated by thoughts of young Hippolytus's loins. "I do not much care for Theseus either, my lady. But can I remind you that this is his court? If you say those words to the wrong person, you could be killed."

She looked down and mumbled, "I'm usually careful. But the gods will protect me—I believe it. Theseus is not the hero everyone thinks him to be. He killed my brother."

"Your brother?" I asked.

"My half brother, Minos. Theseus has told everyone he was a monster, but he was not. He wasn't even armed."

"Minos . . . you mean the Minotaur?" She nodded. "Was he not armed with giant horns on his head?"

She turned away. "You don't understand."

"No," I said, although I was beginning to. "So Theseus killed your brother, and you have come to Athens to take revenge upon him?"

"No," she said, scandalized. "Not revenge. To bear witness. To ensure the gods do their work."

I shook my head. "This theology is too advanced for me, Queen Phaedra." I stood up to stretch my legs, although there was little enough room to do so. As I looked around, I caught sight of the mural on the back wall. I had not seen it for several weeks, and she had made progress.

It was clearly painted by an amateur. Corinth, where I had lived with my husband, had among its populace some fairly competent mural painters, and none of them would have painted this way, the waves of the ocean crashing in all directions as shown by erratic brush strokes, and none of them coming in to the shore. It was physically impossible, if nothing else. And yet there was a charm in it, for all that, visible even in the dim light cast by the flickering flames of an oil lamp. A certain wild faith.

"Did you paint this?" I asked, knowing the answer.

She nodded. "Yes, I did. Painting is my passion."

"Well, well," I said. "You are full of surprises."

She grimaced. "So why did the woman in the story tell the wise king to divide the baby? And why did you kill your children?"

I sighed. "Because I do not have the faith in the gods that you do. Because sometimes, women need to take matters into their own hands. If the Minotaur was your brother, why was he locked in the labyrinth?"

I hadn't thought my answer particularly illuminating, but it seemed to satisfy her. My question, on the other hand, caused her brow to furrow. "That is true. My father said it was for the best, and my father is the son of Zeus. I don't know." She tailed off and bit her lip, ignoring the little speckle of blood she drew, then said, "You know you are hated here? If Theseus finds you, he will kill you."

"Theseus isn't here," I said with more bravado than I felt.

"Why are you still in Athens? Why do you not flee? Or throw yourself on the mercy of your father?" These were good questions, and I studied the mural intently while I composed myself.

"I do not feel the need to flee. Why do you not return to the mercy of your father? Now you have seen the bear pit that is the Athenian court? Oh, I forgot. You want to see revenge enacted, but not by you."

"You do not need to mock me." I remembered my daughter, only four years old, sounding similarly hurt when I laughed at her for professing that Corinth was the best place in the world. The brief memory was a stab through the heart, a luxury I did not permit myself often. Why was I allowing this young woman to get under my skin in this way?

While I was musing on these thoughts, she continued speaking. "In any event, the Athenian court is not the most civilized, I grant you. But I am safe. I am the queen. It is other women I feel for. Women like you."

I turned to face her in horror. "Phaedra, you must never think like that. Never. Being queen will not protect you for the length of time it takes a mosquito to suck your blood from your neck."

She shook her head. I could see she did not believe me. "You only feel that way because you antagonized the gods by taking your own revenge. They do not protect you. They will protect me."

"Child" was all I could manage to say in return. She pouted.

"I think it is time for you to leave," she said, standing up.

I nodded. "Indeed. Sleep well, Your Majesty." But I could not resist, and I turned to face her in the doorway. "I did not take any action out of revenge. My conscience is clear on that part, at least."

I left quickly before she could close her mouth and ask me any further questions. Once outside the room, I wanted to sag down onto the floor and cry. I wanted to weep, to beat my chest, to howl until the gods heard me, and my precious children were returned to my arms. I wanted to raise my head high and stride past all my deriders, the likes of Herakles and Theseus, to spit in their faces and tell them they knew nothing, they understood nothing—they were not mothers. They may be strong enough to bend iron, but not one of them was strong enough to bear my pain.

I did none of these things. I pulled my cloak about my face and skulked back to my rooms, where I snapped at Cassandra and set Agneta to pouring me better wine, and much of it, besides.

Night Chorus

We are living in hell. Who knew that Theseus was the one to impose order?

No room is safe. No man is safe to be near. The loud ones, the quiet ones, the ones who glare, and the ones who smile. Stay away from all of them. Don't ask permission, just leave. By night, if you must.

There is safety in numbers. I will assist you in your master's chambers if you help me clean my master's riding gear. We can begin as soon as they leave for the hunt, and then we will be gone by the time they get back.

When I make the stew for their dinner, I will put a sleeping draught in, to make them all drowsy so they pass out as soon as they reach their rooms.

We cannot rely on any king to look out for us. We will look out for one another. We will survive. We must.

Is anyone looking out for the Cretan princess? Has anyone warned her?

Medea

I went back to see her again. How could I resist? I was drawn to her, like the supposedly almighty Zeus to one of the many women he bedded, enticed by Phaedra's talk of the gods' plan for punishment of Theseus. I didn't believe in the gods myself, but did she? Did she really think there was a divine plan, or was it all an act, a cover for some more sinister scheme? Neither the risk of being caught nor the pain of reliving my own past decisions outweighed my need to know more and to understand.

A few nights later, I crept down the dusty passageways to those dreary rooms. Once again, I found the princess sitting up, staring at her mural. Still, I was pleased not to have to see that surly maid of hers again.

"Your Majesty," I said to her, and she nodded her head.

"Your Majesty," she replied. In anyone else, it would have been a form of insolence.

"Call me Medea," I invited, throwing myself into a chair, or at least doing some approximation of that action in the tiny space we had available. I wondered, and not for the first time, whose idea it had been to provide her with such a huge dining table, taking up most of the small room. No one's, most likely. A table was needed, and one that was not being used had been installed in place. Nobody had spared the matter any more thought than that. "We are cousins, after all."

"Yes," she agreed. "We are cousins. Our mothers may have been close; I don't know."

I doubted it. My mother had been the oldest of five siblings, while hers was the youngest. But sometimes in these instances an older girl will adopt a new baby as her own child, a sort of pet. Perhaps my mother had used up all her maternal instincts caring for her youngest sister. A thought to be wrapped away carefully and examined another time.

"Medea," she said, her mouth pursing around the unfamiliar syllables like that of a boy who has been asked to call his tutor by his first name on reaching adulthood, "I wished to speak to you about something. Are you aware of the night chorus?"

I looked at her blankly. "Is it a play?"

She shook her head, her brow furrowing. "Am I going mad?"

"What is it?" I asked. I felt sorry for her distress, but I still preferred this conversation to our last one.

"I hear women crying at night," she confided.

"Oh, there are lots of women crying at night." I raised and dropped my hand. "It is like a battlefield in the palace. I do not advise that you venture out at night."

"But you do," she pointed out. I opened my mouth to remind her that I was twice her age, old enough to be the mother of most of the boys who were causing so much misery, and I had the reputation of being a witch besides. But she carried on, not interested in any subject other than the one she had raised. "Anyway, it is not normal crying. We are too far from anyone in these rooms to overhear that." I nodded, and she continued. "No, it is like voices calling through my very head, speaking to one another, sometimes over one another, sometimes in unison. That's why I call them the night chorus."

"And what do they say?" I realized that I was leaning forward. There was something compelling about her, I had to admit.

"They detail the atrocities that take place nightly. Warn each other of men to avoid. That sort of thing."

I was sceptical, but I had heard of such a thing before. Women will always find ways of communicating with other women, even if men prefer them not to do so. Especially if men prefer them not to do so.

"And have you heard Hippolytus's name mentioned?" I asked, unable to resist teasing her.

She looked surprised, as though she had not considered it. "No. I haven't. Is that such a surprise? He worships Artemis, does he not?"

"If I had a feather for every man who claims to worship a virgin goddess and yet has his way with the woman who makes his bed, I would grow my own wings and fly far from this court," I said, my tone sharp. It was difficult talking to her. She was so naive. I did not want to see her get hurt.

"I need to do something to stop the night chorus," she said as I started to stand and take my leave.

"Stop it? You mean stop it from communicating?"

"No, I mean stop the atrocities from taking place. I am the queen, am I not?"

I looked at her, her head raised high, even though there was a smear of paint on her face, and the peplos she had thrown over her shoulders was the only one I had ever seen her wear.

"I would wait for Theseus to return," I said at last. "Speak to him then."

She nodded her head, and it was not until I was back in my own rooms that I realized she had done so in order to dismiss me. I sighed and went to bed. I only hoped that whatever philanthropic plan she concocted didn't make things worse for the poor women who had to deal with the aftermath.

Kandake

You volunteered for this.

I sang these words in my head all day. I didn't know if it would keep me sane or drive me mad, but it did stop my complaining. Mostly.

Why did I ask to come here? I had no idea. Was it love for the queen, as she assumed? It certainly wasn't love for her daughter. I had nothing against the girl, but I'd never cared much for children. But Pasiphaë did love her own children, especially the mutated one. Perhaps that was why I had volunteered to accompany her youngest child to Athens, a place I had never been. Now that I was here, I wanted to leave.

I wanted to leave all the time. But I never wished I had stayed in Crete. I had lived in the Cretan palace for almost my whole life, serving the queen. I thought my work would be the same here in Athens, serving her daughter. But at least it would be a new place, one I hadn't seen before.

Were the people different? They were and they weren't. Rougher than Cretans, I would say. Less civilized. More willing to speak their minds and tell you what they thought of you. But Cretans and Athenians alike love a good gossip.

I don't like gossip; I prefer to hold my tongue. Another reason I worked so well for Queen Pasiphaë. There was always plenty of gossip about her. I thought I should be telling people the truth, but she made herself clear. That was not my job. Let them say what they liked. She knew the truth, and working for her, so did I.

But what should I say to these Athenian gossips, convinced that Phaedra was copulating with Hippolytus? What would her mother have wanted? Phaedra was all alone in this strange palace, which if you asked me, looked more like the mud hut I had been born in than a real palace. And if rumors about Hippolytus and Phaedra got back to Theseus, he could have her killed. He'd already killed her brother, after all.

So I did my bit to put the gossips right. Casually, not making a fuss about it. When I went to collect our washing, I would mention that the princess rarely left her rooms and never saw a man. When I cooked our food in the shared kitchen, I would let slip that the princess slept alone every night. These rumors would do nothing to bolster her status as the wife of Theseus, but they were at least true, unlike some of the wilder suppositions I heard involving Phaedra and Hippolytus.

When we had moved our belongings into the palace, I had expected it would be like those early days at Knossos again—that I would find myself sleeping outside on the floor most nights, because the king couldn't resist his attractive young bride. But we had never seen Theseus, and now he had gone away.

I found myself remembering those early days in Knossos more and more. I had been so young, although I hadn't felt it at the time. And so had Queen Pasiphaë. She gave birth to her first son, a beautiful boy. She told me more than once that she and King Minos could not feel more blessed.

And then there was the second son. And the rumors and the cruel laughter and the decisions that I could not possibly understand, being only a poor goatherd's daughter, and not descended from the gods, as Minos told me. Shouted at me, one bad night. I expected I would be dismissed, but Pasiphaë must have put a word in for me.

And after that, she had two beautiful girls. And although I didn't partake of gossip, I always wanted to reply to those who muttered that Queen Pasiphaë was cursed, that I for one would still exchange my life for hers, given the chance. Mutated son or no mutated son. But perhaps that was just me.

It was not just that I didn't believe the rumors about that boy. I knew they could not possibly be true. Firstly, my mistress could not have had intercourse with a bull without my knowing. I am sorry to have to be so crude, but it is the blunt truth. As for all that nonsense about working with Daedalus to create a cow shape for her to sit in: firstly, I don't know when these discussions would have taken place, because the two were never alone together. At a state banquet, with the king and all the court looking on?

Secondly, I had spent my first fifteen years on a farm. Daedalus may have been a clever man (although, like most men, not as clever as he gave himself credit for), but the mechanism wasn't possible, and it wouldn't have fooled the bull, that's for sure. And thirdly, I knew that child. I thought, at one time, that I might have been allowed to take him away with me, away from the palace and the rumors and the cruel glances. But Minos had his own plans for his son—make no mistake, he was his son—and I wasn't asked my opinion.

After that bad night, I agreed that I would continue to work for the queen, but I didn't want anything to do with any more of her babies. And she agreed; I think at that point she didn't expect she would have any more. But she did, the two girls, as I said, and now here I was in Athens, and I might as well have been in Hades.

I did not like that Hippolytus. I wished that I could speak to Phaedra honestly about him, as I knew that her mother would have done, but I just didn't have the words. She thought of me as sullen, I can tell, as her father did before her. And perhaps I did come across as sullen, obstinate, an old woman with her weaving. But I knew a dangerous young man when I saw one, and Hippolytus was dangerous.

Wherever she went, he seemed to be there. She would return and prattle artlessly about her paints and the countryside and the sights she had seen, and always she came back to Hippolytus, Hippolytus on his horse. She would like to paint him, she told me. If I were her mother, I would have thrown her paints into the sea.

☽

One day she came to me. She asked me if I would set up a chance for her and Hippolytus to talk. She made some excuse about asking him to prevent the violence in the court; I could not follow it.

"Kandake, have you noticed that the atmosphere at court has been strained since Theseus left?" she started.

"It is not for me to say, madam." I studiously looked at my sewing.

"But you must have noticed," she protested, jumping up from her chair and pacing about the small room. She was more careful to avoid her mural than the soup that was still on the table, I noticed. I would have a lot of cleaning up to do later.

"Noticed what, madam?" I asked.

"Women are being ill-treated," she said after a pause. "By men."

"Yes," I replied, continuing to sew. "Men have always treated women ill, madam. Common women, I mean."

"But I should do something about it," she said, now tapping her foot in emphasis. Her anger frightened me; I could not see it leading to any good place.

"Please, madam, I cannot advise that. I mean, not that it is my place, but . . ." I could hear myself stuttering and could think of nothing to add except "For your mother's sake . . ."

"My mother would never allow this to happen in her court," she said feelingly.

I did not disagree with that, but I said, "But this is not her court. And Theseus is not your father."

"I think you forget yourself," she said coldly. We were silent for a while, then she exclaimed, "I just want to talk to him. To Hippolytus. If I explain about the suffering the women are experiencing, I feel sure he will stop it. Hippolytus is not his father."

Finally, I understood. She was in love with him. All this nonsense about gaining his assistance was just that: nonsense, an excuse to see him. I said, "He may be shy, you know."

"Shy?" she asked, and laughed bitterly. "I'm not sure about that."

"He's a young man who grew up without a mother and has devoted himself to the virgin goddess. I don't suppose he's ever spent much time around women."

She sat down heavily again as she reflected. Finally, she said, "Then what should I do? I really want to talk to him."

"Perhaps I could approach him and let him know," I suggested, risking another glance at her while I continued with my sewing. This entire section would need reworking anyway. "Perhaps I could ask him to meet you in private."

"Why would he be more likely to talk to you than to me?" she pouted.

I smiled, the wry smile of the older woman. "Because I'm not a pretty young girl, madam."

"Neither am I," she said. "I'm a queen."

"Even so, madam," I said. "It's worth a try, isn't it?"

She nodded.

☽

So I arranged with Hippolytus's maid to take over her duties, and I waited for him with a bowl of soup when he returned from hunting.

He wolfed the soup down without pausing for breath, without looking at me, without even removing his stinking riding gear. I was glad of it, in one way. I had only ever been a lady's maid, and I would not have known where to look if he had stripped.

"Sire," I said when he pushed the bowl back to me.

"What?" he asked. He was already making his way to his bed, a mess of sheets in the corner of the room.

"I am not your usual maid," I began.

"And? What of it? The soup was good. Now let me sleep." And he turned and started tossing his sheets like a wild animal preparing the ground. The stench of these sheets made me gag. I wanted to say what I had to say—and do it quickly.

"I am Queen Phaedra's maid."

He turned to me, his eyes wild. I stepped back and looked at the door. "I have had enough of that woman's name, do you hear me? I am sick of it—the torment—" He stared at me with such a cold fury, I felt myself shiver. He stood up quickly and hissed. "No more. Enough. Enough, enough, enough!" He shouted those last words. I turned and ran for the door, fumbling with the knob.

"Oh, get out," I heard from behind me. "I'm not going to attack you, foolish wom—" He continued speaking, but I did not wait to hear the rest. Instead, I made my way back to Phaedra. By the time I reached her, my pounding heartbeat had returned to normal, and I was able to briefly inform her that Hippolytus had absolutely no interest in meeting with her.

Phaedra

Kandake told me that Hippolytus wouldn't meet with me, and something in her tone told me to drop the idea. I offered libations instead, sure that the gods would see justice done. Hippolytus worshipped Artemis, did he not? I remembered my old tutor telling us how Artemis had transformed a young man who had seen her naked into a stag, then shot him. How much more punishment would she visit upon the men who raped young women?

In the meantime, I was growing bored staying in our rooms. Kandake said she had chores and left me on my own for most of the day. Her conversation was not scintillating, but at least it was better than sitting by myself, staring out at the sea. Sometimes Medea came to visit at night, and it took all my resolve not to beg her to come more often.

One morning, I awoke with a longing to escape the rooms that was so potent, I felt dizzy with it. Kandake had made her usual excuses about needing to wash the linen, and disappeared. I waited until I was sure she would not return for some forgotten item, then I changed my chiton from the drab and dingy one I wore in our chambers to a bright apple green and fluffed up my hair a little. I even pressed a little paint to my mouth. I didn't expect to see anyone, or at least not anyone that mattered, but if I did, I wouldn't like this person to think the queen was not keeping herself looking her best. My mother had always looked immaculate, whether she was receiving dignitaries or cutting flowers in the palace gardens.

I almost skipped down to the stables, the cool air on my shoulders and face reviving me further. I felt as though I had been imprisoned for many months, and now I was released. I deserved a treat, even if it was as small as a trip to the stables.

The stables were a little way from the main court. I had never been before, and I expected them to smell foul. The air was fresh, though, and as I approached the stables, I saw the area was clean and airy, and I found myself taking deep breaths, trying to replace the stench that had clotted my lungs since I'd arrived in Athens.

I stopped when I reached those stables, though. The horses' compartments were arranged in a semicircle around a central patch of grass. On that patch, their backs to me as they examined a horse, stood two of Hippolytus's closest friends. The horse was sweating and pulling away from a third man, who had its hoof in an iron grip. It was no other than Hippolytus himself.

"I don't understand," one of the men said, his tone bordering on whiny. "I checked its hooves before we left, and I haven't felt it pick up any grit."

"He," Hippolytus said, his voice calm but firm. "Your horse is not an object, Philomenes—he is a living being. And one of those statements cannot be true, because there is a huge stone embedded in the very center of the hoof. See here?"

Philomenes leaned closer, then jumped away as the horse veered towards him. Hippolytus and his other friend laughed, and I chuckled a little, too, at his red face.

"Who's there?" Hippolytus's head whipped round, although he did not let go of the horse's hoof. "Show yourself. Anchises, pass me my knife." I gasped, but he continued, "So I can take this stone out. Philomenes will never manage it. I take it that's you, Princess Phaedra, skulking behind walls."

I stepped forward, my face blushing. "I was not skulking," I said. "I did not like to interrupt you."

Hippolytus ignored me as he twisted his knife in the horse's hoof, then sprang to his feet to soothe and stroke its head.

"I will ask my stable boy to look after him for now," he said. "You can ask for him back when you're brave enough to handle him, Philomenes."

Philomenes' face was now a darker, uglier shade of red, and he scowled in a way that made him look most unpleasant, but he did not argue with Hippolytus.

"Now, Queen," Hippolytus said, turning to me. "What can we do for you? We haven't seen you here before."

"I came to see the horses," I said, and bit my lip. It sounded like something a child would say. Philomenes and the other man guffawed.

"And now you have seen them, perhaps you will leave us alone to do our work," Hippolytus said, his tone barely civil.

"Perhaps it wasn't the horses she came to see," Philomenes snickered. He punched his friend in the arm, and his friend laughed again.

"I don't know what you mean," Hippolytus said coldly.

"Hippolytus is a worshipper of Artemis; he seeks no earthly woman," I said. I meant to be helpful, but I could see instantly from the way Hippolytus's brow furrowed that I had missed the mark.

"Even Artemis must turn a blind eye sometimes," Philomenes said.

"Do not disrespect the goddess," Hippolytus snapped.

"I do respect the goddess," Philomenes said, the laughter disappearing from his tone. "I respect the hunt."

"Sire, as we have discussed before, you must worship all of the gods," I inserted. "Artemis is the goddess of the hunt, but Dionysos and Aphrodite have their place, too."

"I have no time for Aphrodite," Hippolytus said. "I have very little time for *you*." He turned back to the stables, but Philomenes was not prepared to let him go.

"Are you telling us, Hippolytus, that you have never paid your respects to Aphrodite? I mean, really, never?"

"That is terrible," I agreed. "You should pour her a libation at once. What did I say?" For the two young men were rolling about with laughter once more.

"The Cretan bull outwits the Athenian owl for a change," Philomenes said, his mouth smirking. Hippolytus refused to look any of us in the eye. He opened the door to one of the stables and led a horse out. He threw his leg over the horse and rode off, calling as he did, "The hunt, gentlemen! You seem to have forgotten what that means."

"Pour her a libation," the friend whose name I did not know said, mocking my higher tones. "That was well aimed, Your Majesty."

"I did not mean to jest," I said, but quietly. Privately, I was just a little pleased to have disturbed Hippolytus. Perhaps I could get the measure of these young men yet, especially if I did not hide myself away in my rooms all the time.

Trypho

Theseus had been gone several moons now, taking with him Pirithous, the one man left in Athens with a steady head on his shoulders. And the resulting mayhem and lawlessness was worse than any of us could have imagined. The court was transformed into a circus carnival. One of the young men rode his horse through the central corridors, and the smell never quite seemed to disappear, no matter how much cleaning was undertaken.

Not to be outdone, another bartered with a peddler for a wild monkey, which was quite the favorite for a day or two, and then was left to roam the halls, stealing food and snapping at anyone that got in its way. It became common to trip up over drunken men snoring loudly wherever they happened to fall, always with a cup of wine in their hands, and usually a spill of urine seeping from their groins. Those of us who considered ourselves more sensible slowly retreated to our own rooms.

I would perambulate from time to time, usually around midday, when the worst offenders were either still sleeping from the night before or riding through the forests in search of mythical beasts. Perhaps inspired by Herakles' recent visit, Hippolytus announced that there would be a quest to find a horse with a horn protruding from its forehead, or some such nonsense. It kept him out of trouble, at least.

My scouts were still sourcing information for me, both within Athens and without, so I knew that Theseus's trip, far from being a disaster a lesser man might have secretly hoped for, was a success. And I was pleased to hear it, because for all my faults (and I have many, I own), my priority has always been Athens. Serving the king had made me rich, but I had never acted in a way that might have jeopardized my nation. So it did give me great satisfaction to hear that one peasant king after another agreed that his position could be strengthened by giving up his title and joining a council to govern the new, wider Athens. The descriptions that Theseus gave of Crete were most compelling in this regard, and I did wonder that he hadn't thought to take the Cretan princess along with him on this journey.

In fact, not only had he not taken her, but he didn't seem to have made any provision for her. I wondered at this, and my mind briefly considered the possibility of offering her accommodation on my own farm until Theseus returned and peace was restored. I quickly dismissed that thought; she was in no real danger as long as she kept to her own quarters. Not enough to warrant the infraction of my own privacy.

I never believed the rumors that my scouts brought to me about a secret affair between Phaedra and Hippolytus. For one, the young man was too closely attached to his horse. But more importantly, I observed the two of them talking, and I saw no signs of any real attraction on her part. Yes, she blushed prettily when he spoke to her, but he was just a boy, and she was his stepmother.

He, on the other hand, bore the brunt of the teasing and gossip, mostly from those apes he called his friends. In vain, he continued to protest his adherence to the goddess Artemis. The princess Phaedra was accused of stealing his heart, and with it, his virtue.

It did happen that I was in the dining hall one evening when one of these discussions was taking place.

Rhesus, a loud and muscular boy, who happened by chance to be the son of an old friend of mine, started the discussion. His voice was slurred with the copious amounts of wine he had been drinking since midday. He raised his wine cup and shouted, more loudly than he realized, "Hippolytus asks you to drink a toast to Queen Phaedra!"

"To Queen Phaedra," responded not only his own table but several surrounding ones as well. Hippolytus's face twisted into that deforming scowl once more.

"I asked for no such thing, and you know it," he said. Although there was a cup of wine in front of him, his voice was steady, as was his hand when he raised it to his mouth. It did not surprise me. Hippolytus loved his sports, not his drink, and he would not carry out any action that would undermine the former, even with his father away.

"Then you do not wish the lady good health? And perhaps her husband slightly worse health?" Rhesus had jumped to his feet, although from the way he was circling, he had already realized it was not his best idea.

"Her husband is my father, you buffoon," Hippolytus said, slamming his knife into the table. If Rhesus had been sober, he would have stopped at this point.

"He's old enough to be her father, you mean. Will you wear horns when you bed her? I've heard Cretan women are turned on by bulls."

"I will not bed her," Hippolytus scowled. "I am sworn—" he began, but Rhesus interrupted.

"Come on, Hipp . . . Hipp . . . old friend, you can't still be serious about all that Artemis nonsense."

Even I couldn't help myself from looking at Hippolytus with frank interest, eager to see how he would respond to this.

"What do you mean—*nonsense?*" His voice was cold, and his hand flicked over the handle of his knife.

"It's one thing to stay away from women when you are young, but men are supposed to bed women. Real men do."

The knife flew through the air so quickly that none of us realized it was moving, until it hit Rhesus in the shoulder. He staggered back, his face pale and a patch of red spreading quickly across his tunic.

"I'm tired of your talk," Hippolytus said, and stood up and stalked from the room. I shivered, watching him go. Once he had gone, Rhesus, too, staggered out, aided by a few of his fellows. I trembled; the incident gave me pause for thought. There was a dangerous scent in the atmosphere, a charge that had not been there before.

Theseus could not return too soon.

Agneta

The very air in the Athenian court was heavy, weighing me down so I couldn't breathe. We had stayed for too long. We had outstayed our welcome, if we were ever welcome in the first place. I tried to make plans, to speak to the people who could get a boat for us, who knew which courts might be open to exiles.

But what was the use when Medea refused to leave? She thought that she had fooled us with her brave acts, spying on Theseus, confronting the princess. She just wanted someone to tell her to stop, to put an end to it all for her. But where would that leave us? Or rather, as I supposed Cassandra would return to her husband, where would it leave me? This court had become perilous since the Cretan princess had arrived, but that was just a coincidence. It was since Theseus had become king, then left us to the mercy of Hippolytus.

I thought I would breathe a little more easily outside, but the Greek climate was too hot for someone with my fair skin, and so I took to wandering in the shady woods that bordered the palace. I had never really gotten used to living in palaces, everyone on top of each other, the locks on the doors doing less to keep predators out than the standing of the inhabitants within. We had lived in houses, one family guarded by walls, and the forest without. Here in the woods, the faint smell of mulch under my feet, and the leafy canopy above, reminded me a little of my home, what feeble memories I had of it anyway.

I had been so young when Jason took me away, a small girl who didn't find a place to hide quickly enough. I knew what happened to girls who fall asleep in the woods, and I was not going to let it happen to me again.

☽

It was the sort of day when it doesn't rain as much as the air seems to leak moisture. The huntsmen had all given up on finding their quarry, and there was much crying and sorrow in the palace as they hunted women instead. I could not bear it anymore. I had to leave, even though it meant risking a cold or a fever from the damp outside.

When I got out of the palace, my head cleared a little. The sun was not visible in a cloudy sky. Water drizzled down into my hair and my eyes, and the ground was turning into mud in front of me. I realized that there was still one horseman who had braved the weather, wheeling and turning on his horse. The Greeks speak of the centaur, half man and half horse, but to me all those spinning limbs only resembled a spider.

He came closer to me, and I wrapped my arms around myself, futile protection against what must come next. My legs seemed to have morphed with the ground; I could have tried to run, but I knew I would only collapse into the sodden earth.

Then I saw another girl, Phaedra, the princess, between me and the horseman, foolishly standing out in the open. The horseman's gaze alighted on her, and he tensed up, as alert as if he had seen a prize deer, or that fabled unicorn.

Her wet tunic clung to her thighs, and her blonde hair swirled around her head. She reminded me of a picture I had seen in the Corinthian court, of the Greek goddess Aphrodite. Or, going back further into my past, a place I never wanted to visit if I could help it, my own goddess, Freyja. The goddess of sex and of death.

The horseman descended from his horse and carefully tied it to a tree. If I had been in any doubt as to his identity, I would have known him instantly from his voice.

"What are you doing?" Hippolytus asked.

"Drawing," Phaedra answered calmly. I was rooted to the spot, as though some Greek god had turned me into a tree, but if I could have, I would have run, and he wasn't even interested in me.

He moved closer to her, forcing her to step backwards towards a tree. She turned and looked over her shoulder, realizing that she was trapped, unless she could push him aside.

"Stay close, Princess," he said, and he dropped his arm onto her shoulder and gripped it like a vice.

"Let me go," she said, indignant. She still didn't realize the danger, I marveled, unable to believe that a woman could live for nearly twenty years and not understand what would happen next.

"You have spent so much time watching me, with my father away. Don't you want to see me up close?" His voice was cruel, nasty. I could see her looking around, but what could I do? If I went down there, he would only hurt us both.

"I said, let me go!" she repeated, and then louder, "I am your queen. Take your hands off me."

"There's no one here to hear you pretend, Princess," he said, and put his hands around her throat, although he did not yet squeeze.

"Your father told you to look after me." She sounded frightened now, but far too late. Was I going to watch him kill her? Why could I not move? I should fetch help, but there was no one who could help her now.

"He did. And I will."

She spat at him. He wiped his face and stared with wonder at his fingers, before staring back at her, pinned in his hand like a butterfly.

"Have you gone mad?" he asked, almost bemused.

It was then she pulled desperately. Hippolytus kept one hand on her throat, brought his other hand round, slowly, casually. He stretched his fingers, then balled his fist and smashed her in the face. I screamed, then slammed my fingers over my mouth. They didn't seem to hear me, though, focused only on each other.

"You should disgust me. Most of the time you do. All of you. You claim to be the granddaughter of Helios?" He was not shouting, even though she was scrabbling against him with all her might. But he was almost casual in his tone, as if he were a lion and she a mouse, unaffected by her attempts to push him away, to claw at his face, his arms. He looked up at the sky now. "Helios, look at your granddaughter now, look at her wicked body which she has flaunted at me, which she taunts me with—like I am her pathetic plaything."

He kept talking as he pushed her down into the mud and then tore her chiton apart. He kept talking as he thrust his muddy hands onto her chest, her torso, and below her waist.

"I have spent my life dealing with women and their temptations. You cannot help yourselves—everywhere you go you disturb the air. And you are the worst of them. Worse even than your beast-loving mother. Yes, I know all about that. We all know about that. Is this what you wanted? Is this all worth it? Will this make you stop?"

He brought up one of his large hands and smashed her face into the ground. I felt I might stop breathing.

His face was close to hers, and his voice was lower, so I could barely hear him. "How could your dirty mother lie with that animal? Are you half animal, too? Is that why all you want to do is rut?"

His horse was panicking now, rearing up and trying to escape the knot he had tied in its reins. The frightened whinnies of the horse rippled through the forest, making it hard for me to hear her words.

"It's a lie," she choked out. "My mother no more laid with a bull than yours did."

"I know how to tame bulls," he hissed. "I learned from my father."

And then he smashed both his fists into her face, and she sank down into the mud.

☽

Afterwards, the entire forest was still. I couldn't hear a single bird call or a mouse scurry past. The exhausted horse had stopped trying to escape and just pawed at the ground, nickering pitifully. Hippolytus pulled himself upright and staggered forward. It hadn't taken long; there was that at least. But she lay so still on the ground, I thought she was dead.

Then he leaned over and howled, howled as if he had been the one hit and kicked and violated. He howled as if he were in intense pain. He doubled over and screamed before dragging his hands through the hair. "By the gods," he shouted. "I had a vow! I had a vow to Artemis. Oh, my sacred goddess, forgive me! It was her fault, not mine. She tempted me. She flung herself into my arms. Forgive me, Goddess, forgive my weakness."

He pulled his tunic together, untied his horse, and began to stumble in the direction of the palace, still weeping and calling Artemis's name. I do not claim to be an expert on those Greek gods, but I could not imagine that Artemis, that any female goddess, would take his side, seeing the body of another woman lying naked on the ground. But the ways of gods are mysterious indeed.

Phaedra moaned, and her arm twitched. She was still alive. The realization was enough to free my legs from the spot, and I ran forward to help her to her feet, slipping in the muddy hollow the horse had worn with its feet. I would guide and support the princess as she limped back to the palace, the only place she could go, although it did not feel like a place of refuge for either of us.

Night Chorus

I clean for Rhesus, and he says that Prince Hippolytus has bedded Queen Phaedra.

Hippolytus? But isn't he sworn to Artemis?

And she is married to his father!

I knew it! I saw the way he looks at her.

Rhesus says that Phaedra tempted Hippolytus, and they lay down together in the field. He says she was so desperate she could not even wait to go indoors. Theseus has been away a long time.

He's been away from her chambers longer than that!

But . . .

Andros says something similar. He says all Cretan women are like that.

But . . .

Phaedra

When it was over, I was violently ill all down my front. I heard loud, gasping sobs from somewhere nearby, and then as light came into focus, I realized that they came from deep inside my chest. Every part of my body ached, even deep inside of me.

I knew I should stand up, but I couldn't bring myself to do it. And then a girl appeared. I thought from the way she dressed that she must be a maid, but I had never seen her before. She was fair, impossibly fair, even compared to me, with skin that seemed almost translucent. I wondered if she was a goddess, but she did not speak, just helped me to my feet and put her arm around me. I was covered in so much mud and bracken that it was difficult to tell, but I might be bleeding. Perhaps I would die. I looked up to the sky, but it was overcast. No heavenly grandfather would be coming to my rescue today.

I was sick again, on my knees this time into a nearby bush. No one had ever touched me like that. It had never even occurred to me that anyone would try. I remembered my earlier self, so happy and innocent. She had even been pleased to see Hippolytus. Pleased! I wanted to cry for her, and then I remembered that I was she, and I would only be crying for myself. As the last of the vomit dripped away, I became aware of a throbbing pain in the back of my head.

I wasn't dead, at least.

My leg muscles seized up in fear at the thought of meeting Hippolytus at the palace, but the girl helped me to take one step, then another.

Like the bull leaper, I had thought I was safe, but I wasn't. She had been so confident, so full of life when she came to my rooms. I wished I could remember her name. She had been impaled on the horns of the bull she had trusted. I had been impaled—but my mind shied away from the thought. The gods had done nothing, but why would I expect them to? They took what they liked. Hades and Persephone. Apollo and Leda. Zeus and my own grandmother.

But thinking of the gods reminded me. Hippolytus was my stepson. I had been entrusted to his care. This was more than rape. This was a complete betrayal of the bonds of kinship, the rules about hospitality. I remembered Theseus sternly telling my mother that xenia applied, knowing that xenia would keep him from being murdered in his bed. Xenia applied here too, and Hippolytus had thwarted it. I gagged again and the girl held me tighter.

I had thought that I was here to bear witness to Theseus's punishment. What if my role was greater than that? What if my body was the instrument to bring the punishment about? The gods surely would not let this atrocity go unpunished. They rained down atrocities upon transgressors, as the bards loved to tell us.

A king called Lycurgus tried to rape his own mother. The gods visited madness upon him, causing him to mistake his own son for a grape vine and chop him to death with an axe. I remembered Hippolytus pushing into me, and wondered whether the gods would have him kill

Theseus, or if Hippolytus would be killed so that Theseus would be forced to live with the pain of losing his son.

With thoughts like these, I almost stopped the choking sobs that wracked my body and threatened to send me weeping to the floor, unable to move again. Each time I imagined the gods destroying Theseus and Hippolytus, I walked a little taller. But then the wounds on my face and deep in my groin made me buckle over again, utterly powerless against the waves of pain that swept through my body.

We stumbled up to the palace. I paused outside the front gates, swaying on my feet. I had come this far. I wasn't strong enough to go farther. But the girl pulled me on, her bony arm sturdier than it appeared. We hobbled through the entrance, and I whipped my head around, too frightened to breathe.

No one was about. By the dimming light, I guessed that they must all be at their meals, and I felt my heart slow down in my chest again. I couldn't imagine eating after what had happened, but I supposed Hippolytus would have no such reservations. Even worse, I reflected, with the now familiar taste of bile rising in my throat, he must be telling his friends about his success.

I wept again, hot, frustrated tears dripping down my cheeks. We made slow progress through the corridors. The girl finally let me go as I staggered into my chambers, where Kandake was waiting for me.

Kandake

Phaedra refused to leave our room for weeks after the attack. I did not know what to say to her, and so I said nothing at all. She deserved better, I knew that, but how could I talk to her about what she had been through? I had never even been with a man.

I knew what had happened as soon as I saw the princess come back limping, her clothes torn and bloody and her hair heavy with mud. I took her into the rooms and gently laid her on the bed. She tried to say something, but I hushed her, stroked her hair, and held her hand. I bathed and dressed her, and then I bundled up her clothes to throw on the fire as soon as I had a chance. I was determined that she wouldn't see them again.

Phaedra looked nothing like her mother, but I still felt as though I had slipped into the past, back into those long-ago days when I had cleansed Phaedra's mother's legs and wiped the sweat from her forehead, cleaned up her little baby boys and handed them over to her. But this time the act that had torn a woman apart had been the violence of a man. There was no gentle nursing to slowly bring her back to life. My heart broke, not just for Phaedra, but for her mother, so very far away.

I knew it wasn't good for her to stay inside all that time. I tried to persuade her to go for a little walk with me, even just up and down the corridor. No chance of bumping into

Hippolytus there, I would say, although I wouldn't mention his name. No chance of bumping into any man. No one ever came this far. And though she knew it to be true, her face would close up, and she would leave the sitting room, with its oversized table and two chairs, which was more of a prison than we'd ever anticipated when we arrived, and return to her bed. And then she would sleep some more.

And that was our life for a good couple of months afterwards. With frustration, I heard the rumors of how Phaedra had tempted Hippolytus, but I could do nothing about those. It concerned me, though, not because of Phaedra's reputation, but because of the danger it would bring when the king came back. I kept my ear to the ground, but I could not hear any rumors of Theseus returning. And in time, I started to realize that was a good thing, because I washed Phaedra's sheets and her clothes as regularly as before, but after that night, when I had washed out enough blood to drain a woman dry, I never saw any stains on either of them. I did not know how to speak to her of it, so I did not know whether she understood, nor if she realized why she was having difficulty keeping her food down. I did suggest that I could speak to Medea the witch, who might have some potions to solve the problem before it was too late, but she shut herself into her own bedchamber, a prison within a prison.

I thought nobody ever came down our corridor, but someone must have. Because we would receive small gifts from time to time, little bouquets of wildflowers, and once or twice a new cake of soap. I brought these in and did not tell Phaedra where they had come from. But I was certain they came from a woman, or even women. Just little treats, from those who understood what she had been through.

Phaedra

As my stomach started to swell, I had to face the truth. I was having a baby. Perhaps even more than one, although Kandake assured me that some women did present larger than others, even for a first child. I hated every minute of it. My ankles hurt, I had a horrid taste in my mouth, and my face had taken on an unnatural sheen.

Neither Kandake nor I spoke of the bigger problem that was awaiting me, although we both often looked out to sea and shared worried glances. Theseus would return to Athens soon, and I was with child by another man. I had been raped, but I didn't know if Theseus would believe that, or even care. It seemed I had two choices. I could tell him the truth, or I could use the excuse women in my situation always reverted to. Eventually, Kandake put it into words.

"Theseus is a follower of the god Poseidon, his father. Perhaps you were sitting by the shore waiting for his return, and were visited by the father instead?"

I was ill at the thought, although at that time I was often ill, so the two may not have been connected.

"Is that what happened to my mother? Is that why she told my father she was bewitched by Aphrodite, infected with love for a bull? It isn't true, is it?"

"Obviously, it isn't true," Kandake scoffed. "Would that even be possible?"

"But Zeus . . ." I started, and then stopped. No, it did not seem possible. "Then why was my brother so deformed? Who was his father?

"When Minos—Prince Minos—was born, he looked like any other baby. Your father was excited to have another son. As the child grew older . . ." She paused for a breath. These were more words than I had ever heard her say in all the time we had been living together. "He began to look different," she continued. "People were starting to talk, so your father built a home for him under the ground. Where he wouldn't be seen."

"So whose child was he?" I asked, but then I realized that I knew the answer. I felt as though my world was spinning; if I hadn't been sitting down, I would have had to find a chair. All my life, I had favored my father over my mother. I'd always thought of him as the fairer parent, the kinder parent. The parent who allowed me to paint. My mother was much stricter, harder to get on with. She didn't seem to like me much. But perhaps all along, she'd been trying to tell me that the world was a cruel place, that men were not to be trusted. For the first time, I could understand why the Amazons lived as they did. And not without a pang of self-pity, I thought that Hippolytus's mother would probably be ashamed if she could know what he'd done. Just as I was ashamed, thinking of my kind, loving father, turning his own son out of his house when he was little more than a child. Medea had asked me why Minos had lived in the labyrinth. I had the answer now, and more understanding than I had ever wanted.

As though reading my mind, Kandake suddenly said, "They put him underground, and he was such a lovely little boy. So kind. I said to your mother, I said, 'Let me take him. We can go back to my parents' farm. My brother will help. You can come and visit him. Just don't put him underground.' She agreed, she was going to go along with it. But your father found out and said it would shame him to have him raised on the farm. But it didn't shame him to lock him in a cave." She stopped.

I looked at her with my mouth open; it was as if a stopper had been removed from an overfilled wine skin. My brother was a full sibling and not a half brother at all. He'd been at least ten years older than me, and I had always enjoyed visiting him underground. Ariadne and I had called him the king of the labyrinth. We'd spent hours learning the paths, making sure we could all find each other without hesitation. He'd asked the kitchen staff to keep my favorite sweets on hand, and he'd stroked my hair when I wasn't feeling well and let me rest on his bed. He'd been kind, as Kandake had said. It wasn't just me; I'd heard the kitchen staff saying they'd rather work for him and earn a smile in private than serve up the most lavish food to be enjoyed by kings in the Great Hall. And yet we had always been told, Ariadne and I, that we were to keep his very existence a secret. We were never to contradict the rumors of a monster in the labyrinth. We were told that the safety of Crete depended on it.

"What did you do, Ariadne," I said softly. Kandake wasn't listening to me anymore, caught in her own miserable memories. Because Ariadne had loved Minos as much as I did, I knew it. For as long as I could remember, I had been running behind my big brother and my big sister, their hands entwined. Together they had tried any number of schemes and games. They had learned to swordfight together, and they had even tried to breed their own chickens. When Minos had expressed sorrow that he could not learn from a tutor, as we did, Ariadne had painstakingly gone over each of her lessons with him, despite being a reluctant student herself. And yet, she had led Theseus straight to him. I could not understand it. I could not forgive it. And I had not been allowed to express any of that anguish in public. Perhaps if I had, I would not have started on the path that led to marriage with Theseus, and Athens. For a long time, Kandake and I sat in silence together.

))

The suggestion that Kandake had made went round and round in my head. If I told Theseus the child was Poseidon's, if I made the claim in public, he wouldn't be able to deny the baby or besmirch my name. I had heard the night chorus talking about Hippolytus and me, but I'd stuck my fingers in my ears, and soon, even without my fingers blocking the noise, I ceased to hear them. I didn't think Theseus would listen to them if he could hear them at all. And as Poseidon was his own father, he might even be forced to adopt the baby as his heir.

Even though I still felt repulsed by my father, I wished that he were there so I could ask him what the best course of action might be. Or better still, so he could put both the baby and me on a boat and spirit us away back to Crete. We could disappear in the night, only to reappear in Crete. We could blame a god for that too. Helios and his chariots of fire, the same golden horses that brought Medea to Athens, or so they said.

If I weren't careful, I would lose my faith, I realized. I was thinking as Medea did. There were no gods after all. Only flawed humans looking for something to pin their faults to. Their exploits they took credit for themselves.

I needed to talk to someone. I didn't want to see my cousin, Medea. I still remembered the scepticism she had brought into my rooms after I was first attacked, and I'd refused to see her again. She had given up trying. Instead, I remembered the old man who had talked with me when I first arrived in Athens. Trypho, his name was. He had been an adviser to the old king, and he had talked so kindly of him. I was sure he would be able to give me the fatherly advice that I needed.

I asked Kandake to arrange a meeting for us in my rooms. I was petrified of leaving them, terrified that I might see Hippolytus. He'd left me for dead; what was to stop him carrying through that intention?

Trypho

I was sitting in my room, drinking wine and reflecting on the general lawlessness at court and Theseus's proposed political machinations, when a maid knocked at the door. I recognized her instantly, although I pretended ignorance. She was Phaedra's maid, Kandake.

"Sir," she said hesitantly, in the beautiful language that even serving maids in Crete spoke. "I come to you with a message from the princess . . . I mean, the queen."

"Yes?" I asked, trying to look unconcerned, even angry that she had interrupted my evening drink. Inside I was fluttering with excitement. All my instincts told me that this was just the opportunity I had been waiting for.

"She would like to meet with you again. For supper, perhaps? Tomorrow night?"

This was most forward and boded very well. Even so, I frowned.

"It isn't convenient, you know. But of course, she is the queen. Very well. But she must come here."

To my surprise, she shook her head. "No. She will not leave her rooms. You must go to her."

Too shocked at being refused to make any objection, I simply nodded my assent. She departed as quietly as she had arrived. I sipped again at my wine and traced the knots on the large wooden table in front of me. A table that I was sure was much nicer than anything in the queen's chamber. My wine was better than anything her maid could arrange, too. And yet she refused to leave her rooms. What was more, I checked with my sources, and they told me that no one had seen her for at least four moons. My curiosity was thoroughly whetted now.

$$\mathbb{D}$$

I am an old man who has never married, and you will forgive me not jumping to the obvious conclusion. But when I went to her chambers that night, carrying a small flagon of wine with me, even I could see instantly why she had not left her rooms.

I did not say anything, but simply bowed my head and said, "Your Majesty," and allowed the maid to show me to my seat. There was barely enough room for me to sit down, as the table had been moved to one side of the room to allow space for the princess's growing bulk.

"Sir, I hope you will excuse all the secrecy and subterfuge," she said in those wonderful lyrical tones of hers. "But as you can see, I am not myself." And she gestured at her stomach helplessly.

"So I see, Madam," I said. I did not want to commit myself further at this stage.

"This is not a happy occasion, you understand," she said, and her eyes filled with tears. While she spoke, her maid had put a plate of food on the table in front of me, and she had poured my wine into a glass. It seemed callous to begin eating, but I took a sip of the wine and nodded sympathetically, encouraging her to say more.

She opened her mouth, then closed it, then opened it once more. Then her face crumpled, and she blurted out, "Hippolytus raped me."

I can't say that I was hugely surprised. Hippolytus had always struck me as one who was devoted to the goddess until his baser instincts were allowed free rein. But I opened my eyes wide and said, "The prince? You poor, poor girl."

She was crying in earnest now. Her maid passed me a cloth which I handed to her, presumably to blow her nose. I patted her hand and tried to remember my self-assigned role as a stand-in parent to this child far from home, even while my mind was busying itself trying to decide how best to use this information.

She was talking again, her voice thick with tears, and I had to strain to understand what she was saying. From what I could make out, she was asking me for advice—whether to pass the baby off as the child of the god Poseidon.

"You could, but Theseus will kill the child," I said before I could stop myself. She looked surprised.

"Even if he thought it was the child of a god? Or if everyone else thought it was the child of a god?"

"Yes, unquestionably," I said. "Theseus is a hard man. Oh, it might not be obvious that he'd killed the child. I imagine there would be a chariot accident or a drowning incident. For you, too, I suspect."

She blinked at me. Here was a girl who was starting to understand the world she lived in.

"Then what should I do?" Her eyes were very blue, and wide open. For a moment I felt overwhelmed with the possibility of leading this innocent young woman astray, of taking advantage of her in the same way every other man in her life had.

If she really had been my daughter, I would have been asking her, or more likely, her maid, if she was past the point where a few herbs would take care of the problem for her. But I sensed that was not the fatherly response she was expecting from me.

"I will have to think," I said slowly. "Will you allow me to take some time to do so?"

"The princess does not have infinite time," her maid cut in, and I thought from the unusual insolence of her behavior, and the worried tone in her voice, that she, too, was mulling over herbs that might cure the princess's upset stomach. But I did not know if that was the right path. I could see a plan forming, but I wanted to formulate it properly, away from those cornflower-blue eyes.

"Take as much time as you need," Phaedra said firmly. "I can wait."

I bowed my head, then stood without eating. "I should leave you to get your rest, Your Majesty. I will eat in my quarters."

"I will prepare a bowl for you," the maid said, but only after Phaedra had glared at her. She didn't like me, I assumed. She wouldn't be the first person who felt that way.

"Thank you, I would appreciate that," I said. "An old bachelor like me seldom gets to taste the delicious meals prepared by ladies' maids."

The flattery did not have any effect, but I hadn't really expected it would. I left the rooms, motioning to her to follow me later with the food. I didn't want to be seen carrying containers of food across the halls, like a common servant.

☽

When I got back to my rooms, I poured another flagon of wine. The princess had bestowed upon me a real gift, a chance to take down Theseus himself, if only I used the information carefully. She trusted me, so I was not concerned about her not taking the course of action I determined upon. But I needed to consider what that action would be.

On the one hand, I thought, as I casually tapped on the table, Theseus loved his son Hippolytus beyond all others. It was incontrovertible; he was proud of the boy, although why, I had no idea. He overlooked in Hippolytus sins that he would never have overlooked in anyone else.

On the other hand, there sat his precious democracy, his chance to be a father of more than a human boy, and his legacy to leave to the world. Without it, he was an unprincipled adventurer who had fathered an unsavory son. Without this new political system, no one in years to come would know about Theseus's cold wit and his clinical mind. Instead, he would be known as Herakles' sidekick, the man who raped an Amazon, who kidnapped girls, and who slayed the Minotaur. He would be in the same category as Jason, as Perakles, as any one of a number of heroes who claimed to be demigods. They made for a fine tale, especially when sung by a good bard, but that was all. And Theseus wanted more. He wanted to be a statesman.

My wine was empty, and I motioned angrily to my servant to refill it. I couldn't afford to be distracted now.

Theseus would have to choose: to rescue his son or to continue with his political career. I remembered what he had said to us about his plan for justice under this new system of rule by the people, and I started to smile.

Would Theseus entrust the life and freedom of his beloved son to a trial, a vote by the men of Athens? Men could be so capricious, and while Hippolytus had his friends, Theseus himself was not well liked. I could see how this would work.

A little cough disturbed me, and I turned to shout at my servant, only to see it wasn't my servant. It was Kandake, Phaedra's maid, clutching her plate of food. I took it from her with a courtly bow, and she turned to go, but then turned back.

"Sir, please, the princess has been through enough."

"I understand," I said. "But she is stronger than you give her credit for."

"Could you not arrange for her to return to Crete?" she pleaded, wringing her hands together. "I hear you have money—and resources. Perhaps you could arrange for a boat . . .?" But the words died on her lips as she watched me. I had revealed too much of myself, but there was nothing I could do about it. She knew that I would not be arranging for a boat.

"I will try to help her," I said softly. "She has asked me for my help, and I will give it to her. This is a dangerous court, and I cannot guarantee her safety, but I will try to help her."

She nodded sadly. There was nothing more she could do. I watched as she left the room, and wondered at these women who came to care so deeply for those they served.

Kandake

I left Trypho's rooms with a nasty taste in my mouth. It wasn't so much that I didn't like the man as it was that I didn't trust him. If Trypho cared so much for women, why wasn't he married? If he was the fatherly type, where were his children?

Phaedra would hear none of this. When I returned to our rooms, she would hear nothing at all, because she was fast asleep. Her face was unlined and worry-free again, for the first time since she had returned from the woods that day. I just wished I shared her relief.

The next morning I expected Trypho to send a messenger to us, so I was taken off-guard when a knock on the door disturbed us over our breakfast, and I opened the door to the man himself. I tried to cover it up by muttering something about getting the princess ready to see visitors.

I sat in my own room on my bed, with the door open a crack, and watched closely. First, Trypho took Phaedra's hands between his own in that way he had, which made me shudder a little but didn't seem to bother her. He paused and looked straight into her eyes. Then he said, "Your Majesty, I have been giving your situation much consideration."

She nodded. Her back was to me, so I couldn't see her face, but I could picture it, her blue eyes wide and trusting, cheeks flushed and her skin glowing with the baby inside her. She said nothing, waiting for him to explain his plan.

"Has Theseus spoken to you of his plan for Athens? Rule by the people—democracy, he calls it?"

She shook her head. Theseus had barely spoken two words to her since we arrived here.

"As part of that plan, Theseus intends to set up a court—not a palace like this one, but a court of law. You understand how, currently, if a crime has been committed, the king sits in court over the accused man and decides his guilt? Well, under the new system, the men of Athens will act as jurors, and they will hear the case and decide whether the accused man is guilty or not." I felt a wetness in my palms and looked down to see I had dug my nails in so tightly that I had drawn blood. I did not like where this was going.

"I would suggest that you throw yourself upon the mercy of this new court and ask them to find Hippolytus guilty."

I gasped sharply, so loudly that Trypho looked at me, his gaze a warning. I said nothing.

"Sir, you misunderstand my relationship with Theseus," Phaedra said. "He will never take my word against his son's."

"But that's the beauty of the new system he wishes to introduce," Trypho said, his eyes glinting with glee. "He won't get to decide. He will have one vote, the same as any other man."

"I see," Phaedra said, but she sounded unconvinced. I did not blame her; I was not convinced myself.

"Everyone knows what Hippolytus is really like. This is your chance to make a stand."

"Yes," she said slowly. "Make a stand. Against Hippolytus. Against every young man who thinks he can take advantage of a helpless woman. And against the man who taught him that would be possible."

"Against Theseus. Against the man who put you in harm's way. Against the king," Trypho said softly, and I saw her head rise.

I thought he would continue to make his point, but he stood up abruptly.

"Madam, I have not yet breakfasted, and I do not believe you have either. These decisions should not be made on an empty stomach. I will leave you to consider your decision. Nothing can be done until Theseus returns home, and he is not expected for several days." We had not known he was expected at all. I visited the kitchens and the laundry rooms daily, after all, and I had not heard anything that suggested Theseus was on his way back. I shivered a little; I did not like this Trypho with his fingers in every pie.

He turned to leave, and Phaedra, heavy as she was, stood up with him.

"Thank you, sir," she said.

"Think carefully," he warned. "A trial will not be an easy prospect, even if most of the court is on your side. It will mean reliving your ordeal. I cannot ask you to do that if you are not strong enough for it."

And why would he ask her to do anything at all? But while he was still here, I could not question him as Phaedra should have done. I waited until he had left, and thought about how best to bring up my objections. I could already see that I would have to speak carefully.

☽

I did not comment on the conversation for as long as I dared; then, later that day, while Phaedra was sitting gazing out the window and I was working on my embroidery, I said, "Forgive me, madam, but are you entirely happy with Trypho's plan?"

Her head whipped round quickly. "And why wouldn't I be, Kandake?"

"You don't think that perhaps he is a little too quick to push you towards a course of action that could cost you more than it could gain?" My tone was hesitant, but I didn't want to anger her.

"I don't think he is pushing me at all, Kandake. I asked him for advice, and he provided it. And anyway, what's my alternative? Pretending a god sired my baby? You heard him—we would both end up dead."

"And who's to say you won't anyway?"

We looked at one another. Her eyes were piercing, her father's eyes, but I held her gaze anyway. She blinked and looked away.

"Well, at least it's a plan," she mumbled.

I took from this conversation that she could be persuaded to try a different plan. I did not have the contacts that Trypho had, but in my short time at the palace, I had made it my business to know who could provide for us, should we need help. I had no money myself, but I could use the name of Minos, known to be wealthy. Whether he would fulfil my promises, I had no idea, but I could throw myself on Pasiphaë's mercy, and besides, once we were out of Athens, it would be harder to cause trouble for us than if we were to stay.

For an errand of this type, the people to speak to are not the maidservants, providing refined services to the wealthy men and women. The women to speak to are the kitchen staff, who cook up the food for the entire palace. These

women are the same the world over, it seems: either large
women with big forearms, or scrawny women with stringy
muscles. Both kinds can lift pots bigger than the average
man, and both kinds will know someone, whether it is a
brother, a male companion, or even an old woman with a
reputation for witchcraft, who can get you what you need,
no matter how illegal it might be.

Too many ladies' maids are rude to the kitchen staff
because they assume that their ladies will always be perfectly behaved and will never need that type of assistance.
But sooner or later, we all fall foul of a law we didn't make.

A few discreet inquiries led to my waiting in a dark hallway in the grimier part of the palace late that night. It wasn't
cold, but I shivered and pulled my peplos closer around me
anyway. I do not want to make it seem as though Crete
were a perfect place, but I knew that I would not have been
so worried in the Cretan palace. Knossos has its dark corners, but there is at least an aura of civility, especially for a
middle-aged woman like me. Athens had no such scruples,
especially with the king away.

I smelled the man before I met him, a fetid mix of alco-
hol and fatty beef wafting down the corridor. He crept
behind, a small rat of a man, sniffing loudly and wiping his
nose on his hand. I gritted my teeth. I'd never thought he
would be savory.

"What do we have here then? Aren't you a little far from
your chambers?" he snarled, and for a moment I was worried that he wasn't my contact and was just an opportunist
who had happened along at the wrong moment. But then I
took hold of myself; surely he wasn't going to start by offering me illegal services.

"Lucia in the kitchen told me I might meet a man here who could provide me with some assistance." I kept my voice firm and reminded myself that I was not a young ingenue like Phaedra, but a mature woman who could hold her own, especially against rodents like this man.

He sniffed loudly and said, "Lucia talks too much. Do you have money?"

"I can get it to you. When the job is done." I held my breath. This was the most precarious part of my plan.

"We will see. What's the job?"

"I work for a certain well-born lady. I need to arrange transport for her and one companion back to the land of her birth. When we arrive there, her father will pay handsomely."

He rocked back on his heels and sniffed again, but I said nothing. I held my breath and resisted the urge to speak further.

"So, if this young lady is the lady I have in mind, her father is not short of funds, am I right?" I nodded. "In that case, why isn't her father sending his own men to bring her home?"

It was a good question, and not one I had thought of, but I made an effort to answer it now.

"It isn't that simple; there are politics involved at that level. If he sends someone to bring her home, that would be a declaration of war."

"But if the young lady goes home of her own accord, that's just to be expected when a pretty girl is married to a man twice her age who hasn't been home much?" I nodded again. "I'm not sure that it won't be war in any event, but war is none of my concern except where there are things to be bought and things to be sold, and there are always more of those in wartime. Very well. I can arrange for a boat for you and your young lady. You will have to leave all your fancy belongings behind, though. There won't be room for them."

I pictured Phaedra's one small trunk, with a handful of chitons and a spare peplos, and tried not to smirk. No princess had ever been sent off with such a pitiful trousseau before.

"That is fine," I answered quietly.

He named his fee; it was more bronze than I had seen in my life, and while I didn't think it was an amount that would cause Minos to lose any sleep, I countered it with an offer of half as much. The little man would expect me to do so, if I really acted with the authority of the king. He gave me a second price a little higher than my counter, but nowhere near the initial amount, and I accepted it gladly.

"You will travel at night. Does anyone watch the lady, do you know?"

"Not as far as I'm aware," I said, shaken by the question. I had never seen any guards or spies, but suddenly, all the walls seemed to have eyes; and all the doors, ears. I felt I had been very naive.

"I will make some checks and inquiries. If you do not hear from me, assume it is safe to leave. Meet us at the palace gates two nights from now, when the moon is at its highest. If anyone accompanies you, there will be no one to meet you, and no boat. Do you understand?"

"I do," I said, although I wasn't sure I did. His next words were clearer.

"I'm helping a young lady to get home to her papa. I have no interest in helping young lovers escape. Do I make myself clear? If there is a young man with you, you will be on your own, and I might have to make good my fee by reporting the young lady to the proper authorities."

He sniffed loudly, and I remembered how the court had been buzzing with rumors about a perceived romance between Hippolytus and Phaedra. The very idea that I might be arranging for the pair to elope was preposterous, ridiculous to me in the extreme, but obviously he had no way of knowing that.

"I can assure you that is not the case," I said coolly.

He tipped his chin to me and sauntered off, leaving behind his foul aroma. I lay against the wall and tried to catch my breath. I may have promised him more money than he would otherwise see in his entire life. But if he could deliver what he promised, it would be more than worth it. I just didn't know if he could. And what was more, I still had to convince Phaedra that this was the right course of action.

Medea

I longed to resume my night walks, but Agneta had made me promise to wait until Theseus, and some sort of order, returned. So instead, I prowled up and down my rooms, unable to find out anything useful and bored out of my mind.

Eventually, Cassandra approached me. "Madam," she said, a courteous tone in her voice that was often absent, "I have news for you. The young men will be hunting tomorrow, and they are not expected back for a week."

I glowered at her; I'd been pent up for so long, even being spoken to caused prickles of irritation to break out across my skin. "Why are you telling me this?"

"We thought you might like to take the opportunity. To walk," Agneta said.

I glared at them both. "I do not need anyone's permission to take a walk. I am not frightened of a gaggle of youths."

They nodded and looked away, busying themselves with their needlework or whatever they occupied themselves with. None of them met my eye. Eventually I conceded.

"But yes, tomorrow night would be a good night to take a stroll. The night is chosen by me independently, you understand, girls?" Neither of them said anything. "You understand, girls?" I repeated more loudly, and they murmured their assent.

☽

The next night saw me swooping about the corridors once more, and I felt much better for it. Despite the heat, I still covered myself with my dark disguise.

As my perambulations took me closer to the princess Phaedra's chambers, I wondered about fleeing to Crete. From what I had heard, King Minos was not a sympathetic individual, but Queen Pasiphaë was my aunt, even if we had never met. I could arrive with news of their daughter, which surely they would be eager to receive. And then once I was there, I could assess the best way to appeal to the king and queen, and ensure my stay lasted a little longer. I started thinking about which of my maids I might take with me. Agneta, without a doubt. Cassandra was useful, but she was Athenian born and bred, and I wasn't sure whether she would want to leave a court in which she had adapted so well for survival.

I let my thoughts flit back and forth, but I never allowed them to alight on Jason. I never thought about him, not since that day I had left the Corinthian court, a nomadic ex-princess with no home, his crocodile sobs ringing in my ears. They hadn't realized I was leaving until I was already on the boat, and the entire court had rushed to the shore to berate me. They'd all fallen for Jason's lies, or at least it suited them to believe him. That father-in-law of his had railed with him, waving his gnarled stick at me and calling down the curses of the gods on me. "Unnatural woman," I believe he shouted. "You are no mother." Well, what sort of father was *he*? His daughter remained with Jason, and at least my children were free of him.

I had slipped out of the court at night, and my ship sailed in the morning, a bright, beautiful morning, with the sun's rays gleaming behind me, dazzling those angry onlookers on the shore. I threw back my head in relief, and the light seemed to emanate from my very being. I bathed in the heat, but it couldn't last. I suppose that bright light seeming to radiate from my boat had given credence to those rumors that the god Helios had engineered my escape. But then my thoughts always came back, not to Jason, but to the small body he clutched in his brawny arms, and my heart clenched to think that he was able to manhandle her even in death.

To think of Jason meant to remember my children, and that I could not do. Or at least, I couldn't do it and remain sane.

Instead, I let my thoughts skip on towards what would be needed for the trip, such as bedding, and the best way to obtain a ship, and other practicalities that would need to be resolved. Bright butterfly thoughts were not meant to rest for too long on darkness. And all the time I made my way closer to the Cretan princess's bedchamber because I would need the most up-to-date news of her to report back to her parents.

I had not seen her for several moons, and my knowledge of her current situation was hazy at best. I could make it up, of course, but it was almost certain that Minos had spies of his own, and if my knowledge did not accord with his, it could bode ill for me.

When I reached Phaedra's chambers, I paused. I had expected her to be asleep, but there were lamps lit, beaming out into the dark night. I heard voices coming from inside: a young woman's light, musical voice and the gruff tones of an older man. I crept as close to the door as I dared, pressing my ear against it.

"Have you considered my proposition, Your Majesty?" the man asked.

"I have," she answered. "And . . ."

"Wait," another voice interrupted. A woman this time, middle-aged. That would have to be the princess's servant. I remembered the scowling, difficult woman. And I thought only my serving girls were this disrespectful.

"Kandake," the princess said, confirming my assumption. "Now is not the time—"

"I have a ship," the older woman said, babbling in her desire to get her words out. "We can discuss the details later, but Your Highness, we can leave. We can return to Crete and to your mother and father."

I wondered if calling her "Your Highness" would be a mistake. I saw a little chink in the door and pressed my eye to it. It gave a surprisingly good view of the room. I could see the man was that old spider Trypho. I couldn't see the maid. And then Phaedra stood up, and I could see from the roundness of her stomach and the sticklike appearance of her arms that she was with child. No wonder the maid wanted to spirit her away. I chided myself for not having returned sooner.

"I am not Your Highness. I am Your Majesty," Phaedra said, confirming my suspicions. "I am the queen of this court, even if no one acts like it. The only queen this court has.

"You would have me run away like a thief in the night," she continued, her voice rising as her rhetoric built. "I have not committed any crimes. I am not an adulteress. I have remained faithful to my husband."

Do continue, I thought. She obliged me. She was in full speech-making mode now.

"I have been cruelly used and cast aside by my own step-son. I tell you, I will have justice. The gods saw what happened, and they will not let this slide. Theseus killed my brother. Now his son has taken my honor. Master Trypho here tells me I can have justice in court. I believe this is what the gods intended to happen."

Trypho applauded.

"So to be very clear, Your Majesty, you intend to ask the court to convict Hippolytus of your rape?"

Her voice rang out, clear and passionate. "I do."

I crept back to my rooms, feeling most pleased with my night's adventuring. I could not have chosen a better night if I had picked it myself. Now I had to decide how to use my newfound information. Would it be more valuable to Theseus or Minos? Or should I bide my time a little longer?

ACT III

THE TRIAL

*P*haedra talks and talks, and Hippolytus can bear no more. He rises to his feet, pushing aside his father's restraining hand.

"She lies," he screams, his voice high pitched, as though he is still a young boy.

But his cry is inaudible, for his friends are already on their feet.

"Liar!"

"Witch!"

"Whore!"

It is as though the words are stones, and Phaedra flinches with each one. The young men hold their fingers to their heads in imitation of bulls, and pretend to stab one another, laughing uproariously. Hippolytus feels the writhing of his stomach subside. She is just a mortal woman. Weak, fallible, one of a long line of unnatural women. Hippolytus has nothing to fear from her.

Then he gasps as he feels a pain in his shoulder. Theseus's fingers are digging into his flesh, his breath hot in his ear.

"Sit down."

Then, when Hippolytus, stunned, does not move:

"Trust me, Hippolytus," his father says. "Sit down, now."

Night Chorus

The king is returning. The king is returning.

His ship has been spotted on the horizon. He will be here in two days.

And what will he make of what he finds here? He wanted a palace like Crete. He will return to a raging bear pit.

We dare not clean properly; we stay out in the open as little as possible.

There are wild animals still roving the corridors.

Hippolytus has led a rampage through the palace.

And has anyone seen the queen? Not since . . . not since then.

No, but judging by the meals her maid has been preparing and the washing that she's been doing, the queen may have a surprise for the king when he returns. A surprise that was six moon cycles in the making.

But he's been gone seven moon cycles now.

This will not end well at all.

Phaedra

When Theseus returned, Trypho and I were ready for him. He had assembled all his fellow Athenian men in the dining hall so he could brag to them of his triumphs. I had waited outside the doors for him to start speaking. And then I had pushed the door open, and walked in, my pace slow and deliberate, my eyes fixed only on Theseus. Trypho had been too delicate to say it, but my stomach, protruding before me, would tell the court everything it needed to know.

Trypho had insisted that I wear a white chiton and braid my hair to resemble none other than Athene herself. He would have had me carry an owl if he could have found one. The chiton was supposed to be loose, but it clung to my round, firm belly, and the court gasped as I slowly walked towards Theseus. I hadn't seen any of the men in months; they were none of them prepared. I couldn't help but steal a glance towards Hippolytus, though Trypho had warned against it. He looked sick.

I felt the baby moving, pushing its foot against my side. I tried every day to dissociate the baby from its conception, but seeing him there, in front of me, still walking and breathing and living his life as though nothing had happened, made me want to push the child out and away from me. I stumbled a little. No one came forward to help me, and I continued my walk to the king. I looked again at Hippolytus, and he turned away, his face blank.

I imagine everyone expected me to engage in supplication, to kneel, throw my arms around his legs, and beg forgiveness from Theseus. Theseus himself certainly did, his hand already outstretched towards my head. But I stopped short of the reach of his arm, drew myself higher, and said instead, "Sire, it is good that you have returned. There has been a serious breach of the laws of xenia, and the filial relationship. Your son has violated me, and now I am with child."

Behind me, I heard the whispering start. This was a serious accusation, and what was more, there were a lot of superstitious men at court. I could hear more than one talking about the poor quality of the harvest that year. Trypho had told me they would, and if they didn't, he would start the whispers himself. And the other word he had warned me would be heard: *Thebes*. The city of Thebes had been visited by plague, he told me, and the popular belief was that it had been caused by the young king's transgressions, marrying his own mother. We would be able to use both concerns to our advantage, Trypho had said.

"Lies!" Hippolytus shouted. He tried to run from the court, but one of his friends gripped his arm. The friend echoed the cry, "Lies!" But his voice was hollow. He knew what Hippolytus had done. They all knew, even if they'd done nothing about it.

Then Trypho himself stepped forward. His voice silky, he said, "Theseus, this is a serious accusation. The boy must be given the chance to prove his innocence, is that not correct, sire?"

Theseus's face had turned white under his tan. I don't flatter myself that it had anything to do with the protection of my virtue. But always two steps ahead, Theseus had seen immediately the path that Trypho was leading him down. His son, his beloved son, was now on trial, and his system of democracy meant he couldn't do anything to save him. Already justice was sweet.

Hippolytus yanked his arm away from his friend, who hissed in what he may have believed was a quiet voice, "You can't run, man—they will think you are guilty." But I saw Hippolytus stare at my stomach. He took a faltering step towards his own father, and said, "*Abba*, I didn't do it." He sounded barely more than a child himself, and I remembered that he was only sixteen years old. But he'd still been able to hurt me.

"Be quiet, Hippolytus," Theseus said. "We will talk in private. Trypho, he's only a boy. Do we need to go through this rigmarole?"

"Certainly not," Trypho said. "You are the king, sire. You can make the decision."

Hippolytus was visibly shaking now, those broad shoulders pressed together. He held out his hand towards me but pulled it back as Theseus glared at him.

"Hippolytus, don't you have . . ." Theseus trailed off, and I bit back a smirk. No one could think of a task that Hippolytus had to do, not even his own father. "Horses to groom?" he finished. "And Phaedra, you look tired. You should lie down."

Trypho had told me that it was likely that I would be sent away. But as I began to lumber back towards the door, I realized that to leave now would mean that Hippolytus and I would be alone together. I remembered those fists, now clenched like a small boy's, smashing into my face, and

I looked around in alarm. The men all seemed oblivious to my plight.

Help came from an unexpected quarter. The door opened a crack, and a maid poked her head around the door. "We're here for the princess," she whispered, her voice barely audible. She looked at the floor, but I recognized her as the girl who had helped me back to the palace after Hippolytus attacked me. The men ignored her, but she opened the door a little wider, and I saw several maids standing there. I waddled towards them. The door shut behind me, and I could hear the men resuming their discussion as though it had had nothing to do with me.

The maids formed a phalanx around me. I glanced to the maid next to me, Kandake. She smiled at me but made no attempt to take my hand. No one spoke. We walked back to my rooms, the maids keeping to my slow pace. From time to time I looked around me in wonder. These women must be the night chorus, or some of them. And yet, though it sounded churlish to say, they were none of them beauties. Most were missing teeth, a few were overweight, and one was so thin you may not have seen her standing sideways. I remembered how Ariadne had been called "Ariadne of the Beautiful Hair," and she'd had so many suitors. But perhaps beauty wasn't all that men looked for in women. Perhaps, when Hippolytus had forced himself upon me, my own looks had been less important than his need to control me. To own me.

When I got back to my rooms, I whispered, "Thank you," and they nodded and crept away.

"Did you arrange that?" I asked Kandake later as she brushed my hair out for bed. But she shook her head.

"No, I was just asked to be a part of it," she said, and continued brushing. A few strokes later, she stopped. "I don't think that Trypho did either."

Neither did I.

❯

Trypho persuaded Theseus that there would be a trial, just as he had assured me he would. Seven days later, I sat and watched my feet, dangling over the rocks into the seawater. A discreet distance away, a guard watched over me. The guard had been Trypho's idea, but he'd persuaded Theseus that it was his own idea. I didn't care; for the first time I felt safe enough to leave my quarters.

I questioned myself all the time now. Why hadn't I listened to Kandake and taken the boat back to Crete? Right now, I could be sitting on a Cretan beach, with three guards I'd known since childhood watching over me. I would be able to dine in the Great Hall again. The young noblemen who had sought my hand in days gone by would be around me, and they would say, "Was it very primitive in Athens, Phae?" and I would reply, "Oh, you have no idea!"

This was always the part where my vision came to a halt. Because if I were surrounded by friends, the young men and women of Knossos and the surrounding palaces, whom I had grown up with, then surely Minos, too, should be alive, waiting for us to go and visit him and tell him about life outside the labyrinth. I had always known that the gods would have their revenge, but I had thought I was here as a witness. I hadn't realized my body was to be the battle-ground on which that revenge was wrought.

Now we were waiting for the men of Athens to be convened so that the trial could be heard. I had been working with Trypho to prepare my story. Trypho was not going to present my case. He had declined, stating that he was too old and not a good rhetorician. Instead, a younger man called Criton would do the honors. I had met him, and I did not like him as much as I liked Trypho, but I trusted that Trypho had my best interests at heart, and Criton would do as good as job as possible. He just struck me as being overly ambitious, and I did not want my case to be used for political advantage. I mentioned as much to Trypho, and he smiled at me kindly.

"But, madam, as long as you win, what does it matter if others gain, too?"

"I suppose so," I conceded. "But his cause seems so base compared to mine."

"You are being a little too precious, Princess," Trypho chided gently. "He will work hard for you, knowing that a success will benefit himself. What more could you ask for? Better that than for him to be simply a do-gooder with nothing to gain."

"Like you, you mean?" I asked slyly, and he laughed.

"Exactly like me, and that is why I cannot represent you in court. I do not have the stomach for the fight. Criton does."

I had accepted defeat at the time. Now, with my feet wet and my mind cooler, I felt I could better articulate my concern. If Criton cared only for his own political promotion, then he could change sides in a heartbeat if there were political motivation to do so.

I wondered whether it was worth raising this with Trypho. I had come to depend on him so much in the past weeks; barely a thought I had went unshared. Kandake, on the other hand, hated him. She made sure to be absent whenever he came to visit.

"I am so sorry," I apologized to him once when he arrived unexpectedly and she stood up and stalked off, muttering something about going to the kitchens to see about dinner. "She is very rude, I know, but I don't have any alternative here."

"Do not worry, Princess," he reassured me. "I understand her position. She thought she had secured her passage home. She did not expect you to be so brave. She's old and homesick, and she sees me as the reason she isn't home now. At least she is being rude to me, and not to you."

It was hypocritical of Trypho to call Kandake old when he must be old enough to be her father, but I said nothing. After all, she had just walked out, unthinkable behavior from a maid back in Crete. My mother would have had her whipped. I did not even know who I could ask to do the whipping.

Now, behind me, the guard cleared his throat. I sighed and reluctantly pulled my feet out of the water, drying them on the small piece of cloth I'd brought with me for that purpose. Theseus had agreed that I might have the time during the day, from when the sun was at the peak of the highest tree until the time it was at the third branch down, alone on the beach. I could stay on the beach later if I liked, but I wouldn't be alone, and the young men had been so unthinkably obscene in my presence, it was easier if I left. Trypho had tried objecting, telling Theseus that it would be better if Hippolytus were required to limit his movements given that I had committed no crime, but Theseus could be pushed only so far where his son was concerned. It was hot and my rooms were stifling, but I kept to them as much as I could, aside from those precious hours when I had the beach to myself.

I placed my sandals on my feet and laced the straps around my ankles, then began to walk back up the beach to the palace.

Night Chorus

What is this trial? Who is this princess, creating all this fuss?

All she has done is rile them up, and now they demand more of us. They sit and listen, and they want more, more, more of us. Hippolytus has become a monster. He and his friends charge about the palace, protesting his innocence to everyone they see, and yet when they get back to their rooms and they see us, they enact the rape all over again.

I felt sorry for her before, but she has made our lives harder. Why could she not be quiet?

Do you even believe her? I heard she had her eye on him from the start.

We all saw her follow him round the court.

She is expecting his child. Maybe she made all this up to convince Theseus that she was not unfaithful while he was away.

Princesses can bring trials. But someone still has to make their beds, and lie in them, too.

Medea

With Theseus back, I walked every night. No one could talk of anything but the trial. Who was telling the truth? Was Phaedra a Cretan whore, unnatural like her mother? Was Hippolytus a raping brute like his father? After all, everyone knew—or if they didn't, others were quick to tell them—that Hippolytus himself was the son of the Amazon queen, raped by Theseus in battle. Everyone had an opinion. The night before the trial, Agneta was waiting for me when I got back to the rooms.

"You are always listening at doors," she accused.

"And you are being insolent," I retorted. "Is this any way to speak to your mistress?"

Her thin shoulders rose and fell like small, bony animals. "So dismiss me."

"I should beat you," I said, but I sat down at the table instead. The princess's attack had almost broken Agneta. It wouldn't take much more to shatter her completely. "What of it? I am listening at doors. Do you have any idea what is happening in this palace?"

She joined me at the table, pushing a glass of wine she had prepared to me. "Yes, I know what is happening in this palace. But I do not see what it has to do with us."

"I haven't worked that out yet," I admitted. "But I am gathering knowledge that will benefit us."

She snorted. "Leaving will benefit us. Madam, they will have your head on a platter if they find you are still here."

"Who will? Theseus? He's a little preoccupied with that wayward wife of his." I sipped the wine. "This is good, thank you."

"I'm hoping it will make you sleep. That wife of his is your cousin. And she is under the gods' protection. You are not. He will make an example of you. He will have you beaten in public. He always hated you, and you will give him an excuse to vent his outrage. Madam, we must go."

She sounded young and desperate, and I felt sorry for her. Sorrow, mixed with an affection that was not quite love. I knew the difference.

"Agneta, my dear," I said, keeping my tone gentle, "if you are worried, I can arrange for you to leave this palace. You could go—"

She turned away from me, which was just as well. I had no idea where she could go. I wouldn't know how to get her back to her family.

"All those punishments you listed, Agneta—do you really think I care?" I tried instead.

"I care for you," she said, her back still to me.

"And I thank you for that. But since my children—since my children—" I stumbled over the words and decided I would just skip ahead instead. "I don't care what happens to me, Agneta. My life is a living torment now. Until I am dead, I will not care what is done to me. And this court intrigue provides me with a little diversion from wishing it were so."

She turned back slowly. "It is a little more than an intrigue. There will be a trial."

"And do you believe justice will be served?" I asked, genuinely curious for her point of view.

"Of course, madam," she said in tones of awe, which made me wonder to whom she had been speaking recently. "It is democracy in action, the rule of the people."

"The rule of the *men*," I corrected her. "And only the freed men at that. Besides . . ." and I reflected on a conversation I had overheard only that night between two jurors, strolling leisurely towards their chambers. They smelt a little boozy, and I felt an irrational stab of hatred that they could walk so freely and carelessly when I was forced to skulk about like a thief.

"What do you make of this trial tomorrow?" one asked. I didn't recognize his voice, nor could I make out his features in the dim light.

"A good opportunity, and nothing more," the other replied. I froze; I might be wrong, but I thought that was Trypho.

"I was surprised that you pushed so hard for a trial. I thought you agreed with me that these rights of common men are just a fairy tale that our king has absorbed from his nursery."

"By all means, I do. As do all right-thinking men. Skiron, you've seen the young buffoons that scamper around with the prince. Should they have a say in the running of our kingdom?"

"Still, Theseus has done a good job bringing the Atticans on side, and he couldn't have done that if he didn't argue so passionately for his democracy."

I inwardly sighed at this point. I found the politics the least interesting part of the court gossip.

"Yes, he's quelled the squabbling masses and the peasants. But once we form an army, it should be clear again that the king of Athens is, in fact, the king. Do you think Minos allows his peasants to vote on important matters? Do you think we can defeat the Cretans if we waste all our time consulting with farm boys and idiots?"

The other man chuckled. "So you do still think as I do, Trypho. In that case, why are you so insistent on this trial?"

There was a pause, as though the man was gathering his thoughts, and then he said, "The young queen should win. Not just because she's telling the truth—surely, she's telling the truth, Skiron. You know Hippolytus is a fiend, and she's got nothing to gain by lying. But how would Theseus live with himself if his beloved son and heir were sentenced to death? What choice would he have but to overturn the entire court system and take back his authority?"

Their voices were getting fainter now as they walked away, but I could still hear Skiron saying, his tone brimming with admiration, "That's genius, Trypho. I will spread the word. The queen is to win."

But I said none of this to Agneta. Instead, I said, "Justice is sometimes a mistreated woman. What should happen isn't always what does happen."

She must have assumed I was thinking of my children again, because she said nothing, but rose and cleared away my wine glass, resting a gentle hand on my shoulder as she did so. I would not have accepted such familiarity from anyone else, not even my young cousin, but Agneta was different. She had no one other than me.

Phaedra

After Trypho had gone, I buried my head in my hands and waited. Kandake opened the bedroom door and came and sat down on the seat Trypho had vacated. She sniffed at the warmth he had left behind; while a lot of our behavior had been an act for Trypho's benefit, Kandake's dislike of the man was real.

"What do you think?" I asked her, hearing my voice crack with fatigue.

"He believes you are an innocent young girl who will do what he wants," she answered. It wasn't quite the question I had intended, but the response was still helpful to me.

"And what do you think I should do?" I asked, being clearer this time, although I thought I knew what her response would be. I was right.

"We need to leave, and quickly. You shouldn't stay here."

It was the same argument she had put to me earlier when I returned from the beach. It made sense. And more than that, the more I heard about the trial process, the more convinced I became that I could not win. Oh, perhaps Hippolytus would be found guilty. But the cost to me and to my unborn child would not be worth the fight. I rested my head in my hands again. I wanted to do the right thing. I wanted to be the fighter that Trypho thought I was, to stand up for his version of justice. I just didn't know if I was strong enough.

"I don't know, Kandake." I sighed. "I wish my mother were here." She looked away at the mention of my mother, and I knew it was because I'd hit on the weak point in her argument. Had my mother not stayed in Crete all these years despite people saying the most awful things about her? She hadn't fled back to her parents with her son, no matter how much she might have wanted to. I blew a raspberry, frustrated with myself and the entire process.

"Why does it have to be me?" I asked suddenly. Kandake looked at me with a frown, not understanding. I elaborated. "We've both heard the night chorus—I know you have, no matter what you might say. Women are being raped all the time in this awful palace. Why don't I persuade one of them to bring a case? Trypho has his justice; Criton has his day in court; I can return home with my child." She said nothing. I had learned by now that if either Trypho or Kandake said nothing, it was because I'd said something that strengthened the other's position. The pair of them had more in common than they realized. It was only fate that made one a senior politician and one a serving maid. Clearly no one could take my place. I was the king's wife, living in Athens under the protection of xenia, the form of hospitality granted and guaranteed by the gods. The jurors might listen to me. They would not listen to a maid who had been taken advantage of by a fellow citizen.

"I hope this baby isn't a girl," I said suddenly. "I hope it is a boy. A boy wouldn't be taken advantage of like this. A boy could fight. A boy wouldn't have had to leave Crete."

"Ah, but a boy might be killed fighting," Kandake said calmly, and we were both silent. I couldn't say what Kandake was thinking, but I was thinking of my two brothers, neither of whom had been fighters and both of whom had been killed by the Athenians.

☽

The new day dawned, and I tried to take comfort from the scorching sun in the sky. Surely nothing could befall a daughter of Helios while the sun bore witness. I took a deep breath, dressed in my most sober chiton and peplos, and made my way to the Great Hall. I set my mouth in a determined expression. Instinctively, I knew that I would have to be as stern and matter of fact as possible if I wanted these men to listen to my words, and not dismiss me as a hysterical woman. There was no room for emotion. No time for tears.

The men had breakfasted elsewhere, I realized when I stepped into the hall. The furniture had been rearranged in preparation: a chair in the front of the room, with benches assembled around it. I was going to have to give my evidence while surrounded by men. For a moment I wished that someone, even Kandake, were with me, but then I reminded myself that I was a queen. I took my seat in the middle of the room and waited.

The older men came in first, stroking beards and muttering quietly to one another. I suspected that they, too, would rather be anywhere other than here. At first they left a space in the center of the front bench, for Theseus, I assumed, but then Trypho came in with several other men I didn't know, and they jostled their way onto the benches, so those men in the middle were forced to give up the gap.

When Theseus came in a few moments later, he looked around in surprise. He said nothing, though, but took his seat quietly on the third bench from the back. We all sat in silence, waiting for the last bench to be filled.

Eventually, we heard the whoops and calls as the young men sallied down the corridor and into the room, bumping their fists and chests against each other in a primal display. They, too, stopped and looked in surprise, and I hid a grin. Clearly their plan had been to arrive early, and sit at the very front to intimidate me, but they hadn't managed to get up early enough. The first, albeit minor, triumph of experience over youth.

After much shouting, arguing, and pushing and shoving, they settled into their places. I snuck a look at Hippolytus himself. He sat on the end of the bench, poised like a coiled snake. One of his friends fell into him, a jokey gesture between friends, but Hippolytus shrugged him off, annoyed. I took comfort from his posture. No matter what anyone else might think, Hippolytus was taking this procedure very seriously indeed, and that could only mean that I had a chance of winning.

Theseus stood up, his lanky frame towering over us all. Briefly, he was silhouetted against the oil lamp on the wall, and I had a moment where I thought it was not Theseus at all, but his father, Poseidon, come to sit in judgement over us all. And then the shadow moved, and I saw it was just Theseus, passing his hand over his face wearily.

"Thank you, everyone, for being here. Thank you, Phaedra, too. *Queen* Phaedra," he added quickly, seeing me open my mouth in automatic response. "Let me briefly summarize how this day will unfold. First, Her Majesty will explain to us the allegations against my son, Prince Hippolytus. If anyone has any questions for Her Majesty, they can put them to her after she has finished speaking. Then Her Majesty will leave us. Hippolytus will then have his chance to rebut her presumptions. After that, we will vote. You have all been given a token"—he held his up, a small wax disc—"and you will scratch two long lines if you believe Hippolytus guilty, a long and a short line if you believe him innocent." He continued speaking, explaining how the votes would be tallied by the court auditor, but my mouth was hanging open, and I had no interest in the mechanics of the voting process. So Hippolytus was to listen to everything I said, and have the chance to question me, but I couldn't be in the room while he was speaking?

"Phaedra?" I realized that Theseus was calling to me. It was time for me to speak. Funny, how I wasn't the one on trial here, and yet it felt as though I were.

Quietly, calmly, never allowing my voice to vary from an even pitch, nor the tears that pushed at my eyelids to fall, I explained to the assembled men what had happened. I avoided emotional language as much as possible. I didn't speak of my fear, except in the most practical terms. I didn't tell them how my entire body had been split open, or how I thought I was going to die in a muddy ditch, or how I hadn't been able to sleep through the night since. Just the facts—bland, unemotional, incontrovertible facts.

Even before I finished what I was saying, one of Hippolytus's friends had leaped to his feet, his shoulders shaking with anger.

"She lies! She lies! How can you sit here and listen to this lying whore?" Hippolytus's other friends took up the cry, "Liar! Liar! Whore! Witch! Liar!"

"Enough," Criton called out. "King Theseus, is this a court or a theatre? Hippolytus will have his turn." Hippolytus himself sat back in his chair and smirked, as though a point had been made in his favor. I tried not to look at that face, tried not to remember his breath panting against my neck. I took a deep breath and focused on Criton's face instead, on a sprinkling of light freckles on the bridge of his nose.

"Do you have anything more to say?" Criton asked me. Tucking my trembling hands under my thighs, I recounted how I had come to in the mud, left for dead, and I'd made my way back to the palace. *Facts,* I kept thinking to myself. *Focus on the facts.* I told them about the mud in my mouth and the blood that flowed from my nose, all the while trying to make it sound as though I was describing nothing more emotional than the weaving of cloth.

It was working, I saw as I risked a glance at the watching men. More than one had shielded his eyes at the mention of the blood, and a few had their legs clamped tightly together. I was getting through to them.

"She can't prove any of this," another of Hippolytus's friends howled. "Nothing! After all he's done for Athens . . . he won the horse race three times running! Three times. By Zeus—"

"Think carefully before you invoke his name," Theseus interrupted. I looked at him, surprised. He still showed no emotion on his face, but his voice had been tense with anger. I didn't blame him; my call on the god was far greater than Hippolytus's. Zeus, my grandfather, the protector of travellers and guests. I recalled, so many moons ago, my mother and Theseus talking about the proper requirements of a host.

"Actually, Selagus raises a good point," Criton remarked. Shocked, the young men hushed and listened to what he had to say. "Your Majesty, when you returned to your chambers, covered in mud and blood, as you say, you surely did not clean yourself?"

Quickly, I realized where his mind had gone. "No," I agreed, shaking my head at the ridiculous idea of it. "My maid cleaned me."

"Then your maid will be able to . . . shall we say testify? Bear witness to the fact that you arrived back at the palace, near death and covered in blood?" His words were far more evocative than mine. Still, I nodded.

Theseus sighed. "Very well, this maid can speak. But we have already heard enough testimony for one day, and I know I'm not the only man here who has other work to carry out. We will reconvene tomorrow."

The men filed out of the courtroom, laughing and slapping one another on the backs. I noticed several of them cross over to speak to Hippolytus while others still turned their faces from him. I could not tell whether we were winning or losing. I remained where I was, sitting still, or so I thought. When I looked down at my hands, I saw they were shaking.

Kandake

Trypho came to visit us regularly, and I began to really dislike him. Phaedra should have left Athens. She should be home in Crete, with her parents. They had dealt with one baby who wasn't what they wanted. They would manage with another.

But I had not realized just how bad things were until one day when I went to the shared laundry facilities. I liked to try to keep Phaedra's bedding nice, because I knew she had so much trouble sleeping. The bigger she got, the more she heaved about in the night, and her sheets became tangled and sweaty. Her mother had been the same. Every few days I took a little bundle of sheets and clothes down to the washing room and pummelled them with stones and fresh water until they were clean.

I did the same as I always had that day, finding a clear space in the room to work. I was focusing, as I always did at this point, on not thinking about Crete. In Crete there were the basins with running water that flushed away the dirt, boards to rub clothes against to get the cloth fully clean, not to mention my team of women who worked beneath me. In Crete, I hadn't actually done any washing myself in several years. I tried to pick up a bucket, only to have it knocked out of my hands.

I thought I had been clumsy, so I looked up to see which woman I needed to apologize to. I realized I was wrong when I looked about me; not one woman, but four or five stood ranged above me, their arms akimbo, their faces dark.

I swallowed, but I did not speak. I had been coming to the room for several moons now; I was not aware of any special rules that I had broken. So I waited for them to tell me their issue.

"You work for that Phaedra, don't you?" one of them asked. She was a short, wiry woman with dark hair that grew thickly on her head and also on her face.

"The queen?" I asked, seeing where this was going. "Yes, I do." I straightened up.

I wasn't afraid. Should I have been? They were only women, after all. Yes, they outnumbered me, and I could be in for a drubbing. But I knew they weren't going to rape me, and they weren't going to kill me.

"Her washing isn't welcome here," another woman hissed. I suppressed a smile; this was a ridiculous concept.

"Then where am I supposed to wash it?" I asked. "In the ocean?"

"In the o-cean?" the hairy woman repeated, mocking my accent. They were all young, I saw, and that again gave me confidence. I was old enough to be their mother.

"Why don't you want her washing done here?" I tried. I stepped towards a woman who so far hadn't said much. Out of the corner of my eye, I saw other women in the laundry, just watching.

"It's horrible," she said, bursting into tears. "Since she brought that trial, Amphedes has done nothing but push himself into me, night after night. He used to ignore me when he'd been out riding, at least, but now it never stops."

"Shut up, Ani," the hairy woman said.

"But it's true," another woman said. "We want that trial to stop. So Hippolytus took her once? He's taken me every night since. And he makes me sit there and watch him pray to the goddess afterwards. He makes me tell the goddess it was all my fault."

The cries were coming from all over the laundry now. I put my hands up.

"Ladies," I said, "I don't want the queen to take part in this trial either. She is with child—"

"I hope it dies," the woman who cleaned for Hippolytus snarled.

"But I do not think it can be stopped now," I continued as though she had not spoken. "And at least if she wins, someone might listen to you all too. There might be justice for all of us."

They broke off now, moving away, arguing amongst themselves. I sighed and picked up a stone.

"You don't believe that, do you?" a small voice near me whispered. I looked about and saw that girl who worked for Medea, the one who had brought Phaedra back that awful night. She had dropped her own washing and was clutching the bucket to her chest as though she might be sick into it.

"Perhaps," I said cautiously. "Don't you?"

She shook her head. "I told Medea we need to leave. We aren't safe here."

I looked at her small body, more child than woman. "Are we safe anywhere?" I asked dully. "We are only women, after all."

Trypho

Court went as well as could be expected, I suppose, but I was glad that we were not relying on our legal prowess to win this battle. Criton's performance bordered on the apathetic, so I wondered whether Phaedra was right and he had been bought off. Hippolytus stormed and raged, and his party of young bucks cheered and booed as though they were at a wrestling match. Still, it was behavior that impressed some of the older men, confirming that Hippolytus was nothing more than a high-spirited young boy, and any crime he had been accused of was little more than a boy's prank.

And as for Phaedra herself? Well, she conducted herself with dignity, I would give her that much. But the story she told clearly took a toll on her, and her face was white by the time she had finished, causing at least one man to mutter that he could not imagine bedding her when the palace was full of beautiful maids. Theseus referred to her as "Her Majesty" so sarcastically throughout that no member of the court was in any doubt that he did not consider her either the queen of the court or his wife. All in all, a most unsatisfactory day. And now Criton thought it was a good idea to call an actual maid to the stand, and that dreadful woman Kandake, too.

I saw Criton walking up ahead of me and called out to him. He patiently stopped and waited for me, and then, when I got closer, said quietly, "I am going to visit our queen. I suppose you would like to come, too?"

I nodded. We walked without speaking until we had left the rest of the jurors behind us. Then I exploded at him.

"What was that performance today? You are supposed to be on our side, are you not?"

"I was not aware you had chosen a side," he said, his hazel eyes glinting at me. "I thought you were acting in the best interests of Athens."

I snorted. I may have used those words when speaking to the king, but I did not want to hear them parroted back to me by a youngster like Criton.

"Trypho, our case is not strong," he said. "Antagonizing the court will not help matters."

"You are used to appearing before the king," I replied. "You are trying to remain in Theseus's good graces. Theseus has only one vote here."

"Did you know that they call Minos the king of honor and justice?" he asked, ignoring my comment. "He is famed for his ability to sit as a fair and impartial judge."

"And?" I asked, a little rudely, I admit.

"Theseus does not share that reputation. But I believe he would like to. I know you think of me as inexperienced, Trypho, but I have been trying cases before Athenian kings for ten years now."

"There you go again," I said, lowering my voice as we entered the corridor that would take us to Phaedra's quarters. "You are not trying a case before a king."

"Whether king or commoner, no one likes to be browbeaten to a verdict," he said, ducking his head to walk under a beam. I managed it easily, which did not assist my bad mood. "You have to lead your judge gently to the right verdict, so gently that he believes it was his idea to begin with.

We do not have a strong case, but if we tread carefully, we can lead the jurors to the right verdict."

"I hope you are right," I said, and then was quiet as we knocked on the princess's door. She opened the door to us herself, her face still white. I took her hand.

"My dear," I said gently, "you have completed a terrible ordeal today. The worst is now behind you."

"That is not strictly true," Criton said in his usual drawling tones. "She can still be cross-examined. There is no point in glossing over the matter," he said to me as I glared at him. "If she is not prepared then she could stumble."

"Perhaps we should come inside and not discuss this on the doorstep," I said hastily. We entered the chambers, and too late I remembered that this so-called queen had only two chairs at her disposal. Criton had already taken one, and I would dearly like the other, but one glance at Phaedra's ashen face convinced me that she should take it. I ushered her into the seat, and she did not protest. It was not a good sign, I knew.

"Have you eaten, Your Majesty?" I asked. She shook her head.

"Kandake is making me some Cretan delicacies. But I don't have the stomach for them."

I remembered Cretan delicacies and shuddered.

"Would you like me to have my servant bring you some yogurt and honey? It is simple food, but sometimes it is what is needed after an ordeal."

I could see by her face that she was sorely tempted, but she shook her head again. "I would not like to hurt Kandake's feelings."

"Yes, absolutely, not if she is going to give evidence tomorrow," Criton said, leaning forward and rubbing his hands together. I could see that these homely matters were boring him, and he would rather be discussing his case.

"Must she?" Phaedra asked. "She is a maid, after all. She worked for my mother for many years. I am not sure she will be comfortable speaking in front of so many men."

"I do not see how we can win this case otherwise," Criton said, crossing his right leg over his left and leaning back. Phaedra recoiled, then recovered.

"But I feel I have a duty to her. She's only here because of me. She shouldn't have to give evidence."

"I'm sure her experience will not be as harsh as yours," I interjected quickly. "She only has to give an account of what she saw, after all. She does not have to relive the experience."

Phaedra still looked unconvinced, but Criton and I repeated to her the need for this evidence in support of our case, and in the end she nodded her head.

"Will you need to prepare with her?" she asked Criton.

"I will, but we can meet early in the morning. The court will not convene until midday."

"That should make all those young bucks happy," I said morosely. "They do like their sleep."

"As do I," Criton said, and stood up and stretched. "And you, madam, need sleep more than any of us. Please do try to sleep well. I know you have been through a terrible ordeal, but you are still young. Sleep heals most wounds at your age, I have found."

There did not seem to be much I could add to that, so I simply pressed her hands between mine and muttered, "It is nearly over." Then we departed, and I went straight back to my own chambers for the sleepless night of the aged.

Phaedra

After Criton and Trypho had left, I paced back and forth nervously. The sounds of Hippolytus's friends still echoed in my head, calling me such awful, unspeakable names. How had my mother survived for so many years, being accused of such things, and worse? I did not think I could last another day in court.

And to inflict the process on Kandake was inhumane. It was all very well for Trypho and Criton to be so nonchalant about her appearance. They were men of the world. They were used to speaking in the agora. Kandake was not. I should have protected her from this. I had been a terrible queen.

While I was remonstrating with myself, I heard a knock at the door. I composed my features into a more positive expression before I opened the door, expecting to see Trypho had returned without Criton. I suspected that he hadn't been happy with his performance either. But instead, to my complete astonishment, there stood Theseus.

I heard footsteps walking away outside; clearly the guard was leaving, whether because he was told to do so by Theseus or because he wanted no part of whatever was going to happen in here. I wanted to run after him and beg him to stay. But what would the point of that be? He wasn't going to defend me against Theseus. He wouldn't even bear witness for me against Theseus. I had been on my own since Trypho left, and I hadn't even realized it.

I had been standing, staring at Theseus, no doubt with my mouth open slightly like a country girl, and I recovered myself and motioned to him to come in. He did so, and then it was his turn to look about him in embarrassment.

"Welcome to my humble dwelling, sir," I said pointedly, and he flushed. "Please, do take a seat—this one or this one, as you please."

"I am sorry," he said. "I had not realized your rooms were so sparsely furnished. It is not what you are used to in Crete."

I remembered the queen's suite, with its murals, soft cushions, and above all, fellow women about. Talking, laughing, completely relaxed. And I thought of how Theseus's voice became thin and bitter whenever he mentioned Crete, and I knew that he had realized my rooms were so sparsely furnished, or at the very least, he had chosen not to care.

"It is no reflection on you, sir," I lied, and smiled tightly. "Please, sit."

We both drew up a chair to that monstrosity of a table, and I waited for him to begin.

"This trial," he said, and then stopped. I said nothing. He began again. "This trial cannot continue."

I frowned. "Then call an end to it, sir. You are the king, are you not?"

"It isn't that simple," he said curtly, and looked about the rooms. "Have you considered what you will do when the trial is complete?"

"It rather depends on whether Hippolytus is convicted or not," I said, my turn to be curt. We had not exchanged so many words since we had been married. He looked exasperated, and I remembered him accusing me of being mute on the boat. It felt like a lifetime ago.

"But what if he is? You will still have his baby to care for," he said.

"Then you believe me?" I asked.

"It doesn't matter whether I believe you or not," he said, and half rose to his feet. I think he intended to start pacing, as a good rhetorician does, but the ugly table blocked his path. I was glad it was good for something.

"It matters to me," I said. "Sir, why have you come here?"

"This trial needs to come to an end before we reach a verdict," he said. "I'm here to make you an offer. Safe passage back to Athens for you, your unborn child, and your maid."

"Is that all? You think I could not have that already?" I asked, the words breaking out of me despite myself.

He looked at me, his gray eyes as cold as ever. "Then why have you not taken that option? Why do you intend to destroy my son?"

"Did you not destroy my entire family?" I asked. He looked at me, puzzled. "My brother, my sister. You turned my sister against my family, and you killed my brother."

"Your brother . . .? You mean that creature? I did your father a favor, destroying that beast."

"Minos was not a beast." I managed to squeeze the words out. I turned and stared at the opposite wall, willing the tears not to fall.

"Your father?" I shook my head and watched as understanding dawned. "You mean the freak? By Zeus, Minos named him after himself? Still, I suppose of the two of us, Minos's boy was probably less of a monster. What about him?"

"You killed him in cold blood . . ." My voice was faint, weak sounding.

"Yes, indeed I killed him. That whore of a sister of yours made me promise I would be kind, and I was. One quick blow. Not quite what she intended, but she knew the sort of man I am."

"Ariadne didn't know you were going to kill him?"

"I don't know how she failed to work it out," he said, sounding more like Hippolytus than I'd ever heard him. A sulky boy, things not going his way. "Of course I was going to kill him. She told me that he never actually hurt any-one—well, that's not what they say about him in Athens! Bloody fool. He wasn't even armed. Tried to reason with me. He should have fled. Or better still, fought back. At least your sister tried to fight back." He looked at me again, stopped short by the look of utter horror on my face.

We stared at each other in silence for a moment as I digested the impact of those words.

"She lives with Dionysos, in the hall of the gods," I said at last.

He snorted.

I couldn't breathe. I was going to die. I was going to die from lack of breath, murdered by Theseus as surely as if he had put his hands round my neck himself. "You told my parents," I tried. "You told the whole court that Dionysos chose her."

"I could hardly say her body was lying in the bottom of my boat. By the gods, you are young, but you aren't a child, Phaedra. You must have known, just as your parents did."

I remembered the vision of Ariadne, the handprints around her neck. She had told me to beware of Theseus. I remembered my mother saying that three of her children had died at the hands of the Athenians. He was right. I had known.

"What happened to her?" I asked. "Please, it can't hurt you to tell me now."

He sighed. "No, I suppose not. There's not that much to tell. She helped me to find my path to the center of the labyrinth, in return for which she intended to come back to Athens with me. She laid the path, then hid in my boat. But she wasn't happy to find out that the beast was dead." I winced as he called my brother a beast. He saw me, but he carried on speaking. "She tried to launch herself at me. Said she was going to tell your father everything. She would have destroyed me, and Athens with me."

"You mean—"

"I mean I put my hands around her throat and throttled her until she was dead."

He stared at me, defying me to confront him, as my sister had done. But there was a table between us, and a baby weighing down my stomach.

"What is it that you want, Phaedra? Will you destroy Hippolytus, me, and yourself? Be reasonable." His tone was still exasperated, but I turned around slowly.

"Why should I be?" They were the words of a petulant child, but I did not care. I did want to see them both destroyed, it was true.

"Because you have a child to consider." I gasped a little. He saw that he had wounded me. "You think I am uncaring, I can see. You blame me for your siblings' deaths. And maybe you are right—who knows? But there is one thing I care greatly for, and that is my son. I would do anything for him, Phaedra."

"Why is your son more important than me? Why is he allowed to attack me? Why can he—" The words caught in my throat, and I had to look away. "Why can he rape me? Where is the justice in that?"

"How long did it last? Long enough for the sun to journey across the sky? I doubt it. I doubt it took a fraction of that time. And you will—" He reached across the table, caught my chin, and forced me to face him. "Look at me when I speak to you. You want to destroy Hippolytus's entire life for the sake of a few moments of discomfort?"

A few moments of discomfort? I couldn't reply to him; he was holding my jaw too tightly. And perhaps that was for the best, because I didn't know what I would say to him. Was it discomfort when I felt that pain deep inside of me, rough and unrelenting? Was it discomfort when he left me for dead? Was it discomfort when I discovered that I was bearing the child of a man I never wished to see in my life again, distending my stomach and weakening my legs, so every step reminded me of him? Was it discomfort that I could never again walk freely among men without wondering whether one of them was harboring thoughts of raping me, without knowing that any one of them could overpower me and use me as he saw fit?

Something of my panting breath and burning eyes must have conveyed my feelings, my thoughts to Theseus, because he loosened his grip on me and moved a step away.

We looked at each other. I studied those cold, gray eyes; that hard, long nose; and the cruel, thin lips. Was this what my child would look like?

As though reading my mind, Theseus said, "Perhaps at this moment you look at your stomach, and all you see is the person you hate. But when that little baby comes out . . . it changes you. It changed me."

I studied him. I did not think that this was the politician speaking. I placed a hand on my stomach. I was dreading a monster, a boy who reminded me of Hippolytus or Theseus. But what if it were a little girl with Ariadne's face? Or what if it were a little boy with Minos's good nature? This was my child.

"So what are you offering me? Safe passage is not enough," I warned.

"Legitimacy, then. What if I announce that the child is mine, not Hippolytus's? It is plausible. We are married, after all."

"You were away," I said slowly. He shrugged.

"In time, no one will remember that. Do you think Aegeus remembered which year he visited my mother? We will dress the tale up a little. Everyone likes a good story."

"And where will we go? Will I have to move into your chambers?" I withdrew at the prospect.

He shook his head. "No, that does not suit me. We will arrange for you to move to finer quarters of your own. Perhaps in the palace, or perhaps we will have a separate dwelling built. You can staff it yourself. I would expect you to attend state banquets and the like, but nothing more."

This was the settlement I should have driven from the start. Before I even left Crete. I had gained nothing. Nothing except the sour taste of knowledge I would sooner not have.

My sister's murderer sat across from me, drumming his fingers lightly on the table. I glanced across at the small shrine I had made. I had been petitioning Dionysos to intervene as the husband of my sister. I'd have to change that, ask him instead to intervene as one whose name had been used in a lie. The words were already forming in my head, and I could almost feel the jug of oil beneath my fingers. I itched for Theseus to leave, so I could continue with my prayers.

"I'm sorry," I said, rushing the words out. "I understand what you are saying, but I would not be respecting the gods if I withdrew my claim. The gods will see justice done, and I will witness it."

I thought he would argue with me, but he did not.

"Very well," he said. "You may regret this choice, but it is your choice to make." He passed a hand over the mural, almost absentmindedly.

"This child is your grandchild," I said as he was leaving.

"I know," he said. "A second chance. I would not have been so generous in my offer were it not so."

He strode down the corridor. After a brief pause, the guard returned. He resumed his post without looking at me. I closed the door, and picked up a bottle of oil, then put it down again. It seemed very heavy in my hand all of a sudden. But what else could I do? I began to prepare my oils for the offering I intended to make to the gods, pausing now and again only to brush the tears from my eyes and cheeks.

Kandake

I did not want to give evidence. What good would it do? Men weren't going to listen to me, an old serving woman. Minos hadn't, all those years ago. I tried to tell Trypho and Criton, but they did not listen. I wanted to tell Phaedra—I did. But I couldn't look her in the eye and tell her I could not give evidence, not after what she had been through.

Whenever I tried to speak to Trypho and Criton, my tongue seized up and my palms started sweating. I had never done such a thing before. I had never even been alone in a room with two men before. Oh, they were nice enough, said encouraging words to me, told me it would be easier in court. But how could it be? When there would be not two men, but a hundred? All staring at me. Some shouting. Phaedra had told me what it was like.

That night, as we were about to fall asleep, I asked Phaedra, one more time, if we could simply leave and make our way back to Crete, where we could all be under the king's protection. She said nothing. Perhaps I had misjudged my timing, and she was already asleep.

☽

The next morning Trypho and Criton came to our rooms early to take me to the courtroom. They said they were here to give me support, but I knew they thought if they did not come, I would run away. I hadn't planned on running away, but with one on either side of me, their arms tucked under my sweaty armpits, I wished I had.

When I reached the room, a roar of laughter rang out. I looked around for support, but all I could see was men. I sat on the chair that Criton pulled out for me, and lowered my head. It would be over soon. It wouldn't be as bad as what Phaedra had gone through.

Theseus called for order several times. Finally, everyone was quiet except one voice, a male one, who was still speaking, saying, "At least this one has no fear of being raped. I'd sooner screw a donkey . . ." His voice died away, as though he were embarrassed, but I didn't see what he had to be embarrassed about. I wished I could crawl away, all the way back to Crete if I could.

"Madam," Criton started, his voice gentle. There were a few interruptions—"She's no madam, she's a maid," that sort of thing—but he ignored them. "Can you tell us of a time when your mistress returned to you in, shall we say, not a very good state? As though she had been attacked?"

I froze, even though we had rehearsed this. What did he mean? Did he want me to talk about Phaedra, how she was bleeding? I heard more jeers, although I did not want to look up. Criton repeated the question, sounding irritated. "Could you tell us what happened in the summer months, when Phaedra came back to your rooms after she'd been with Hippolytus? What condition was the queen in?"

"Bleeding," I mumbled. "Hurt. You know . . . there."

All around me I heard hoots of laughter.

"Criton, this is ridiculous," I heard Theseus say. "This woman can barely speak Greek. Is she going to tell us anything the queen did not already say?"

"Did it look to you as though she had been a willing partner?" Criton asked quickly.

I shook my head, then spoke up. "No." I risked looking up at the men surrounding me. They were all so large; they took up so much space. I could smell their hot breath and the odor of horses. They lounged about with their legs splayed. I wanted to curl myself into a tiny ball, but I didn't. I pictured Phaedra, too frightened to even leave our rooms for months. I raised my head and looked straight at the king. "She was in a lot of pain. She was sobbing. She could have died. I don't think she wanted that."

"Thank you. Hippolytus, do you have any questions for Kandake?" He pronounced my name wrong. He emphasized the *Kan*, instead of the *da*.

"No," Hippolytus called. "She's a maid—she's lied for her mistress. I've never seen her before, and I hope to never see her again."

There was a murmur of agreement in the room, but I wasn't listening. I thought back to the time I took him his meal, asked him if he would meet with the queen. He had seen me then. Except, of course, he hadn't. We all looked the same to him.

☽

Theseus called for a break, and the men left the room. They jostled and pushed me as they left the room, so I found myself bumped this way and that. I was going to be covered in bruises. I buried my head in my hands and waited. When the room was quiet, I looked around for Criton and Trypho, but they'd left with the rest of them. Sighing, I heaved myself to my feet. At least it was over.

I rose to my feet carefully, hearing my joints creak. I couldn't have cooked supper in the time we'd been in that room, but it had felt like a lifetime. Looking around me, I could see no one, so I crept to the door. I was already planning in my head what I needed to do, my real work. Prepare lunch for Phaedra. It was time I changed the bedding. There was no time to rest. I was ticking items off in my head when I saw them. Three of them, three men. All young enough to be my sons. All waiting for me. And I knew what was going to happen. I knew I would not be washing any sheets this afternoon, or perhaps ever again.

Phaedra

Trypho and Criton told me that I could not be in the court-room when Kandake was being questioned. So instead, I waited in the room for her. I paced up and down beside my bed as best I could, a little breathless and off balance with my newly large belly. I wished there was something more I could do, make her favorite food, perhaps, but I had no idea what it would be or how to go about preparing for it. I wished we had embraced before she left, but Trypho and Criton had taken her away so quickly, there hadn't been time. And that was proba-bly for the best; I didn't want to embarrass her.

Eventually, I heard voices outside approaching my rooms. Two male voices, one berating the other. I listened carefully.

"What was the point of that, Criton? A total waste of time, and it made us look incompetent."

"Are you leading this trial, or am I?"

"Be quiet—" And the voices hushed as they came closer to the door. I began to chew on a little loose flap of skin by my finger. They wouldn't tell me the truth, but it did not sound as though it had gone well. I should have told them she was not to testify. My mouth flooded with a sharp taste; the finger had started to bleed.

There was a tap on the door, and I moved to open it, then stood back to allow them to come in. First Trypho and then Criton took up what were becoming their accustomed positions on either side of the table. They both began to speak to me, then glared at one another. I looked out into the corridor.

"I don't understand," I said, ignoring their attempts to brief me. "Where is she?"

If Kandake weren't missing, their expressions would have been comical.

"You escorted her to the courtroom, but you didn't bring her back?" I exploded.

"Your Majesty," Trypho said, but he didn't seem to have any words to follow up with.

"I'm sure she will be back soon," Criton said, his voice oily. He started to say something about duties and kitchens, but I wasn't listening. I burst out into the corridor and lumbered down it, hurrying as best I could. I called for her until my voice was hoarse, but I couldn't see her. I asked every maid I passed, but they all shook their heads. Eventually Trypho caught up with me.

"She will be back, Phaedra," he said, taking my arm gently. "But you will make yourself ill like this. Shall I ask my sources to look out for her?"

I nodded. I felt a fool; I didn't even know where the laundry room was, and yet I knew Kandake spent most of her time there. And the kitchens scared me, so hot and staffed with coarse, common women. But I knew the dangers that lurked outside our doors, knew why she should have come straight back. I allowed myself to be led back to my rooms, all the while silently berating my companion for not having taken more care.

That night, when Kandake had still not returned, I knelt in front of my makeshift shrine. It looked cheap and poor, so obviously cobbled together by an amateur. But I had to trust that the gods would see my ardor. They would understand that I had made the most of the limited resources.

"Oh, gods," I said out loud, as there was no one else there to hear me. "Oh, Zeus, father of the gods and my grandfather, please, respect the principles that you stand for. We, my maid and I, are guests here. And we have been treated so badly. Please, let there be no more atrocities. Let Kandake be safe. Let there be a good reason that she has not returned. And let her come back unharmed."

It was not the most elegant wording, but it was heartfelt. And I added, "And then let us go home, please." And in response, the sky flashed brightly, and a rumble thundered through the sky. A lightning bolt, I thought, my eyes still seeing stars. Zeus's symbol. I pulled myself to my feet, no longer an easy task, and stumbled to bed. I slept soundly that night for the first time since I had come to Athens.

☽

The next morning, there was still no sign of Kandake, but I could not search for her. Hippolytus was due to give evidence. I was not permitted to be in the courtroom, but Trypho arranged for me to hide in a small alcove. It was a tight fit, and I had to pull my legs underneath me and balance my hands against the walls. I had no idea whether I could hold my bladder, so unpredictable lately, for the entirety of the hearing, so I drank nothing all morning, and stuffed torn up sheets into my skirts. A chink in the wall gave me a perfect view of the courtroom and the seat that Hippolytus would take. I held my breath while I waited as what sounded like footsteps approached my alcove, but they went away again, and I did not know who it might have been.

Eventually, I heard the men assemble into the room. There was much guffawing, stomping, and calls to one another across the room. The entire mood seemed to have lifted, I thought angrily. No inconvenient women to disturb their peace of mind by complaining about rape today.

"Hippolytus," I heard a familiar voice begin. Theseus. I should have known that Theseus would serve as counsel for his son, but it still shocked me. Somewhere, deep in my core, I'd hoped he would remain more neutral than that. "You have heard what the queen accuses you of. Is it true?"

A long sigh. I pressed my eye to the chink and saw Hippolytus actually yawning. "Of course, it is not true, Father. The queen is my stepmother. I would never dishonor you and the gods by having any sort of intercourse with her." He sounded bored, the passage having been learned by rote. Did that help my case or hinder it? I couldn't know. I couldn't see the faces of the men who were to pass judgement on Hippolytus. On us both.

"Then what happened?"

"The queen begged me to have intercourse with her. She was desperate to lie with me. Me, a disciple of the goddess Artemis!" There was a murmur of confirmation after this statement, and I had to stuff my fingers into my mouth to stop myself from crying out. "She was like a dog in heat," Hippolytus continued, the smirk on his face suggesting that he was enjoying himself now. There were some muted snickers.

"Hippolytus, enough," Theseus said sharply. Hippolytus was quiet. "So did you agree to her demands?"

"I most certainly did not," Hippolytus said hotly. His face had gone red, I noticed. At first I was amused by his childish attitude, but then I thought how he hadn't been embarrassed when he bared his manhood and forced himself upon me.

"Thank you. Criton, did you have any questions for Hippolytus? He has answered to my satisfaction." I heard soft footsteps as Theseus returned to his seat, then the sound of Criton scraping back his chair and standing up.

"Indeed, Theseus, he may have answered to your satisfaction, but can I remind everyone that, in accordance with your own wishes, you have only one vote?" There were more murmurings, but I could not tell whether they were in agreement or not. Criton did not wait for an answer, but continued swiftly: "Hippolytus, why do you think the queen made these demands of you?"

There was a pause. I could see Hippolytus look about him helplessly. He had not been coached on this question.

"She is a foreigner here. She is a princess of the court of Crete. She is a fine-born woman. Why would she behave like a common slattern?" Criton asked. I felt sick. He hadn't told me he would take this tack. Again, I had to restrain myself from shouting, "This isn't about being fine born. You have a whole court of women here that you abuse nightly." There was a small chip in the stone in front of me, so I rubbed my finger up and down it, trying to calm my breathing.

"I don't know. Why don't you ask her?" Hippolytus sounded sulky.

"And you say you did not have intercourse with her? Then whose baby is she carrying?"

"Some god's? How would I know. She's nothing to do with me." Surely they could all hear he was lying. Surely they could all hear in his weaselly words his entitled attitude? Hippolytus took what he wanted. Everyone knew that.

"What would you do with a horse that wouldn't jump as you like?" Criton's voice was smooth and in control.

A small snort. "It would depend on why it wasn't jumping. I'd try to examine it, see how I could persuade it. I take care of my horses."

"And a maid who wouldn't clean your room as you like?"

"Beat her." No hesitation there.

"And an attractive young woman who got in your way? Who flaunted herself in front of you? What would she deserve?"

"She'd get what was coming to her. I mean, from the goddess. The goddess would punish her. Not me." He was looking about him again, searching for assistance.

"Thank you. Theseus, Hippolytus has also answered all the questions to my satisfaction now. Are you insistent that he must stay for the summing up?"

"I'm not staying," Hippolytus huffed.

"You are," Theseus said, but Hippolytus had already risen to his feet.

"You have reminded me that I have horses to care for. Call me back when there is a verdict." He walked out, his steps echoing through the halls.

"Your Majesty," I heard Trypho say, the first words he had spoken during that morning's procedures, "do you wish to continue this process without him?"

Theseus was silent, and I imagined him staring Trypho down. Finally he said, "We had better. The sooner we begin, the sooner we can finish, after all."

"Very well," Criton said. He stepped into the space vacated by Hippolytus, allowing me to see his face. His expression was calm and urbane, as though he were discussing nothing more exciting than the weather. "Gentlemen, the king has given you the power to decide what has happened here. You have seen the queen, a polite, demure lady, who is with child. She claims that Hippolytus forced himself on her in contravention of the laws of nature. And you have seen Hippolytus, a callow, callous youth, who could not even bear to sit down long enough to respect this court that has been convened before us. One of them is lying. If you believe it is the queen, vote to acquit Hippolytus. If she is speaking the truth, find him guilty. Remember, the king has given you this power, and he wishes you to use it wisely and honestly."

I heard his chair move again as he sat down.

"You all know my son," Theseus said. "His character speaks for himself. I have nothing further to add."

"Then I suggest we vote," Criton said, his voice a little surprised for the first time that morning.

One by one, the men stood up and deposited a token into the waiting basket. No one spoke; no one dared. I heard the tokens being deposited on the floor, and a man I didn't know intoned the count. I could barely breathe. For the first time I wondered what would happen to me if they chose to believe Hippolytus. Being sent back to Crete was probably more than I could hope for.

"Guilty . . . guilty . . . guilty. Gentlemen, you have found Hippolytus guilty of the rape of the queen, his stepmother, by forty votes to twenty-five."

For a moment the silence remained, an uncomfortable blanket over our heads. Then the losers realized what had happened, and quarrels began to break out. I cringed away from the noise. I was so tired of the company of men.

"Silence," Theseus called. "Bring Hippolytus back in to hear this verdict."

There was a scuffle as the guards pulled him back into the room and thrust him in front of the jury. Everyone must be focused on Hippolytus. I took the risk and pushed open the little door to my cupboard so I could see more clearly.

"Hippolytus, the court of assembled gentlemen has found you guilty," Theseus said quietly. "Do you have anything more to say?"

Hippolytus slumped for a moment. I don't think he had believed this moment would happen. He relaxed his broad arm muscles, and Theseus motioned to the guards to release their tight grip. They did so and stepped away carefully.

Hippolytus remained staring at the floor for a moment. He looked at his father and murmured, "*Abba*?" Again, the diminutive, the little boy's voice coming out of the nearly grown man. Theseus raised his hands, a gesture of care. Perhaps a reminder of a previous conversation. Then Hippolytus pulled himself up to his full height—the only man in the room who was nearly as tall as his father—took a deep, visible breath, and said, more calmly than I would have believed, "This is a travesty of justice, but I accept the verdict of the court. I will not stay to hear your punishment." And he whirled around, pushing past the guards, and stormed out of the room. Even the guards tasked with keeping him prisoner were too stunned to do much other than watch him leave.

"Theseus—" Trypho began, but Theseus cut him off.

"I'm not interested, Trypho. You've had your court. You've proven him guilty. What more do you want? The skin off his back? He's still a prince."

Trypho looked as though he were going to consider pushing the point, but instead he said, "As you wish, Your Majesty."

Theseus's chest swelled up, and for a moment I thought he might punch the elderly statesman. But instead, he sat down on the bench and placed his head in his hands. He seemed to be mulling his options over, because in a couple of minutes, while they all waited in an awkward silence, he said, "Clear the room."

The men departed, obvious signs of relief on every face. As they moved away from the Great Hall, I could hear them starting to speak to one another again, no doubt keen to examine in depth everything that they had participated in and witnessed. If they'd been women, we would have called it gossiping.

☽

Theseus waited until they had all left, and then he lifted his head. "Phaedra, you can come out now."

I thought about remaining where I was, but I could see there was no point. I struggled out of the alcove, trying not to overbalance. He did not offer me any assistance.

Finally, I stood in front of him. I put one hand on my back to ease the strain, and it must have caused something, a memory of another pregnant woman perhaps, because now he did stand up and push a chair in front of me. I shook my head. "I'd rather stand. I have been crouched over for too long."

"It is not too late, Phaedra," he said. "You can still retract your statement. You can stay here, or you can return to Crete. It is all one to me now."

"I will not. I will stay to see Hippolytus punished. Then the gods will deal with me as they see fit." I kept my voice even, but some of the jubilation rang out. We had lost so much, but we had still won.

"Punished? Foolish woman. Shall I tell you what will happen to Hippolytus?" he sneered, raising his upper lip. I could feel my chest growing cold, as though he had reached in and gripped my heart. The child inside me was kicking wildly.

"He will be executed," I said. "The gods will see it is so."

"He is to be sent to his mother's people," Theseus said. "They will take care of him. I understand they prefer to be on horseback, too. He can spend a year, perhaps two years there. And by the time he returns, he will be much more matured, and the court will welcome him back with open arms. He will be my heir."

That this was clearly to be a non-punishment was not lost on me, but I was paralyzed by the first thing Theseus had said. "His mother's people? But . . ."

"Yes, the Amazons. They have already agreed to take him, out of respect for their lost queen."

"But they are women," I said. I waited for him to disagree, to tell me I had misunderstood.

"So? I have paid handsomely. He will be safe, for all he is a man."

I felt again that man's hands around my neck, forcing me down into the mud.

"Sire, do not send him to women," I begged.

"They are hardly defenseless," he scoffed. He started to stride to the door. "Of course, you will not be here when he returns, unless you have retracted that statement."

"What have you told them?" I called after him, holding one last flicker of hope. "Do they know why he is being sent away from Athens?"

"I've told them he's too sensitive. Loves his horse too much, won't speak to anyone else. He knows he's to be on his best behavior."

So the rapist was to be sent to a tribe of unsuspecting women. True, they were the Amazons, but they would be unprepared. They thought they were receiving their deceased ruler's son, a shy boy who cared for animals. How long before they knew the truth, and which girl would have to pay to reveal it to them? Did the Amazons even have a night chorus, living so far from men?

"Work on that retraction statement," Theseus said brusquely, interrupting my thoughts. "I'm going to find my son."

He left, and I was alone. I wanted to throw myself down and weep, but I couldn't give myself that luxury. I was still reeling from what Theseus had said. How could this be the gods' intention? That Hippolytus was to go unpunished? That Theseus was to suffer no loss? And worse, that Hippolytus was to be released into a community of women where he could treat them as badly as he liked?

I felt hollow; this was not what I had believed the gods had in mind. I stumbled back towards our rooms, trying to imagine what would happen next. Would he try to injure an Amazon, who would shoot him? Was that the sort of punishment that Artemis intended? Would he need to seek shelter on his journey and be murdered by his host? These thoughts did not give me the comfort they once had.

I could feel an uncomfortable realization bubbling through my stomach, prodding me in my side. It was so real that I put a hand down and stopped short as I felt the heel of a foot. My baby, making himself known. Giving his mother hope. I pressed it quickly then hurried on, not wanting to be seen by anyone. This moment was just for me.

After what felt like an eternity traversing the corridors, I arrived at our rooms. I pushed open the door, desperate to get inside, to lie on my bed and watch that little foot dancing in my womb. Something was wrong, though. I stopped in confusion. A small piece of meat sat on the table. Was it an offering? Kandake had mentioned to me how the women had brought me small gifts after I was attacked. But wouldn't they have cooked it first? This small chunk was still raw, the blood seeping into the table. No woman had done that. The baby stilled inside me, the foot retreated. I forced myself to step into the rooms, past the oversized table, and to open the door to my bedroom.

For a single moment, I saw in front of me the bull leaper, her body slumped over the horns of the bull, the single trail of blood running down her side. Then my eyes cleared, and I saw instead a much older woman, her body thicker and her hands rough from a lifetime's work, slumped against the bed. Her skin had a bluish tinge to it. Her mouth gaped, and I could see the jagged edges where the piece of meat on the table had been cut away.

I didn't hurry. There was no point. I crept towards her, then took one cold hand in my own.

Kandake would not be going home.

"There is no justice," I said, not caring who heard me. I remembered the lightning bolt, a symbol, I'd thought, of a god who would protect us. "There are no gods." I paused. I repeated it, louder, "There are no gods!" Nothing happened.

I had wasted so much time. I had waited and waited for the gods to provide vengeance, only now I realized that Medea had been right all along. There were no gods. If you wanted something done, what was it she had said? *Sometimes a mother needs to take action herself.*"

I wasn't quite a mother—not yet—but the time had come for me to act. My mother had said, "They have taken all of my children now." I remembered Ariadne when she appeared to me in the boat, handprints around her neck. I remembered the stinking pile of entrails that emerged from my brother's body and the way that even other Cretans had turned away, as though he were an animal carcass instead of a slain human being. My parents had told me that I needed to curb my rage, to be the perfect princess, to rely on the gods to take any necessary actions. But I saw now that they were wrong. I repeated to myself, "Androgeus, Minos, Ariadne," again and again, like a mantra. Androgeus, killed by old Aegeus when he was traveling Attica, just a boy and a tourist. Minos, a peaceful man with an unusual deformity, killed trying to reason with Theseus. And Ariadne—oh, my sister! How could I have doubted her? Her reputation destroyed along with her body. I didn't call her name, but Kandake's cold body lay next to me, and even if she hadn't been the daughter of a king or the granddaughter of gods, she deserved her revenge, too.

If I were to succeed in what I had to do, soon Phaedra, too, would be a name for the bards to entertain drunken men with, of that I had no doubt. But I wanted to make Theseus hurt first. The children of Minos would not die unavenged.

EXODUS

FURIES

The jurors deliver their verdict, and they hold their breath. Hipploytus has been found guilty. From her alcove, Medea swallows a gasp. Trypho hears the word echo about the room, but he cannot grasp it, cannot stay its fluttering wings and clutch at its meaning.

These are ordinary men, not heroes or kings, and yet this single word has more power than a red-hot stake through the eye of a Cyclops, a mirror before a gorgon, a sword through the side of a horned beast in a labyrinth.

They cannot know it yet, but the legacy of this day will see Athens rise. Soon the Attican kings will send gifts—money, even—to build a strong sea fleet. Clever men, talented men, will flock to ply their wares and use their skills, to share in the largess that seems only to grow.

But for now, someone must fall. It should be Hippolytus, but his father is still the king. And more than that, assembled on their benches, they feel as though they have been watching a play, and its final act is yet to be revealed. As their thoughts turn from Hippolytus, the pious prince condemned, to Theseus, this king among citizens, hero amongst men, and finally to Phaedra, the foreign girl in the place of an Athenian queen—not one man amongst these jurors can say who that will be.

Phaedra

I crossed to my room and pulled my paints from below my bed. I swirled my fingers in the black paint and then stood up in front of my mural, paint dripping from my fingers like blood, a wild woman, a Bacchae. I took a deep breath, and I called to the gods.

"I am Phaedra, the daughter of King Minos and Queen Pasiphaë. My grandfather, the sun god Helios, allowed crimes to be committed against me when he was not able to see! My great-grandfather, king of all Olympian gods, Zeus, has allowed the enemies of Crete, his chosen city, beloved by him and sacred to him, to destroy Crete's children."

I took another breath, then called, louder than before, "The sea god Poseidon, brother of my great-grandfather, allowed Hippolytus to swear false oaths in his name. Helios, Zeus, Poseidon, I will have the vengeance you should have taken! I do not care whether you exist or not. I will wait for you no longer."

Then in a frenzy, I set to painting the wall, not quietly and carefully, as I had done before, but with passion and strength. Paint dripped down my best chiton. It dyed my hair when I impatiently pushed hanks out of my eyes, and it ran down my face when I brushed sweat off my forehead. Eventually, I sat back down, panting a little, and stared at the picture. I hadn't had any real thoughts in mind as to what I was going to paint, choosing to work on instinct, but now I could see what I had done, and I approved. Rising out of that deep blue Athenian sea, still no longer, was a monster, a sea bull with giant horns and beefy flanks. A sea bull? Say rather, a Cretan bull.

At the bottom of my trunk lay the double-headed axe, the labrys, for which our labyrinth is named. The labrys, the symbol of Crete and a gift from my father. I pulled it out and weighed it in my hands. It was solid, but not so heavy I couldn't lift it. I touched my fingers to the blades and was pleased to see the time the axe had spent lying neglected in Athens hadn't blunted it.

Twirling the double-headed axe in my hands, I left the rooms and strode through the palace. I passed a gaggle of maids in the middle of cleaning the floors. They gaped, then fled at the sight of me, although they had nothing to fear. I didn't see any men; they might all be drinking somewhere, discussing the events of the day as though they were no more than a play, a drama for them to watch. A single guard shouted at me to stop, but he dropped back when he saw the axe in my hands, and perhaps the mad glare that was in my eyes.

I left the palace and continued down towards the shore. Now I passed ordinary Athenians, farmers and peasants. I remembered the peasant who'd insulted my mother, and brandished my axe at the crowd. The crowd parted hurriedly to get out of my way. I laughed out loud. I was huge now, a goddess of new life, the baby kicking and protesting within me, but my mind was clear.

I had to find and kill its father.

When I reached the beach, a crowd was gathering behind me. I bellowed and roared and hoisted the axe in the air.

"She's gone mad!" I heard a child shout.

The sea in front of me was the most vibrant I had ever seen it, a bright blue color completely unlike the muddy glaze of my paints. I wasn't skulking in shadows and cupboards any longer; I could see the world clearly before me. The sun shone in the sky above me, and once I would have taken that for an omen, but now I was going to continue with my task no matter what. I was Herakles, I was Perikles, I was any one of those great heroes. My hair whipped in my face and the salt of the sea stung my eyes, but with my axe in my hands I finally knew what it was to be an Amazon.

I saw Hippolytus in the distance but getting closer and closer, driving his horse through the surf towards me. I raised the axe in greeting to him. The surf pounded in my ears, drowning out the noise of the crowd. Only Hippolytus and I existed in this moment, bound together forever by his evil deeds and my hatred of his father.

He cantered towards me, chin raised in defiance. But something was wrong: he knew it and I knew it. He no longer had that centaur's grace, the torso of a man melded to the body of a horse. His horse was frightened and unwilling, and I intended to take advantage of that. I charged at the horse, waving my axe. He tried to sidestep me, but fighting bulls is not as easy as he thought. I remembered the little bull leaper, so confident, so adept, yet landing straight on the bull's horns. Now it was Hippolytus's turn to fail at the expertise he held so dear. His horse reared and threw him into the air before galloping off along the shore. We all watched as his body flipped and turned and crashed down, not into the sea, but onto the rocks.

I judged his neck was broken without me even touching him, but I needed to be sure. I lifted my double-headed axe, and I was the sea bull, the monster, the Cretan bull, come to have my vengeance on the house of Theseus. The sea drummed in my ears, driving me on. I looked down at his crumpled body in front of my feet. Was this what I had looked like to him, I wondered, when he had left me for dead? I remembered the dull thud as his foot slammed into my side. I hadn't even winced, numbed to any further pain by the brutalities he had inflicted upon me. I could have done the same, kicked him like he was a mangy cur, but it felt undignified, beneath me.

Instead, I brought my axe down onto Hippolytus's neck, the sharp axe parting his neck from his head as though his body were made of sea foam. I felt my eyes roll back in my head, and I passed out.

When I came to, I was lying on my bed. Groggily, I tried to raise myself, and I couldn't. I was bound in iron chains. I looked across the room, and saw my sister, Ariadne, bending over my chest.

Night Chorus

I bring news. Hippolytus is dead!

No!

Good!

How? Was it a riding accident?

You could say that. He fell from his horse.

I won't be crying any tears, that's for sure.

*Me neither. But how could Hippolytus fall? He is—was—
the best rider in Athens. In all of Greece.*

It was the queen. I heard she took an axe to him.

*I heard she was a witch, like her cousin before her, and she
caused a giant beast to rise from the sea.*

A giant beast?

An axe?

Does it matter? Hippolytus is dead.

Does Theseus know?

But what will happen to the queen now?

Theseus will kill her, for sure.

She's carrying Hippolytus's child.

*It doesn't matter. Theseus will kill her as soon as it is born.
Not long now.*

Medea

"Ariadne?" I heard her voice say groggily behind me. I straightened up and spun round, slightly embarrassed to be caught rifling through her belongings.

"No, it is Medea," I said. We had not spoken in so long.

She nodded. "I had forgotten how much you look like my sister. I miss her."

I didn't know what to say to that. "I believe your sister is . . . still traveling with the god Dionysos."

"Do you? Believe it, I mean? I don't. I don't believe in stories anymore." Her voice, although weak, was assured. "I saw her, you know. On the boat. Or at least I thought I did. It must have been a mirage. She told me to beware Theseus. I should have listened. What are you doing here?"

"Here in Athens, or here in your room?" I prevaricated. When I made my ungodly deal with Theseus, I imagined she would be afraid, timid, needing guidance. I did not see there was much I could offer her.

"Either. Are you going to tell me the truth now, Medea? About how you killed your children to spite your husband?"

I flushed. "I thought you did not believe in stories anymore, Phaedra."

In answer, she just shut her eyes, and remained still for so long she might have gone to sleep. But after a while, she said, without opening her eyes, "So I am a prisoner of Theseus, am I?"

284

"What else would you expect? You killed his son."

Her eyes flew open. "Hippolytus is dead?"

"Yes, he is. Don't you remember? You killed him." I watched her closely. It would not be unheard of to lose one's memory after such events.

She shook her head. "No, I was painting. Look" she gestured to the wall across from me, which was indeed covered with paint, although the paint was slashed across the wall in such a haphazard fashion I would be hard-pressed to name the subject.

"I see that someone has been painting at some point, but you cannot prove that you were painting while the prince was being killed," I pointed out, reasonably enough.

"Ah, but my maid could tell you. The painting was unfinished before, and it is finished now. Kandake will say—" and she broke off into loud sobs.

Trypho had told me about the ugly fate that befell her maid, one too terrible for even that surly old crone. After the trial I had been skulking in my rooms, a flagon of wine ready to settle my nerves, but before I could drink it, I had been disturbed by a knock on the door, and Trypho had walked in without waiting to be called.

"Apologies, madam, for my intrusion," he had said in that silky, untrustworthy voice of his. "But perhaps you will be more congenial if I replace your wine with mine." He produced a glass out of nowhere, and, like a priest making a libation, he filled it from the flask he carried in his pocket.

Behind us, I heard the startled giggles of my girls, unused to hearing me challenged over my beloved wine. I was tempted to require them to act as taste testers, but I did not truly believe it was poisoned in any way, and it would only infuriate Trypho. I sipped at the wine, a better beverage than the one I had been about to drink. It warmed my mouth and slipped down my throat. I could feel my shoulders drop and my breathing become more even. But I still didn't trust him.

"This is very kind of you, sir, but I do not believe you came to educate my palate," I hinted.

"No, madam, I am sure your palate does not require my education, although your budget may require assistance." He smiled, a cold smile that did not reach his eyes. I was fast reassessing my opinion of the man. That did not mean I liked him any more.

"So why are you here?" I asked bluntly. The titters in the background stopped suddenly; my girls knew that I was not to be toyed with when I employed that tone.

"Isn't a better question why you are here?" he asked. "Does the king, for instance, know that he has been harboring a fugitive ever since his father died?"

I drank the rest of my wine in one mouthful. "Blackmail is very boring. If that is why you are here, then tell me what it is you want, and leave. I certainly won't give it to you, but at least I need not waste any more of my day on you."

He smiled wolfishly at me. "Spending time with me is a waste? Interesting. I've been spending a lot of my time lately with a young cousin of yours, and she did not consider it a waste at all."

I almost laughed. "And yet from all I have seen, it was not the most profitable use of her time. Young fool. What has this to do with me?"

"Everything, I hope. You know that the princess has murdered Hippolytus?"

I did not know that, and it annoyed me. Why did I not know it? I tried not to let my irritation show, but like an oyster, I was forced to cough up a pearl.

"How?"

"She used a weapon unique to Crete—a double-headed axe. Have you heard of it?" His tone was so dry, he could be asking me if I'd heard of a new tool for cutting meat.

"No, but it seems appropriate. I still do not see what this has to do with me."

"I have not yet told Theseus that you are still here, but I will." I opened my mouth to object, and he raised a finger. "Hear me out. I feel an obligation towards your young cousin. Perhaps I led her down a path that was not right for her. Perhaps I am becoming soft in my old age." He muttered the last sentence under his breath, and I did not think it was meant for me. But then, perhaps that was what I was supposed to think.

"*I* am not becoming soft in *my* old age," I retorted. "What does any of this have to do with me? I need to go and pack my bags before the king finds me here."

"The king does not want to see Phaedra again. He is grieving for the loss of his beloved son. He does want to see his grandchild, though. Perhaps you could broker a deal with Phaedra, under which she gives up the child when it is born in return for safe passage. You could then raise the child for her. She is your family after all."

The man had gone mad. I stared at him with my mouth agape. "Why would I want to do that? Raise my cousin's child? Are you insane?"

For the first time, his self-possession seemed to diminish. "Because . . . you lost your own children."

"I did not *lose* my children. They were not bags or hats, belongings that I misplaced somewhere," I said when I finally recovered my tongue. "And children are not interchangeable possessions, no matter what Theseus may think. One child cannot be replaced by another, especially not when the other child is not even yours. You should go now." I stood up, knocking over the wine. I didn't care. It was time for me to leave this court.

"Please," Trypho gabbled, now looking most disconcerted. "I did not mean to offend you. I accept my words were clumsy. I do not have children of my own."

"Then raise Phaedra's." I cut across him. We did not have guards, but I thought my girls and I could bundle him out of the room, and we could be packed and gone by the time he had summoned anyone. I looked about for Cassandra, who had strong upper arms and was never afraid of causing a scene.

"Please, let us forget that part of the plan. But I need you to reason with Phaedra for me. I cannot persuade her myself," he said.

I stood for a moment, my breath raw, then I sat back down again. "Very well. And what will be my reward?"

"What would you like? Safe passage home? Secured comfort here? I must warn you, I do not believe that Theseus is a man who will allow you to remain indefinitely. If that is the deal negotiated, there are ways of bringing an agreement to a swift end."

His voice had started to slow down again; he was on firmer ground here. His words were reasonable too; I would not trust Theseus as far as I could throw him. I let the thoughts swirl around my head like clouds.

"What do you recommend? Where could I obtain safe passage to? I am Medea, the murderess, after all."

He leaned back in his chair. "I would not recommend any court. I would suggest that you ask for a grant of land, a small homestead, and men to assist you in managing it. Retire to the country."

I laughed. "Retire? I am barely forty years old."

"But you are not, shall we say, active anymore? You creep about the court at night, watching others. What sort of a life is that?"

I flushed. I had not realized that anyone knew what I was doing. Perhaps I had underestimated this old fool, but he had not read me correctly either.

"Perhaps it is a very feeble one, but better that than living on a farm."

"Colchis, then? Your father is no longer living, but you have a brother who might take you in. Or Thebes? I understand the kingdom of Thebes is in complete disarray. If chaos is what you like, there is enough there to occupy your mind for several years."

I thought about it. If I sailed to Colchis, I would be returning in disgrace. But in Thebes, I could brew my potions to convince the gullible that I was a sorceress with the ear of the gods.

"Thebes," I said.

"Very well. I will speak to Theseus: safe passage and an envoy for you to Thebes, in return for which you will persuade the princess Phaedra that it is in her own best interests to leave the child and return to Crete."

"My deal cannot be contingent on hers," I warned him, seeing the peril clearly. "If she will not agree to it, I cannot be held responsible."

"Understood and agreed. You think she will not agree? Interesting."

"What mother would?" I asked simply.

He rapped his fingers on the table. "Phaedra is not yet a mother. She is a young girl who is suffering the unwanted consequences of a violent act."

"Yes," I agreed. "And yet you may find that by now, she is also a mother."

☽

I looked down now at the girl in question. She had rested her hands on her stomach, and her left hand stroked her belly unconsciously from time to time. Did she already have that all-consuming passion, that burning need to do the best by her child, no matter what the consequences? Could she do what I had done? I've been told many times since that most women could not—*would* not—and I do not believe it. Any mother would do what I did if she found herself seated on my throne.

"I am sorry about your maid," I said now. "I have had many good maids over the years, and you always feel the loss." She was staring at me in disbelief; perhaps my words had not been carefully chosen. I tried again. "But now, you must think about yourself, and if you wish, your unborn child."

"If I wish?" she asked. "Why would I not wish?"

So it had happened already with the quickening inside of her. That desire to see the child as something other than the product of a monstrous father.

"Good," I said. "There was a worry that you did not care for the child. As you do, you will want only the best for this child."

She closed her eyes; perhaps she was tired of the sound of my voice. I was making hard work of this, but all I could see in front of me was my own passage on a boat, a trip to a new court, a chance to start again. There was nothing left for either of us here, but only one of us knew it.

"What are you talking about?" she asked. "Please, whatever it might be, just say it. I do not have the patience for riddles."

"Theseus desires to raise the child as his own," I said, shrugging. "It is his grandson— or granddaughter. He will raise the child as his new heir, if a boy, and marry her well, if a girl. He will spare no expenses."

"And what will happen to me?" she asked.

I drummed my fingers on the windowsill.

"You will be offered safe passage back to Crete."

"And if I refuse?"

It felt as though all the air had been sucked out of the room. I had asked Trypho what I should say at this point. He had looked at me and said of the girl whom he professed to care for and feel responsibility for, "Don't sugarcoat it. She needs to know the truth."

"Then you will remain chained to this bed until you give birth, at which point you will be killed and your body tossed into the sea to be devoured by the sea beasts. Your father will be told that you died in childbirth."

She closed her eyes. "And Theseus will take the baby." Her tone was weary, making her sound much older than her years.

"Yes." I agreed with her; there did not seem much point in doing otherwise. I looked out the window. These were small and damp rooms, but they had a beautiful view of the sea. I wanted to be out of here now, away from this cursed place.

She laughed, a hollow, humorless laugh. There was no other sort in Athens. There was no genuine mirth here. "I was going to ask you what you would do, having been a mother yourself, but you are the byword for the very opposite of motherly love."

"That shows how little you know," I snapped. I regretted it instantly. I had built an entire persona, as she said, out of being the opposite of motherly love. I had never defended my actions. To do so might destroy me.

"Really?" she asked now, like a boy with a stick poking a beast. "But you have never denied killing your own children. Now will you tell me why?"

What did it matter? I was leaving anyway. And I did not believe this girl would make it to Crete, no matter what Trypho said.

"There are worse things to do to children than kill them. Worse things that can happen to them. A mother's job is to protect her children, however she can."

There. It was out. I had said it.

She was staring at me now, wide-eyed. All pretense at being half asleep or bored by my words was gone. "Like the true mother, you mean. In your story about the king."

It took me a moment to catch up.

"Oh. You mean the eastern king. The one who threatened to divide the baby."

"This is what you meant, isn't it? That the real mother is not the one who could give the baby up. The real mother is the one who cannot let her baby live without her. Not if she knows the false mother intends a fate worse than death." She sagged back onto her pillow.

"Yes," I agreed. "That is one interpretation, Phaedra. But it's just a story. There probably wasn't even a baby to begin with."

"But what could be worse than death?" she asked. "Not for the baby. For your children?"

I bit my lip. I still did not want to cry in front of her. "There are many things worse than death, especially for young girls with fathers who choose both brides and maids who are much younger than themselves."

Her skin was white, and I could see she had understood. "But you . . . could you not get them out any other way?"

"I tried," I said. "Believe me, I tried." In the end, I did the only thing I could. I appealed to Jason to allow me one more evening with my children before I was banished from them forever. I hugged them goodnight and I fed them a warm drink containing a potion of my own making. The irony. I was known as Medea the sorceress, but I had never brought anyone back to life. All I could do was provide a kind death. And having done so for my own beautiful, unhappy little girls, I had sentenced myself to a living death.

"What should I do?" she asked now slowly. "I do not want to leave my child with Theseus."

"I do not see that you have a choice," I said. "And besides, Theseus is not Jason. Your child will be safe."

"Yes, but raised by the same man who raised Hippolytus," she said.

"You have no choice," I repeated. She sank back down onto her pillows and began to cry. I let myself out, every step I took reminding me of how worthless I had become.

As I trudged back down the corridor, I met with Trypho going in the opposite direction.

"Have you told her?" he asked.

"Yes," I replied. "I do not think she will take the offer."

"No? Ah well. If you had not given her such an unpalatable offer, I would not be able to present her with a more attractive one. Your ship sails at midnight. Do not miss it. There won't be another one." He turned and walked back to his chambers, whistling under his breath. I spared no more time wondering about Phaedra. It was time to go.

Trypho

Theseus remained by Hippolytus's side until he finally crossed the River Styx, and during that time, rumors traveled unhindered. When I asked one of my sources, who had not been present at the event, what he heard had happened, I was presented with the most unusual story.

"The prince, may the gods rest his soul, left the palace and was racing his chariot along the cliff edge, as he has done so many times before. Except this time"—and his voice broke slightly—"this time a giant bull made of sea foam raised itself out of the sea. The peasants nearby, working in the fields, said that Hippolytus did not falter, prince among men as he was, but his horse . . ." Here he broke off completely. Another man took up the story.

"His horse was alarmed and lost its footing on the cliff path, plunging down into the ocean and taking the chariot and rider with him. Hippolytus, may Hades preserve his soul, was dashed to death on the rocks."

"Did he . . . did he die straight away?" I asked. I didn't know what else to say.

"No, he did not. He lay crying for his father and for his grandfather, Poseidon. Theseus rushed to him as soon as the news reached the palace, and he was able to comfort him in his dying moments. His last words were to reiterate his innocence against the evil lies that witch created about him." And here the man glared, presumably in the direction of Phaedra's chambers, with pure hatred, the likes of which I had never seen before. And yet, I could have sworn this man voted against Hippolytus only days previously.

As I say, it really was quite something to hear. My best guess is that the confusion arose because of the weapon Phaedra carried, the labrys. Not many Athenians knew what it was, but we all knew that a bull-headed monster was imprisoned in the maze named for it. And so the story developed.

For my part, my plan could not have worked any better. There was no question of a second trial. Theseus ordered Phaedra to be chained to her bed, and the guards set to and did it. The rule of the people had been overridden. The king reigned supreme, and where a king reigned supreme, there was a role for the trusted advisers who had always been by the king's side. Theseus's own closest associates were too busy mourning their beloved democracy to give much thought to the business of running a city.

I bided my time, though. Paid a few men to make sure my name was being mentioned at the right moments and kept to my own chambers. It didn't do to appear too eager, especially with the young prince dead. Another victory for the entire court, though no one dared to say it to Theseus's face. With their ringleader removed, the young men sharpened up and paid more heed to the words their fathers were telling them.

Yes, it all could not have been more satisfactory were it not for the fact that the princess Phaedra was chained to a bed. We are not a culture of pacifists in Athens, and the violence of her actions did not disturb me. Had Hippolytus not left her for dead first, after all? But still, a niggling voice at the back of my head told me that I had set a sequence of events in motion, and an innocent young woman was paying the price. And at some point, although I could not tell you when, exactly, I started to concoct plans to rescue her.

She could not live in the city anymore. Theseus would have her killed as soon as he could. I was surprised he had not done so already, but he was grieving, and the rumors were that he wanted the unborn child she was carrying, a last memento of Hippolytus. A rather grisly memento, but I do not have children, and the sentiments of those who do is foreign to me. Could she return to Crete? I found myself listing reasons that would be a bad idea; the loss of face, as she returned as a fallen woman and a murderess. Perhaps her father would feel the need to start a war against Athens, a war that Athens would almost certainly lose. What sort of a statesman would I be if I could prevent the loss of the lives of many of my countrymen but failed to do so?

Yet if she were not to return to Crete, where could she go? Thebes was in utter chaos at present; she could probably pass unnoticed, but it did not seem a suitable place for a young lady with her breeding to live. And after all she had been through, she needed somewhere quieter. Somewhere she could live anonymously and raise her child.

In fact, somewhere like my own estate, hidden away from prying eyes, yet close enough to Athens to travel there easily.

Once the idea had entered my head, it proved impossible to dismiss. I could introduce her as my niece, the child as my great-nephew and the heir to my estate. (Somehow, it occurred to me, we had all decided this child was a boy. It seemed inevitable that this ill-begotten child would inherit something of importance.)

I would have to convince Phaedra of the sense of my plan. I was confident I could spirit her away, but less confident that I could keep her without her consent. And more to the point, I did not want her to be a prisoner on my estate rather than being a prisoner of Theseus's. I wanted her to be happy. I was starting to have visions of Phaedra sitting under a tree, watching the boy play while I looked on and smiled benevolently.

I needed to show her the folly of any other course of action. Medea proved disappointingly easy to convince on this point. I never even needed to go near Theseus; just the hint that I might was enough to persuade her to work with me and to present to Phaedra a proposal, supposedly supported by Theseus, which I knew that Phaedra would never accept.

I hadn't talked to Theseus. No one had. He had thrown himself into deep mourning, putting out the word that he was not to be disturbed. But Medea did not know that. I did not know how skillful she might be as a liar, so she thought that she told the truth.

The plan went as I expected it to. Medea presented her unpalatable suggestions to Phaedra and told me that she was not receptive to them. I arranged for a boat for Medea—again, not sanctioned by Theseus, but she did not need to know that, and money acted in lieu of a kingly name in securing her safe passage. I was excited now, seeing my bucolic vision coming ever closer to me, and I did not want anyone to undermine the possibility of its coming true.

But before I could visit Phaedra myself, I was summoned to see Theseus. The king, although I had never been able to think of him as such. I would have to now. He would take up his kingly mantle, and I would advise him until my death.

I visited Theseus in his bedchamber. The room was bare, with little in the way of creature comforts. In fact, it startled me how much it resembled the poor rooms he had given to Phaedra, although in this instance, I suspected it was his desire to focus on his mission that led him to deny himself soft cushions.

"Sir," I said, bowing my head and trying not to show the alarm I felt. Theseus, always a lean man, seemed to have dwindled away to a shadow. His cheekbones were like sharp lines across his face, and his eyes had sunken down into his skull. His arms were stringy, not muscular, and his hair was long and gray. As fantastic as it might seem, I looked at him and wondered if I were not too late, and he was dead already.

"Trypho," he said. "My father's adviser."

This was not the most promising start to the conversation, but I inclined my head.

"You have been working with that woman—don't deny it," he added, raising a finger. In fact, I had not intended to deny it.

"You mean your wife, sire?"

He closed his eyes. "Why did I ever enter into such an arrangement? I thought I would do better this time, you know. I reflected over the mistakes I had made in the past: Hippolytus's mother, Phaedra's sister. The big mistake I made was in taking princesses and treating them like my own property. I wouldn't do that again. I needed the hostage, but I could treat her properly. Marry her. Bring her to Athens. Set her up in her own apartment, without my unwanted attentions. I could use the maids for that, after all. And look how she repaid me."

He opened his eyes and gazed at me. I remained silent.

"Did you hear what happened on the day of our wedding? Of course you did—you hear everything. A young girl, even younger than my son, was set to leap over a bull that must have been twice my height and as big as this room. She was impaled on its horns. By the gods, it left a terrible mess. The Cretans knew it was a bad omen. I just wonder why we let our young people destroy themselves in this way. We are supposed to be the adults, Trypho. We are supposed to be the adults."

He sighed. I still said nothing. This was a performance, a rehearsed speech.

"You say nothing. Very well. You are a staunch monarchist, are you not, Trypho?"

"I am loyal to my king," I said cautiously, feeling my way around the answer he was looking for.

"And if your king wishes to cease being the omnipotent king? To what or to whom are you loyal then, Trypho? Were you loyal to my father when he leaped to his death, thinking he left his kingdom in the hands of Hippolytus, a teenage boy?"

I glanced down at him in his bed, but I still said nothing. If Theseus had only known it, this was the kingliest behaviour I had seen from him. His father often used to berate me thus. It is the prerogative of kings. And besides, if I let him speak, he would reach his point soon enough.

Sure enough, he sighed. "Have you seen her? Phaedra, I mean."

"No, sire, I have not," I said, answering his direct question. He looked surprised.

"I was hoping you could tell me how you found her. Never mind. Tell me, adviser to the king, what should I do with her?"

I paused, considering my words carefully. I did not know his intention in asking me the question. It could have been to assess my wisdom and intelligence. It could also have been a test of where my loyalties lay. Keeping these possibilities in mind, I decided the best course of action was to speak honestly. "You should offer her the possibility of a kind death. You have to punish her—you must—but she is still your wife, and a woman."

"Would she take it? You mean hemlock, I imagine, or a similar herb?"

"Yes, she might. She is deeply unhappy, and she could be made to see reason."

He turned and gazed into space, at nothing, as far as I could see. When he turned back to me his eyes were glassy and he seemed to have moved to a completely different train of thought.

"You don't have children, do you Trypho?"

"No," I said, a little sharply; I was growing tired of answering this question, and I did not see why everyone seemed so concerned about my childless state.

"Right now, you think I am a weak man. You see me, lying on my bed, a man stripped of the most precious part of his world, and you think that I am weak, and your fight is over. There will not be another trial, another chance to do things correctly and with justice. I want revenge, not justice. That woman killed the most important person in my world. I will call on the gods, the Furies, the Kindly Ones, on every good spirit and bad one known to man, and I will see her dead." He raised himself up, sitting now on the edge of the bed. "You think she killed a teenage boy, a layabout, one who rode and played and added little to the life at court. But that is because you are not a father. She didn't just kill that boy. She killed the tiny baby I once cradled in my arms, holding my breath so as not to wake him. She killed the man he could have become—all the men he could have become. As his father, I used to watch him carefully for signs. Perhaps he would be a famous equestrian. Perhaps he would quest with Herakles—perhaps he would *be* the Herakles of his generation. Perhaps he would settle down and govern Athens with me. I could see so many possibilities. And she killed all of them."

He was on his feet now, towering above me. I kept my face passive. I did not allow myself to feel fear.

"And to you, this represents a victory. Democracy is dead, you and your cronies say. Theseus will have the vengeance of a king over the woman who killed his son. My boy, my baby, my son means nothing to you except as a tool to weaken me, to bend me to your will. And you are right, Trypho, I am weak. Phaedra will be executed without trial, without the vote of the citizens, on nothing more than my say-so, because I can. But I will not always be weak like this. I have no other sons to lose. I have nothing else to lose. And when I am ready, I will devote myself entirely to the establishment of democracy, a system under which every man may have his say, and corrupt advisers like you may not profit and grow fat off the vanity and indecision of weak kings like my father."

I was bending backwards now, instinctively trying to move away from him even though my feet were rooted to the spot. We eyed each other up, king and subject, madman and sane one. His eyes glinted, while mine flickered from side to side in search of a reprieve.

"Sire," I said, finally, "you are the king, and you can establish whatever system you choose. That is your prerogative, whether you like it or not. But please, do not believe that I only advised your father in order to profit. I care for Athens, too."

He snorted, but at least he stepped away. His shoulders slumped over, and he slouched back towards his bed, the interview complete. Like any king, he knew how to dismiss me. But I had one last question.

"What of Phaedra, sir? May I offer her the kind death?"

"You can offer it," he said heavily, "but she must have the child first. I do not wish to see him at present, but he will be my heir. I will arrange a tutor for him. Tell her I will look after him well."

I nodded and left the room. I kept my features as bland and expressionless as over, but my heart was singing. I knew that Phaedra would not agree to giving up the child, but children die before they are fully born every day, and I had no qualms in reporting so to the king. Most importantly, I could now tell the court that she had accepted the hemlock, and the body had been shipped back to Crete. Or thrown into the ocean. Or whatever I decided to say had happened to it. Really, I was feeling quite giddy. I would need to keep her hidden for a little while, but no one knew where my property was. I would send word to the servants to prepare rooms for my niece and her child. Much nicer ones than the ones she had here. There was much work to be done.

Phaedra

Everyone was dead. My manacles had been loosened to allow me to sit up in bed, but I wished they hadn't bothered. Everyone I cared about was dead. My brother was dead. My sister was dead. No gods had spirited her away. She did not live on Olympus. She was dead.

I tried to rest my hand on my stomach, the gesture that had comforted me for eight moons now, but I couldn't reach. I looked down instead and saw none of the usual rippling and stretching I had become accustomed to. Hippolytus was dead. Had his son died with him, or was he just sleeping? I tried to move about as much as possible, to shake the baby into moving again, but the chains were not loose enough.

Had it been worthwhile, killing Hippolytus? If Theseus was feeling even a fraction of the pain that I felt now, then yes, I thought. Yes, it had been worthwhile. I did not need to wait for gods to seek revenge any longer. I had taken care of it myself.

I considered Medea's proposal. It was completely unacceptable to me, as I suspected she had known. To hand over my baby to the monster Theseus? I would sooner toss him into the sea. And what if it were a girl? She would never be safe in this Athenian court, not without a mother to protect her. And what would my life be like, wandering from court to court, like Medea? With no one wanting to take me in. I might suffer another fit of madness and kill their sons. And all the while, wondering what was happening to my child. My child, whom I still could not feel.

I couldn't move my arms and legs. I couldn't find the strength to sit up and look around. And yet, I had never felt stronger. I knew what I had to do next. I had to protect my child in the best way I could.

Trypho

After I had spoken to Theseus, I returned to my rooms and summoned a few associates of mine, intending to make the necessary arrangements. My heart was light, and I hummed a few bars under my breath. The summer had been long, hot, and heavy, but cooler weather was ahead of us, and the farm was the perfect place to spend the winter. I had a small olive grove on one side of the property, so we pressed our own oils. And I always knew where to get the best wines.

While I was dallying over such pleasant thoughts, a young man burst into my rooms. He did not knock, and I sprang to my feet.

"You?" I said, recognizing him. "Who is guarding the princess Phaedra?" I looked at him, at the red dye seeping into his clothes, and I understood then, but I didn't want to. I raced to the princess's rooms, shouting obscenities at the guard all the way. When I arrived, even the most delusional of men would have seen that it was too late.

Phaedra lay on the bed, her throat slashed open, her arms still chained to her sides. Blood soaked the sheets. Her large stomach seemed to have slumped to one side, and in this position, I saw what I had not seen before, how thin and bony her arms and legs had become. Her nose rose sharply from her face. When she had arrived in Athens she had been a chubby-faced teenager. She left us as an emaciated crone.

For one foolish moment, I wanted to throw myself down onto the bed, burst into tears, and beg her forgiveness. I had failed her. I had used her as a pawn, and for what? Theseus still intended to be the father of democracy, and he was a good thirty years younger than I. I was a decrepit old man, good for nothing.

I turned on the guard. "Who did this?"

He recoiled at my voice, although he could have restrained me as easily as a child. But his nerves were clearly shattered. "She did," he said, and started blubbering.

"She's chained to the bed. Speak sense, fool," I replied.

"She asked me to come closer to give her some wine," he said, then sobbed again. I could see pottery shards dripping down the side of the bed, a waterfall of fragments that glittered as they caught the light.

"She managed to take her own life with a goblet?" I asked incredulously.

He shook his head and cried some more. "As I leaned over her to give her the cup, she grabbed my sword. I thought she was going to swing it at me, but . . ." He mimed slitting his own throat, a grotesque gesture in the circumstances. I wondered how much of the story he was leaving out—whether his own lack of judgement and protocol had been caused by the fact that his hands were trying to be somewhere they shouldn't. Phaedra was heavily pregnant and a murderess, but she was still a woman. In any event, I did not need to understand the truth. It was enough that he had allowed her to take his sword. His commander would see him executed by the end of the day, tears or no tears.

I, though, turned to the princess and looked at her sad, still face. I felt a few tears well up in my own eyes, although

I did not allow them to drop. I saw my visions of a happy family playing on my farm disappear into the blood and gore that coated Phaedra's bed. It had been so close, and yet so very far away.

I did not allow myself to wallow for long, though. I took a deep breath and turned to the guard. "Fetch Theseus."

"But . . ." he stammered. I could understand that he had no idea how to finish that objection: But Theseus was in mourning? But Theseus was the king? But Theseus was a man wronged, whom he dared not approach? More than one messenger has been killed by an angry ruler.

"Fetch Theseus," I repeated, and this time he scampered off. My tone must have convinced him that he was in as much danger here as he was in Theseus's chambers. And soon enough, the man himself entered the room.

I could see immediately that the news had rejuvenated him. His walk could almost be described as jaunty as he sauntered into the room.

"What have we here, Trypho?" he asked. "It seems this one wasn't a witch after all."

"No, sire," I said quietly. "And it would appear both Hippolytus and Phaedra have left us, to be judged in a final reckoning, not by man."

"Not by man," Theseus mused. He walked around the bed, careful not to touch the princess. "Fine. I did not want the task, and now I do not have it."

There didn't seem to be much I could say to that, so I bowed my head.

"We need to make some sort of narrative," I said after a moment's silence, my mind already whirring. "If I may suggest, tell the bards that she was bewitched by a goddess—Aphrodite, I suppose—into trying to seduce your son. When that didn't work, she accused him of rape. Now her guilty conscience has gotten the better of her, and she's killed herself." Theseus looked surprised. For a moment, I had forgotten that we were not completely on the same side. "My job is to guard the king," I said apologetically. "I cannot forsake that role now. I'm too old."

Theseus nodded. "It is a sensible plan. Why Aphrodite?"

"Didn't your son swear to forsake women and worship only Artemis? It seems like the actions of a jealous goddess to me."

Theseus shook his head. "Make it be so. And in the meantime, we should send her body back to Crete."

"Sire, you cannot," I objected. I gestured at her stomach. "That alone would be a declaration of war."

He nodded. "Yes, I see your point. Very well. We will bury her here in Athens. I will arrange for word to be sent to Crete. I will tell them she was beloved. I suspect it may even have been true, for a fleeting second."

He meant me, I realized with a start. "Yes, sire. A very fast-of-foot second."

He laughed. "Ah, Trypho. You are a man of your times, more's the pity. But I need to continue my work. There's a war coming, you know."

"A war?" I asked, disturbed. None of my sources had told me about this. "Over what? A woman?"

"A woman. A trade route. A precious metal or a piece of cloth. It doesn't matter; it won't matter. It may not even be in my lifetime, but I can feel a change in the air. There are too many kings in Greece. Too many hungry men looking for power and glory. It will all come to a head soon. And Athens is a small and weak little kingdom. I intend to leave it much stronger, even if I currently have no heir to leave it to."

He turned and walked away, his shoulders already straightening and his steps lighter than before. I waited a few more moments by the corpse of Phaedra, but she had taken her secrets to the grave with her. Frowning, I followed the king.

Night Chorus

Aieeeeeee

Aieeeeeee

*She is dead. The princess is dead. She dies by her own
hand.*

So it is true.

It is true.

*They are saying that the goddess Aphrodite forced her to
seduce Hippolytus because he was devoted to her sister
Artemis.*

These aristocrats. They blame everything on gods.

So did Aphrodite also force Hippolytus to rape me?

Will Theseus marry again?

*I'm not sure. Perhaps not. He's very devoted to his
democracy now. He doesn't have an heir so he may as well
pass rule of Athens to the people.*

You mean the men.

The men, yes.

The heroes.

I have to go. I have beds to make and dishes to wash, and I want to do them before my master wakes and sees me.

If they are the heroes, does that make us the heroines? We keep going, we persevere, we ask for nothing, and we get even less.

Where are our stories?

Xenethippe

It took a while for news to reach me in Crete.

It had proved fairly simple to get off the boat bound for Athens. We hid in a backwater off the Cretan harbor for a week, then met up with the Athenian warship.

As we made our way back to Crete, I told Theseus I had seen the dead body of the girl, the older princess, in the hold. It was in both our interests for him to let me go; otherwise, I would tell the king and all the court what I had seen. Fortunately, Theseus agreed with me, although to be on the safe side, he had locked me into an antechamber in the Cretan palace.

Kitos had burst into the room to release me, a demonstration of heroics that I appreciated a little more than I showed at the time. Part of me really had thought that Theseus had left me there to die. I was shocked to find out that Theseus had taken the younger princess, though, and for a long time I wondered if I had done the right thing, saving myself instead of going straight to the king.

I had joined the guards alongside Kitos, and it soon became common knowledge that we were betrothed. At first I was a little embarrassed because I wanted to be known by my merits, not my marital status. But it turned out not to be such a bad thing because, despite training from dawn until long after the sun went down every evening, I must have been in Crete only a couple of moon cycles before I became with child.

I was suspended from training until the baby arrived, although I assured everyone that I would be back as soon as he or she was born. And at first I was, but by this time Kitos and I were married, and he had earned a couple of promotions, and the captain of the guards offered us a small house just outside the palace to live in. It made sense for Kitos to continue working as a guard and for me to stay home with our children.

However, living outside of the palace does mean that I am dependent on Kitos for news, and he is not one for gossip. One day, though, he came home with a long face, and before I could ask, he said, "Xenethippe"—he never abbreviates my name—"I have sad news from Athens for you."

I jumped to my feet, startling Tharsia, who was sleeping in my lap. "Is it my parents?"

"Oh no," he said, looking guilty, then taking the baby to soothe her. "I am sorry. I did not think how that would come across. It is not your family. Just someone you met, briefly."

"Someone I met briefly in Athens? That could be anyone," I said, a little irritated now. I took Tharsia back again, ignoring her cry of protest about being passed back and forth like a jar of wine.

"I'm telling this very badly, aren't I?" he said ruefully, and I smiled reluctantly. "Let me begin from the beginning. Princess Phaedra, who married Theseus, has died."

I looked at him in shock. I had never quite forgotten her, the pretty princess who had led us to safety. She dwelt somewhere in the back of my mind now, filled as it was with my daily duties taking care of the children, but every so often I spared a thought for her. I had hoped against hope that she might be happy in the Athenian court.

"How did it happen?"

Kitos paused. "They say she died in childbirth," he said eventually.

I pulled Tharsia closer to me, ignoring her bleats of objection. I had been lucky; neither of my births had been especially complicated, although after each I had sworn never to do anything that might cause that much pain ever again. But then I thought on Kitos's words. He was always a careful speaker, and the pause at the beginning should have put me on alert from the start.

"They say? Who is they? And what really happened?" I asked, loosening my clothing to give Tharsia what she wanted.

"Xenethippe, it is fortunate that we do not dwell in court, if you will say things like that. The official story is that the princess died in childbirth. It does not do to be seen to be questioning these matters."

"Right. But there is no one here except my husband and me, unless you think that our infant will inform on me to the captain of the guards. Or perhaps she reports directly to the king?"

We stared at one another, and then I dropped my eyes. "I am sorry, Kitos. But I did meet the princess. It was only briefly, but she . . . she was kind to us, when so few people were. I would like to know what happened to her, please."

He nodded. "I know. Very well, but you must not repeat it. The rumors coming out of the Athenian court state that

she seduced her own stepson, Theseus's son, under the influence of the goddess Aphrodite. When the stepson spurned
her, she killed herself in anguish."

I opened my eyes wide. "It sounds like something from
a bard's tale. Under the influence of the goddess? Really?
And do you believe this?"

He looked worried and crossed the room to stare out of
the window. When he turned back to look at me, his brow
was furrowed.

"I agree, there is something not right about this. The
king has ordered that no one is to speak of his daughter
again. She is to be buried in Athens."

I felt sorry for her, to be buried in a strange land,
although it crossed my mind briefly that the same fate
awaited me. But that was different; I had a husband here,
and two children, and by the time I died, I wouldn't miss
Athens that much at all. Phaedra had left us barely two
years ago, and it did not seem that she had been particularly
happy.

"She was kind to me," I repeated helplessly.

Kitos crossed the room and put his arms around me.
Tharsia wriggled against my chest but did not lose her grip.
"Then I suggest that you try and remember her as you knew
her. I'm sorry I told you anything."

"I'm glad you did," I said. "I will offer up a libation to
the household gods in her name tonight."

He nodded, satisfied, and moved away to take care of
the chores that were neglected when he was working in the
palace. I remembered those two carefree princesses, and
how I had envied them so much, with their pretty hair and
their plump skin. And yet both were now dead, and I held

my wriggling infant in the home that belonged to us. I thought of saying something to Kitos, about the mysterious ways of the gods. Instead, I finished feeding Tharsia, held her tightly for a second or two, then put her into her crib and began to make dinner for my family, as though it were just an ordinary day.

Author's Note

Greek myths are often treated as separate stories, even though certain key characters, like Theseus, may turn up in various tales. I have always been struck by the fact that the Phaedra who Theseus married was the sister of the Minotaur, the beast he killed, and of Ariadne, the woman he abandoned on an island after she had assisted him with this feat. Further, Hippolytus is described as being killed by a bull from the sea, a symbol of Crete. Taking these factors into account, it does not seem so surprising that Phaedra would be the cause of his son's death, and yet the two stories are rarely connected.

Plutarch in his *Greek Lives* credits Theseus with the role of the founder of Athens by virtue of his successful campaign to transform Athens into the capital of Attica, persuading the local kings to unite, and creating a democracy instead of a monarchy. Plutarch acknowledges that Theseus's various marriages and dealings with women, including the abandonment of Ariadne, are not to his credit, and indeed, the kidnapping of Helen as a child (long before she met Paris and set in motion the events that led to the Trojan War) causes the fall of Attica and the exile and death of Theseus.

Sources generally agree that Herakles was fond of children, and it seems reasonable to me that a man who loved children would have been like an uncle or a godfather to his friend and ally's motherless son.

I have taken certain liberties with the original sources. I have amended the traditional narrative so that the tributes are sent annually instead of every seven years. Although my invented male characters have known Greek names, my invented female characters have invented names, to reflect the lack of stories about women of their class. I have compressed the timeline of the myth about the Minotaur and the story of Phaedra and Hippolytus. Usually the story of Phaedra and Hippolytus takes place about twenty years later, when Phaedra is much more mature (and it is her brother who arranges the marriage, not her father). Phaedra has two children with Theseus, so he certainly did not treat her as a hostage only. At first I felt guilty for making these changes to make the stories fit my narrative, but then in my research I came across the following quote:

> Greek tragedy almost invariably drew on stories about the distant heroic age of Greece, the period which in historical terms we now call the Late Bronze Age or "The Mycenaean Age," those few generations of mighty exploits, turmoil and splendor, which were the setting of most traditional Greek heroic song, both in epic and lyric. But these stories were not history, nor were they canonized in any definitive collection of "Greek myths." Their oral transmission "at mother's knee" was no doubt subject to the huge variations which characterize nearly all such oral traditions, variations of emphasis and the mood no less than of narrative content (whatever "deep structures" the reductionist sage may claim to detect). It is likely, in any case, that the tragedians drew predominantly on

literary sources. Here, too, there was almost limitless variation, the product of centuries of rearrangement and invention, a process that the tragedians themselves continued. Not even the myths of the *Iliad* and *Odyssey* are definitive.

—Oliver Taplin, "Emotion and Meaning in Greek Tragedy" in *Oxford Readings in Greek Tragedy* (1983)

I do not claim to match the tragedians in skill, narrative, or craft. However, I am pleased to think of myself as continuing their tradition, one that was already centuries old by the time they came to write, of rearranging and reinventing the myths that so many of us continue to hold dear.

The main Greek source for Phaedra's story is Euripides' *Hippolytus*, which contains the story Trypho invents at the end of my Phaedra. However, for sheer sensationalism, I would recommend Seneca's *Phaedra* to the reader, an altogether bloodier affair, some of the language of which I adapted for Hippolytus's rape of Phaedra.

Finally, I am indebted to *The Palace of Crete* (Graham, 1962) and *Palaces of Minoan Crete* (Cadogan, 1976) which gave me a sense of the beauty and majesty of Knossos, including the still-impressive running water. Any errors— or flights of fancy—are my own.

Enjoyed the read?

We'd love to hear your thoughts!

crookedlanebooks.com/feedback

Acknowledgments

I have been extremely fortunate in the support, guidance, and assistance I have received not only in writing Phaedra's story but in all my writing endeavors.

First, I have to thank my superstar agent, Nelle Andrew, without whose steadfast commitment and unflinching high standards this novel wouldn't exist. Some debts can never be repaid, but I am forever grateful. I am also thankful for the assistance of her wonderful team at Rachel Mills Literary Ltd., and in particular Charlotte Bowerman, Alexandra Cliff, and Kim Meridja.

Thank you to the team at Alcove Books. Tara Gavin's eagle eye and expertise gave my initial draft the rigorous shake-up it needed, and the book is infinitely stronger as a result. Andrew Davis designed the beautiful cover. Madeline Rathle (marketing), Dulce Botello (marketing), Melissa Rechter (production), Matthew Martz (publisher), and Rebecca Nelson (publishing and production assistant) all worked tirelessly to bring Phaedra's story to the US market.

Thank you also to the team at Sphere, my UK publisher. Rosanna Forte's editorial vision was exactly what was needed, and again, she was supported by a fantastic team including Emily Moran (marketing), Stephanie Melrose (publicity), Hannah Wood (cover design), Ben McConnell (managing editorial), Tom Webster (production), and Caitriona Row and Lucy Hine (sales).

I have always loved the Greek myths, but I owe my love of classical studies as a discipline to Ms. Heath of Mt. Roskill Grammar School. I have had many great teachers in my life, but special thanks go to my creative writing teachers, Professor Albert Wendt, Professor Witi Ihimaera, Barbara Rogan, Doctor Sarah Burton, and Professor Jem Poster. Thank you also to all my fellow creative writing students, from whom I have learned so much. And thank you to Clare Worley, once a fellow student, now a dear friend.

Thank you to my family, my mum, my dad, and sister Emily, who provided the initial support and encouragement and gave me the confidence to work toward my dream. Steven, my beloved husband, has supported me consistently, believed in me unwaveringly, and sacrificed his own time generously to allow me to write. And finally, thanks to my cherished "production babies," Amelia Joan and Lucian John, who make life infinitely more wonderful every day. I love you all.

Discussion Questions

1. Phaedra believes she led a charmed life in Crete before relocating to Athens. Do you agree with her? What are the key distinctions between Crete and Athens, and can you see any cracks beneath the surface of the Cretan palace?

2. Care of children is a theme that recurs throughout the novel: Minos, Theseus, Medea, and ultimately Phaedra herself all make difficult decisions in order to protect their children. Do you find yourself empathizing with any of these parents?

3. Similarly, both King Minos and King Theseus are prepared to make personal sacrifices for political expediency. Are their actions justified?

4. At the heart of the novel is a court case that pits one character's word against another's. Which character do you find more compelling? Does this change throughout the novel?

5. The novel is grounded in mythological beliefs and ancient sources, but the author also extrapolates from those beliefs (for example, while the Greek historian Plutarch names Theseus as the father of democracy, there is no known connection between Theseus and the founding of the law courts). How did you react to these extrapolations? How did this compare to other retellings you have read?

6. It is often said that history is written by the winners, and at the conclusion of the novel, Trypho and Theseus plot together to create the version that would be passed down the generations, eventually being formalized in the play by Euripides. The Greeks recognized the possibility for alternate versions of the myth (such as a popular version that maintained Helen never went to Troy and instead was spirited to Egypt for the duration of the Trojan War!). Which version of Phaedra's story do you consider more realistic?

7. Do you see any modern parallels with Phaedra's story?

8. If you were able to time-travel, would you choose to visit ancient Greece? Why or why not?

9. Phaedra is initially presented as a young and innocent, if somewhat arrogant, character. How does she change throughout the novel?

10. Trypho is mystified by the behavior of women throughout the novel. In particular, he does not understand the loyalty of the women who serve their mistresses. Given that Trypho's role is supposed to be to serve the king, is he being hypocritical, or is his relationship with the king more complex?

11. The novel opens with a quotation from the Roman poet Ovid considering the distinction between heroes and heroines. Do you agree with this distinction? To what extent do any of the characters in the novel, particularly Phaedra herself, attain heroic status?